STICK OR TWIST

STICK OR TWIST

Diane Janes

Severn House Large Print
London & New York

This first large print edition published 2017
in Great Britain and the USA by
SEVERN HOUSE PUBLISHERS LTD of
19 Cedar Road, Sutton, Surrey, England, SM2 5DA.
First world regular print edition published 2016 by
Severn House Publishers Ltd.

British Library Cataloguing in Publication Data
A CIP catalogue record for this title is available from the British Library.

ISBN-13: 9780727895554

Severn House Publishers support the Forest Stewardship Council™
[FSC™], the leading international forest certification organisation. All
our titles that are printed on FSC certified paper carry the FSC logo.

MIX
Paper from
responsible sources
FSC   FSC® C013056
www.fsc.org

Typeset by Palimpsest Book Production Ltd.,
Falkirk, Stirlingshire, Scotland.
Printed and bound in Great Britain by
T J International, Padstow, Cornwall.

For
Sam and Ash

Part One

One

The bundle of seaweed which was sliding to and fro in the shallows made Stefan think of rotting corpses. Or maybe he had been thinking along those lines, even before he noticed the slimy, brown, blistered tendrils, twisting helplessly, a foot or so from dry land. He knew the stuff was destined to be abandoned by the retreating tide, left to stink on the sand until the sea advanced a few hours later to reclaim it.

The beach was deserted as usual. A series of long, low lines of sparkling froth rolled up the low-tide sands, picture-postcard perfect, wanting only the addition of a couple of kids bent over a sandcastle, buckets and spades in hand, to render it an ideal advert for the Cornish holiday trade. None of this crossed Stefan's mind as he stood contemplating the little bay, with his hood up and his hands dug deep in his pockets. In spite of the sun glittering on the water, it was early in the day and a sharp breeze was coming in off the Atlantic. He took a couple of strides toward the water's edge and returned his full attention to the purpose of the recce. It looked safe enough to bring a boat in here at high water, providing you kept well clear of the rocks at either headland, where the presence of semi-submerged hazards was betrayed by a disturbance in the water.

The place was isolated enough, no doubt about that. He glanced over his shoulder at the cliffs which reared up behind him, a series of tumbled, mud-coloured pinnacles and folds, where the land was steadily losing its battle with erosion from above and the relentless battering delivered by the sea. As he took them in, the sun was completely lost behind a cloud, so that when he turned back towards the water, he fancied that the whole beach had taken on a more sinister aspect. Yes, he thought, once you had lured your target down here, you would be very unlucky to be seen by anyone from above.

Funny how the place had a completely different atmosphere when it was devoid of sunshine. Cornwall traded on atmosphere. The very names along the nearby coast, Deadman's Cove, and Hell's Mouth (mentioned on the internet as a favourite local suicide spot – bet the tourist board didn't mention that in the brochure) bore witness to a past replete with wreckers and smugglers, who thought nothing of removing anyone who stood in their way. Not that he had ever interested himself in that sort of historical stuff. His own exploration of the coast had been strictly practical. It had been vital to find the right location.

Popular beaches, with ready access to car parking, had to be avoided. From his point of view, far too many locations had had to be ruled out owing to their easy accessibility for evening barbeques and midnight dips. Either that or they were completely inaccessible, with cliffs rearing to impossible heights – the daddy of them all on this stretch, the unimaginatively named High Cliff, which topped off at more than seven hundred feet and overlooked a beach known as The Strangles, where the infamous currents made it far too dangerous to swim.

If this little cove had a name then Stefan was unaware of it. Anonymous Bay – that was how he would think of it. No beach concessions, no car park, no nearby habitation, save for the one property which was part of the plan anyway, and a steep enough descent to discourage all but the most determined from attempting to explore. Off the beaten track, not overlooked from above unless you strayed right over to the cliff edge, and accessible by boat. It ticked all the boxes, as they said on those daytime TV property programmes.

He turned away from the sea and strode back up the beach, the sound of his footfalls increasing as his boots encountered the shingle and larger stones. Spring tides had mostly washed away the evidence of recent cliff falls, but some larger stuff remained: big lumps of earth, ranging from the size of house bricks to lumps as high as a man, littered the base of the cliff. He guessed that the largest of them were the result of particularly substantial collapses, or maybe they were part of the original land, left standing when all about them had fallen. Whatever . . . any one of them would be sufficient to secure a mooring rope.

He bent down and selected a flat rock with a jagged edge from among some of the smaller stuff, balanced it on his hand and regarded it speculatively.

'Looking for fossils?'

Stefan whirled around violently and all but struck out at the stranger, whose approach had been completely masked by the sound of the nearby waves.

'Steady on, there.' The man, though well out of reach, took a precautionary step backwards, his hiking boots slipping and scrunching in the gravel. 'Sorry about that. Did I startle you?'

'No. Yes.' Stefan attempted to regain his customary composure while making some swift calculations. The guy was probably pushing seventy, but evidently fit. Clad in typical hiking gear and carrying a small rucksack. From his accent he was clearly not a local and he appeared to be alone.

Many lone walkers, on encountering a complete stranger, in an otherwise deserted spot, are content to pass by with no more than a nod, respecting a mutual desire for solitude, but the newcomer wasn't one of them. 'Doing the coastal path, are you?'

'No.'

'Fossils, is it? Beachcombing?'

'Just out for a walk.'

'Interesting place,' the older man continued. 'If I hadn't noticed you down here, I'm not sure that I would have tried the path. It's a bit steep in places.' He paused but when Stefan offered nothing in return, he continued, 'Worth it, though. I like to get down by the sea. What do you think of it?'

He was one of those garrulous old fools, Stefan decided, who thinks that everyone longs to chat

6

and just needs a bit of encouragement to join in the conversation. The question was, would he remember meeting Stefan, if the beach made the news, in as little as a few weeks' time? Aloud he said, 'It's just a beach.'

'Well,' the older man gave a chiding sort of laugh, 'you wouldn't say that if you'd grown up in the middle of a town as I did, and never been to the seaside until you were well on into your teens.'

The longer the conversation went on, the more chance there was of him fixing the place and the person he had encountered in his mind. Stefan was very conscious of the rock, still balanced in his hand. Could he make it look like an accident? People did fall from cliffs. There was some spectacular footage on the internet of idiots just stepping off while admiring the view or taking a selfie.

'Do you live round here?'

The bloke just didn't give up, did he? The trouble was that the discovery of a body on the beach would only serve to draw attention to the place, no doubt attracting macabre sightseers for weeks to come. Not at night, of course, which was when the plan would finally come to fruition.

'No. I'm on holiday.' Stefan turned away abruptly, making it clear that any interaction was at an end. He headed back to the place where the steep, zigzag path descended the cliffs, and began to climb it without looking back. On balance, he thought, he would have to take the chance that the bloke wouldn't remember him, or their conversation, such as it had been. Not until he was about halfway up did he glance down at the beach, and to his relief, he saw that the old boy was at the water's edge, facing out to sea, not taking the slightest interest in his retreat.

That was good. He probably just thought Stefan rude or moody and would quickly forget him. Old people didn't remember stuff anyway. If he saw anything in the papers, he wouldn't connect it. The beach didn't even have a name. Anonymous Bay.

He couldn't afford mess-ups. This time there would be no mistakes. When he reached the top of the path, he strode purposefully past the outcrop of stone which marked the start of the descent, then across the rough grass, threading his way between the banks of gorse. The sound of the sea receded, mingling with the passage of the wind, until they merged one into another and he could no longer differentiate between them.

Two

Mark was concentrating on the road when the phone rang, so he couldn't see the caller ID, but naturally he recognized her voice right away.

'Is it a good time?' she asked. 'I just wanted to say one last goodbye, before I catch my flight.'

'Of course,' he said. 'It's always a good time when you call.'

'I've been thinking of you every minute, and

wishing I didn't have to go. I'm nearly at the airport now. It's such a beautiful day. The sky is this fantastic, cloudless blue and the aeroplane trails are criss-crossing. In fact, one of them just made a big kiss in the sky – just as you picked up the phone.'

He laughed. 'You're an incurable romantic, Jude.'

'I shouldn't be.'

He was instantly aware of the sadness which had entered her voice. 'Of course you should be,' he said quickly. 'Everyone should be.'

'After what happened last time . . .'

'I want to make you forget all that.'

'I know. I'm sorry. It's just that . . . he's still out there somewhere.' Her voice, which had been so bright at the outset of the conversation, now took on an all too familiar note, which made her sound as if she was on the edge of tears.

'He's not going to hurt you again. You have me now.'

'It's so hard, sometimes . . .' Her voice had dropped to almost a whisper.

'I do understand.' He consciously tried to sound warmer, softening his voice. If he could only get her to completely trust him. 'I want you to put all that behind you.'

'Of course. I'm sorry,' she said again, adding after the slightest of pauses, 'I shall miss you.'

'I wish you'd let me come with you. I could easily have taken the time. I know you don't like being alone.'

'I'll be OK. I know the hotel. I've stayed there before. It's only business. Dull stuff. I'll soon be

9

home . . . and with these clear skies, it's going to be a lovely flight.'

He let her chatter on for a while, allowing time for her mood to lighten. The point would surely come soon when she would open up a little more and allow him to know something about her 'business interests', once he had completely gained her trust. In the meantime he made no attempt to draw her out regarding the nature of her errand to Spain, but instead listened patiently as she moved on to the inevitable topics of the regular traveller, complaining about all the nonsense, the necessity of being at the airport so many hours in advance, and having to take off your shoes, like you were some kind of terrorist – as if!

Only when she had finally paused for breath, her good humour restored, did he say, 'I had a visit from your brother.'

He let the remark hang in the air, conjuring a period of silence, tangible as a veil of fog or a shower of rain, thickening between them while he waited for her to speak.

'What? Robin came to see you? When? Why?'

'He was checking up on me.'

'Oh dear. Oh no. I wish he wouldn't do things like that.'

'It is a bit insulting, Jude.'

'I'm so sorry. It's . . . I suppose, well . . . because of last time.'

'I realize that. But isn't it rather unfair to assume that I'm some kind of rogue abductor; it's the same principle as airport security, isn't it – one nitwit tries to conceal a bomb in his shoe, so everyone has to remove their footwear forever more?'

'It's the money,' she said sadly. 'Money's a curse. You know. *You* must understand that. Don't tell me there have never been any girls who came after you just because . . .' She allowed the sentence to trail off.

'I'd like to think that any girl who came after me was enchanted by my big brown eyes and ensnared by the size of—'

'That's not something she'd know about on an initial acquaintance.'

'Hey – you didn't let me finish.'

'No – but you weren't going to say bank balance, were you?' She laughed and he joined in, expertly negotiating the M25 slip road, as he did so.

'Maybe I was.'

'No you weren't. Only shallow idiots brag about how much they have. Not People Like Us as Mummy used to say . . . well, what I mean is that some of us . . . Anyway, money's the root of all evil. At least that's what they say.'

'Who's they? Not the people who spend their Saturday's shopping for shoes, I'll bet. Money's a contradiction, with the advantages mostly outweighing the disadvantages. You know that scene in *Fiddler on the Roof*?'

'Which scene?'

'One of the characters, Perchik, says, "Money is the world's curse", then Tevye says, "May the Lord curse me with it, and may I never recover."'

She joined in with his laughter, even though she had no idea what he was talking about. 'I have to go now. I'm at the terminal and I need to pay for the cab.'

'Goodbye, darling. Have a safe flight. Happy travels.' He made a kissing noise down the phone.

Sometimes she could be very hard work. He wondered how long was it going to take for her to *really* trust him? He didn't want to put her off by rushing things, but then again, he didn't have that much time.

Three

Though it hadn't been exactly *Life on Mars* when Graham Ling joined the force, the CID had scarcely been teetotal. In that pre-PC, pre-Elf and Safety, and God alone knew what other initiatives and acronym-ridden time, you could still enjoy a fag without standing furtively in a freezing cold doorway. Lingo, (or 'Old Lingo' as he knew some of them called him) accepted as well as any man that things had moved on, and that in many ways they had improved for the better, but he couldn't help experiencing an occasional pang of nostalgia for those far-off days, when he had superstitiously taken home a beer mat from the celebrations which had marked the completion of every successful job. Sometimes he missed the days of the noisy boys from E Division, roaring at the jokes you couldn't make in any other company, and he found that this nostalgia for times past seemed at its strongest when your best DS was approaching with a tray of oversize paper cups, containing concoctions bearing names like Skinny Latte, which back in the day was more likely to have been the nickname of a local working girl, than something a detective constable ordered to drink.

The lad behind the tray – who was not exactly a lad, as he was approaching thirty – though some days this seemed very young indeed to the fast-approaching-retirement Ling – was Peter Betts. Graham Ling liked Bettsy, in spite of the daft haircut which made him look like Tin Tin, and his pretensions with an electric guitar. As if a copper in CID was ever going to have the time that you needed to put in to playing in a band. He rated Peter Betts a very good detective. A thinker, with the kind of mind which occasionally threw up sparks of sheer inspiration. The sort of guy who as well as being insatiably curious, stubborn and tenacious, was capable of looking beyond the obvious. One day he would end up leading a team of his own – always provided that the uncertain world of music didn't seduce him first.

Ling watched as Betts worked his way around the group, handing the first of the coffee cups to Hannah McMahon. Life in the old-style, macho constabulary would have been all but impossible for a woman with looks like that, he reflected. Even her obvious attempts to desexualize herself and be one of the lads – no obvious perfume, the willingness, nay enthusiasm for discussing foot-ball, and her figure always concealed beneath a smart, self-imposed uniform of trousers and jackets – could not hide the fact that Hannah could easily have been the pin-up of the entire force, if those girly calendars had still been allowed. If anything, Hannah's modest dress sense and preference for being addressed by the androgynous appellation, McMahon, rendered her all the more desirable. 'Touch me not'. Working with McMahon helped you to understand why Victorian males could get worked up over a glimpse of a shapely ankle. Speculation, suggestion, anticipation could be everything. Not, he told himself, that he would ever have been interested – even twenty years ago – not least because he suspected that in private, McMahon could turn out to be a right handful and too smart by half.

All that aside, Hannah was a good girl, he thought. A safe pair of hands, who understood the proper way to do things, the budgetary constraints which bound them, and the methodical approach so vital in evidence gathering, if there was going to be a successful prosecution – but so far as Ling was concerned, she couldn't touch young Bettsy when it came to those sudden moments of inspiration. He had never known Hannah to come up with an idea that everyone else had missed. She was essentially very good at all the painstaking, basically boring stuff, he thought: the CCTV footage which had to be collected and checked, the routine enquiries to be made, the following up of leads, but it was Bettsy who could think outside the box, as they liked to say these days. There was a lad whose thought processes were not tied hand and foot to the straight track – a man who looked around the corners, as it were.

It had been Peter Betts whose comment that, 'this bloke must know his train timetables back to front', followed immediately by, 'are any of our suspects connected to the railways?' had directly led them to the satisfactory resolution of Operation March Hare. And it was that sort of unexpected inspiration which Ling had been hoping for when he decided to gather this small group together for what amounted to little more than an informal chat about the Thackeray kidnap. At its height there had been more than a hundred officers involved in the investigation in one way or another, but today Ling had focussed on just the core of this team: Hannah McMahon, Joel McPartland, Jerry Wilkins and Peter Betts; though it was Bettsy in whom the DI was investing particular hopes. He was aware that Peter Betts had taken a particularly keen interest in the Thackeray case (Hannah McMahon had once joked that it was because he fancied the victim).

Though still officially open, the enquiry had effectively reached a dead end, with no fresh leads to follow, and all personnel gradually transferred to work on other cases They had, of course, spent many hours chewing it over already, but with his retirement less than a year away, it irked Graham Ling to leave any unfinished business. He had a good record – some would say a great record. True, the Tyler murder had never been officially put to bed, but with the death of his main suspect in an RTA, it was never likely to be. Fate occasionally dealt you an impossible

15

hand and you had to take it. The Thackeray kidnap was different. There was no road traffic accident to blame – nor any suspect identified. The case had run up against one brick wall after another.

So here they were, forgetting for an hour or so, those other major enquiries on their desks and chewing over the Thackeray case one more time.

'I've never managed to get a handle on this bloke,' Ling resumed the discussion as soon as the various coffees, pastries and sundry assortment of other goodies had been distributed, and everyone had settled down. 'He's not your usual run-of-the-mill offender.'

'I don't think the profiler came up with anything particularly concrete,' put in Hannah McMahon.

'Well he wouldn't, would he? It was all the usual generalities and psychobabble.' Joel McPartland took a dubious view of the supposed science of criminal profiling, and knew that his boss felt the same way.

'It always struck me as kind of odd,' Jerry Wilkins said, 'that he never took the chance to have sex with her, one last time, before he finished her off.'

'But he didn't finish her off,' Hannah objected. 'She got away from him.'

'So you reckon he was saving up for the moment, and might have had her just before he killed her. While she was tied up in the back of the van.'

'Really, Jerry. You shouldn't impute every suspect with your own perverted notions regarding sexual congress.' Hannah took a sip of her drink

16

and grinned, to show she meant nothing by the remark.

'I'd guess that Laddo was way too smart to leave us his DNA by having sex with Jude Thackeray, just before murdering her,' put in Joel, whose deep voice gave an air of finality to his pronouncements. Joel was a huge guy, with Afro-Caribbean origins, who had in the past proved a brilliant asset for plainclothes operations, because he looked far more like a night club bouncer than most people's stereotypical idea of a copper. 'From what the victim said, there had been plenty of consensual sex up until a couple of days before he took her prisoner.'

'Perhaps he didn't much fancy her, once he'd tied her up, tortured her and shoved her in that cupboard under the stairs for twenty-four hours,' said Hannah, with a touch of sarcasm. 'Presumably bondage isn't every man's dream.'

'What I find odd,' Peter Betts spoke for the first time since returning with the coffees, 'is the way this guy was sometimes very smart, then sometimes really dumb.'

Ling who had been listening to what was said, while consuming a bacon-filled croissant, now paused in the act of taking another bite and prompted, 'Meaning?'

'He covered his tracks in all sorts of ways, then stopped at the garage to buy some diesel and got picked up on their CCTV. It's a clumsy mistake. He could easily have filled up the van any time beforehand, and used a garage several miles away – but he actually stopped at the garage closest to the crime scene, *with Jude Thackeray tied up in*

17

the back. That's got to be reckless. He must have known that pretty much all garage forecourts are covered by CCTV, and that we're going to check the ones on the route between the house where she was held captive and the place where he intended to dispose of her.'

'I'm not so sure . . .' Hannah hesitated. 'Don't forget that she wasn't meant to get away. He couldn't have foreseen that she would escape, and therefore that we'd be looking for him so quickly. He intended to kill her and dump her body in the woods. If he'd managed to carry that through, it might have been weeks before anyone found her, with no guarantee that she would be reported missing right away. It could have been several days before the alarm was raised and a lot longer than that before we had a body.'

'Anyway, as it turned out, it wasn't that dumb,' Jerry put in. 'Because even when that footage was shown on national TV, no one recognized the guy.'

'Something to do with the way he kept his head down and had a hoodie pulled down over his face,' Joel put in, taking his own turn at sarcasm.

'I don't understand how a girl like that was taken in so easily. Why didn't she smell a rat when he kept making excuses not to meet her friends? The only person close to Jude Thackeray who ever set eyes on the bloke was her brother, and he wasn't a lot of help.'

'Perhaps she didn't realize – I think she said they seemed like good excuses. "He always found some reason," is what she said.'

'Apart from the garage, he was pretty good at

18

avoiding CCTV. He withdrew her money from cashpoints without getting caught on any CCTV, and he left his mobile off, so there was no chance of tracking his movements that way.'

'That's the sort of thing I mean,' Peter Betts put in. 'He's savvy enough to be aware of phone tracking, so he gets himself a pay-as-you-go mobile, and the only time he uses it is when she calls him, or he calls her and those calls don't happen very often and are all in random places which don't form any sort of pattern and don't lead us anywhere. Who the hell has a mobile phone that's constantly switched off?'

'My mother,' said Jerry, with feeling.

'Apart from Jerry's mother. Basically this guy must be using some other phone that we don't know about for all his other calls. He buys the pay-as-you-go mobile and activates it just days before he first makes contact with Jude Thackeray. He never calls anyone but her with it. He never receives any calls on it except from her. When he uses the phone to call her, he's always in some nice out-of-the-way spot, which we can't match up to any CCTV. It's the same when she calls him. He really only has the phone switched on when he's around her – in places where we already know that he is – her cottage, her car.'

'You'd think she would have found it weird,' Hannah mused. 'Most people I know are on their mobiles all the time, texting and tweeting and checking Facebook.'

'And he wasn't into photographs either. No selfies. No images of him at all.'

19

'And again, she never notices at the time, how unusual that is,' said Joel.

'According to Jude Thackeray, he wasn't into social media and said that he thought Twitter was moronic.'

'Some would say he has a point,' Graham Ling said with feeling. 'You know, there's got to be something else. I want to run a mini-review. Shake up the bag and see if anything falls out.' He winced at hearing himself use a hoist-it-up-the-flagpole-and-see-who-salutes type expression. 'It's been more than six months,' he continued. 'There must be something more that we can work on, other than that bloody CCTV from the garage forecourt. Everyone makes mistakes.'

'He did,' Hannah said quietly. 'He let her get away.'

Four

'Jude . . . Jude . . .' Mark repeated her name with increasing determination, trying to sound calm, even as she thrashed and fought beside him. 'Jude, darling. It's me. It's Mark. Please . . . come on, you're safe. I'm here. It's me, Jude. It's Mark.'

It was her first night back from Spain, and he had arranged a candlelit dinner, before making love to her in his bed. He had attempted to gently probe for details of her mysterious errand in Spain, but when she remained tight-lipped about it – as she did regarding all financial matters – he had backed off at once. Overall he thought the evening had gone very well, but now, in the early hours of the morning, she had startled him out of a deep sleep, crying out and thrashing about, as if in the grip of some terrible demons. He continued to repeat her name, trying to calm her until she was fully awake. They had been here before and the nightmares were inevitably followed by a tearful, apologetic interlude.

'I'm sorry, I'm so sorry.' She was always apologizing, as if enduring the aftershocks of a past trauma were in some way a weakness – an indulgence like getting too drunk, or being caught out in another man's bed.

'Shall I switch on the lights? Get you something to drink?'

'No, thank you. Just, please, hold me.'

It wasn't completely dark in the bedroom, because she always had to have a nightlight, to keep at bay the terrors which lurked in darkened rooms, but he couldn't see her face, because she had nestled into his chest. He could, however, feel her trembling.

'It was the same dream,' she confided, uninvited. 'I was in the back of the van, lying on the polythene sheet, and my hands were tied behind me, and I could feel the pain in my wrists, just like it was, so real, so real . . . and I could see the spare pairs of plastic gloves and the wire noose he was going to use to strangle me. Then he stopped the van and came round the back, just like it all happened in real life. He was wearing the black clothes and the mask, just the same as he did that night and I remember thinking how weird that

21

was, because of course we both knew that I knew who he was and what he looked like. He opened the van door, then he said something under his breath and closed it again, and – this is hard to explain – although I didn't exactly know that I was dreaming, I somehow knew that the van door shouldn't be shut properly, because that was how I was going to manage to get away from him, but when I wriggled across to the door, it *was* closed, and I was trapped in the back of the van. I tried to scream and the gag cut into the sides of my mouth and then he came back . . .'

She was sobbing now. Mark tried to silence her, hugging her close and repeating her name, but she continued regardless of him.

'He dragged me out of the van and put the wire noose over my head.' Her whole body was vibrating with sobs as she relived the moment. 'He forced me to walk away from the van, into the trees with this thing around my neck and a knife in my back.'

'Shush, shush. But that didn't happen, did it? You got away. My brave, beautiful girl got away – and now you're safe, with me.'

Five

'I hate to say this, Jude, but I'm not sure. One or two things about him just don't stack up.'

'You're wrong, Rob. I know you're wrong.' Jude paused in the act of drinking her coffee and

22

tousled Rob's hair in an affectionate gesture. 'He told me that you'd been to "interview him", as he put it, and he took it really well, all things considered.'

'And what constitutes "really well"?'

'Well, obviously he didn't like it. I mean, no one likes being checked up on by Big Brother, do they? But he wasn't phased – not the way he would have been, if he had something to hide.'

'It's very easy to construct a plausible front.'

'But why would he?'

'Oh *come on,* Jude. Get with the programme, for God's sake.'

'I'm not clear what it has to do with God,' she said.

'You know what I mean.'

'Look – he's independently wealthy—'

'How can you be *absolutely* sure about that?'

'For heaven's sake. He's made it abundantly clear that he doesn't need my money. He never lets me pay for anything. It's positively retro the way he always insists on picking up the bills. And he's completely fallen for me – head over heels. He's so patient, when I suffer from flashbacks and things – honestly, you wouldn't believe it.'

'It's all happened far too quickly.' Rob continued to dissent. 'A whirlwind romance. You only met him a couple of months ago and he's talking about marrying you. Doesn't that strike you as a bit sudden? Isn't there even the tiniest bit of déjà vu about it?'

'Actually it strikes me as a wonderful piece of luck. Who could have foreseen it?'

23

There was a pause. He caught her eye but she stared him down.

'He says he wants to protect me, and give me a sense of security.'

'Well he would say that, wouldn't he? If he's a fake.'

'He's not a fake. I'm telling you, he's the genuine article.' She stood up and collected the now empty mugs from the table.

'You've fallen for him, that's the trouble.' He couldn't keep the anger out of his voice.

'Rubbish.' She laughed and bent down to kiss him on the top of the head in passing. 'I promise you that I am not letting my feelings override my personal judgement. I've found the right man in Mark Medlicott. He's the dream ticket.'

'I'm going to do some more checking up – here and there – wherever I can.'

'Rob—' she walked around the sofa in order to face him – 'please be careful. I don't want you to mess this up.'

He was not very good at suppressing his mood. 'We have to be sure,' he said, unconsciously clenching and unclenching a fist, as he spoke. 'Remember he knew who you were right away.'

'That could apply to anyone. The case was all over the newspapers. "Heiress kidnapped" was the headline in the *Daily Mail*. The *Mirror* called me a "spoiled little rich girl", if I recall.'

'They would. If the *Socialist Worker* covered the case, it was probably to demand that wealthy parasites like you be instantly rounded up and shot. But my point is that after nationwide publicity, you naturally became a target for conmen.'

'We've been through all this before,' she said wearily. 'A conman would assume that I don't make a good target second time around, because I'm wary. I'm on the police radar . . .'

'But it won't have taken him long to realize that you don't have any personal security. There's no bodyguard. No active police monitoring.'

'You're being too suspicious.' Her tone was persuasive, almost pleading.

'I'm being cautious. Do you want to end up in the back of a van, trussed hand and foot, with a gag in your mouth?'

'Lightning doesn't strike twice,' she snapped back at him. 'And please don't remind me. I've had to relive that episode too many times. You have no idea what it's like, or what I went through that night.' She was holding his gaze again, staring him out.

'I'm sorry, but I'm still going to do some more digging. For both our sakes.' It was his turn now to adopt a pleading note.

'For goodness sake, Rob, please don't interfere. I know what I'm doing.'

Six

Detective Constable Peter Betts was lying full length on the king-size bed, his eyes closed, trying to ward off the truth as portrayed by his digital clock. He didn't want to get up for work, because just at that moment, he didn't want to go anywhere or do anything. What he needed was time to think. He couldn't think properly at work, because work represented other kinds of thinking, which usually required all his concentration. Just now he needed to think about the email he had picked up the previous evening. An unexpected message which he had yet to answer. He had been thinking about the message when he had fallen asleep the night before (ever since first starting shift work, he had never lost the ability to drop off the moment his head touched the pillow) and it had been the first thing to enter his head when he had woken up that morning.

The very fact that he had to think about his reply at all was what worried him most. He had always wanted to be a policeman. When the other little kids had been into Postman Pat and Thomas the Tank Engine, he had eschewed the idea of a future career in the Post Office or on the railways, and attended his local playgroup proudly sporting a plastic policeman's helmet, acquired on a day trip to London. As he was gradually allowed access to more and more grown-up television programmes, he had fallen in love with the idea all over again. Unlike the other kids, his heroes had never been the fast-talking, sharp-shooting Bruce Willis types. No, Bettsy, as he had been known even then, had preferred to identify with the crusty old Brits like Frost and Morse, who though they occasionally gave chase, or had to physically restrain a suspect, usually arrived at a solution by brain power in the end.

Getting accepted for the police had been his dream. By the time he was old enough to apply, he had long known that the police forces of television drama were well divorced from the police forces of reality, but even so, nothing had ever dimmed that original ambition. Peter Betts had always wanted to be a detective. And now he was one.

In his teenage years, when everyone else was doing weed and making music, he had – albeit very briefly – considered a change of direction. He'd smoked the occasional spliff and become a more than half decent guitarist, whose vocal skills were well above average. He had been in a band at school – well who hadn't? And later on, local bands had sometimes sought his services, and yes, it was true, once or twice he had wavered. Why not become a musician? He had no aspirations to write his own music, but that didn't matter, because his skill and passion lay in covering old standards, and plenty of people had told him that there was work for young, lively, talented musicians with a wide traditional repertoire and no ties.

The police force had always won, but he had retained his connections with a few musical mates, and continued to fill in for people at the occasional gig, and this in turn had led him the closest he had come so far to having any ties. He had originally been introduced to Ginny when the guitarist in Shuffle 'n' Deal fell ill and a replacement was needed at short notice. He had been on eight till four at the time, which made him available for their Saturday-night gig, for which he'd been recommended by a friend of a friend. Ginny was the band's vocalist, and had

27

viewed his arrival as stand-in at a last-minute rehearsal with undisguised alarm. 'A copper?' she had exclaimed on learning that he wasn't even a proper, full-time, professional musician. 'You're having me on? Please tell me that you're not serious?'

Later on that evening, their perfect harmonizing during 'Bye Bye Love' had excited him – albeit in a different way – nearly as much as had sleeping with her in the early hours of the next morning. Ginny had been the least serious, yet most serious, relationship he had ever had. They had enjoyed going to bed together, yet suffered no illusions about being in love.

At the same time, Ginny had been the first and only person who had ever seriously dented his assurance in his own destiny. She wasn't the sort of person to be impressed by job security or a good pension. She didn't factor in the particular reward which comes of undertaking a socially important job, and doing it responsibly and well. What she did understand was the unique joy of creating great music. Security, social responsibility, steady salary – none of it came close. 'We're great together,' she had said – and he had known from the get-go that she was right. He had continued to fill in at the band's gigs, work rotations permitting, until their regular guitarist had made a full recovery. (Shingles, Ginny had explained. Extremely nasty.) There had even been some vague talk of him ousting Jared, the unfortunate shingles-sufferer, and even vaguer suggestions of himself and Ginny breaking away, to form their own

28

band. 'I've got the contacts,' she had said. 'We wouldn't be short of work.'

The police force had won out. In spite of the tensions, the pressures, the cutbacks, the nonsense government directives, he loved his job, he told her, at which she had shaken her head in disbelief. It was the same night that they had received a standing ovation – come off stage on a complete high, Ginny's eyes shining, Baz, the drummer, laughing like he was drunk. That sort of applause was a buzz like no other. It had only been a corporate bash, not exactly the Royal Albert Hall and small beer to a great many bands, but when Ginny's eyes met his across the four feet of stage which separated them, he knew that she was asking him what the police force had to offer, which could ever possibly compete with that feeling?

Shuffle 'n' Deal had been offered a contract to work on a cruise ship soon afterwards. Six months gigging around the Caribbean, playing sets each evening and during the daytime too, when the ship was at sea, with time off for sightseeing and soaking up the sun on their days in port. He had found it hard to say goodbye to Ginny – not so much to the Ginny who had sometimes shared his bed, and whose untidiness and ill-informed views had begun to grate, but rather to Ginny the performer, with whom singing and playing had never been sweeter. Subsequently he had often found himself wondering what she and the band were doing, particularly when he was wading through mounds of paper work, or hanging about in court, waiting for an assault on his credibility from some smart-ass barrister. Ginny had cheerfully informed him that she wasn't good at keeping in touch, but they had maintained a desultory contact by email, and it was vaguely understood that they would at the very least meet up for a drink when she got home. Ginny's typing and spelling were so execrable that some of her messages lent themselves to multiple interpretations and occasionally verged on the incomprehensible, but in spite of this there had been no difficulty whatsoever about understanding her most recent communication.

> *Pleaz think abut this. We v been ofered anoter 6 mnth contract same ship starting Janurary. Jared still mising Annie and not intrested. We alked and we want you.*
> *No need to anser rigtaway.*
> *Luv Ginny xx*

A year ago, he wouldn't even have hesitated before sending a politely worded refusal. He had always been absolutely confident about where his future lay, so the very fact that he now had to think about it was worrying. He loved his job, didn't he? He was good at it. It represented ambitions fulfilled, while continuing to offer goals which he had yet to achieve. Was it merely because he could hear the English summer rain hitting the window panes that the thought of spending six months belting out 'Johnny Be Good' by night and slumming on golden sandy beaches by day, sounded so seductive? In a moment of weakness, he had checked the ship's itinerary online and discovered that the contract coincided with a round-the-world cruise: New York, San Francisco, New Zealand, Australia, Hong Kong, Japan . . . He had never been further than a package to Rhodes.

You couldn't just drop out of CID for six months or a year, then drop back in again. Leaving was a big step.

It gave him a jolt to recognize that he was actually thinking about it. He'd never done anything wild. There had been no gap year, no sowing wild oats, or going off travelling. If he wasn't careful, he would be approaching fifty, and a sad old copper like DI Ling.

That was unfair. Lingo was not sad. He was a good bloke. Peter liked and respected him. But did he want to be him? Did he want to spend the best years of his life chasing after fuckwits who stole cars, robbed the local Cash'n'Carry, or got too drunk to find their way home and ended up decking somebody? How many more perverts, fantasists, morons and murderers would it take for him to become so dislocated from ordinary life, that he suspected everyone of being secretly up to something? How many more tons of useless new regulations? How many more pointless evaluations, awareness days and other hoop-jumping exercises?

In the shower he found himself humming 'Johnny Be Good'. He stopped immediately, as if caught in some unspeakable act. He reminded himself that he was doing what he wanted to do – and it was worthwhile. Ridding the streets of the baddies, making society a safer place, getting

31

justice for people who'd been wronged – that was what he was ultimately about. Last year he had been part of Operation Nimble, which had ended with a trio of hardened, violent, career criminals being handed sentences which would keep them out of everyone's hair for the next decade. Ling and his team had been justifiably jubilant. No other job could ever offer that level of camaraderie, or satisfaction. Or of frustration. At first he had taken them hard, those acquittals after months of painstaking work. Graham Ling had taken him aside the first time it happened. 'No use raging against the system,' he had said. 'Always remember that there's no such thing as a safe conviction, unless the defendant has been given the best possible defence. It wasn't our day today, kid, and that's sometimes the way it is.'

The face of Jude Thackeray rose up in his mind, unbidden. The team talk a couple of days before had taken them precisely nowhere, but Lingo had decided that someone should take a more detailed look, assigning Peter himself, and Hannah McMahon to the task, giving them a week to look through the information and talk everything through again, just in case there was something sitting in the files that had been missed. He had known Lingo employ the technique once before, half-jokingly referring to it as a 'warm case review'.

Peter understood the way that Lingo felt about the Thackeray case, because it was a feeling that he shared. It represented one of the team's biggest frustrations: literally thousands of man hours spent on an investigation which had come up with basically nothing. No arrest, no credible suspects, even. If he stayed in the force, how many Jude Thackerays was he going to let down in the next twenty-five years?

The Thackeray woman's face – pale, bruised and distraught, the way he had first seen it – gave way to Ginny's face, leaning in towards the mic, as if she was about to kiss it, her lips parting in readiness to sing.

Seven

'You have reached your destination.'

'Thanks Pam.' Mark only addressed his Sat Nav aloud when there was no one else in the car to hear him. Quite apart from anything else, he didn't want to have to explain why he called her Pam, after a primary school teacher that he had never quite forgiven, or the way it amused him to imagine prim-voiced Mrs Dangerfield, trapped somewhere in the dark confines beneath the bonnet of his car, eternally condemned to issue directions, while remaining uncharacteristically cool and patient, when he defied her with the occasional wrong turn.

Of course, he hadn't actually reached his destination, because he knew that in this rural part of East Anglia the postcode would cover a long stretch of road, and the property he had come to see might be anywhere for several hundred yards in either direction, or even off down an adjacent lane. He slowed the car a fraction more, scanning the name plates which stood at the end of each drive. Some places were visible from the road and could be ruled out immediately, because he knew from the old press photographs pretty much what Jude's house looked like from the road. The photos had already given him an idea of the property's potential worth, but he wanted to confirm it for himself. It would give him more confidence about what he had to do, particularly after the conversation with Chaz two days ago.

'I only need another couple of months.' As he uttered the words, he had recognized something of the tone which he had been wont to use for Mrs Dangerfield. 'It wasn't me, Miss, honest.' Wheedling and weak. It was sickening to find himself still pleading with people at his age and after all the hard work he had put in, all the successes which had led to the money, which had in turn led to playing for higher and higher stakes.

People naturally assumed that his father had backed him when he set up in the property game, but after financing Mark's education, his father had been unwilling to offer anything at all unless it was repaid by hours of long, hard graft, learning the ropes in the family business, en-route to a directorship alongside his elder brothers. To his father's undisguised annoyance, Mark had never considered the substantial perks and salary this would eventually bring sufficiently attractive to outweigh the disadvantages of working alongside his father and brothers for the rest of his life, so he had turned his back on three generations in engineering and instead used his name, connections and wits to build up, then sell on, a property holding company, and it had all been going brilliantly until a spell of bad luck and misjudged investments had all but wiped him out.

If his father or mother had still been alive, he could have gone cap in hand, but she had succumbed to cancer while he had still been in his teens, and with the old man gone as well, he hadn't fancied his chances with Monty and Michael. They had always presented a united front against him, those fitter, smarter, bigger brothers, tormenting him throughout childhood, sneering at his initial schemes for independence, and then resenting his successful escape south. Quite apart from anything else, he could never bring himself to give them the satisfaction of knowing that the house of cards had fallen about his ears.

It had almost come to that, as the unpaid bills had mounted up and the creditors began to circle, but then a friend had introduced him to Chaz, and it had been like an answer to a prayer. Chaz understood perfectly how a chap could get into trouble temporarily and need a little bit of help in the form of a large cash advance. The arrangement would be discreet, without need of references, or paperwork. 'A gentleman's agreement' had been the words used.

Chaz did not advance any cash himself, but he had what he described as 'various useful contacts', which included an unnamed friend, who needed someone plausible to turn up at various race meetings and place a few big bets on races where the outcome was a sure thing. In exchange for this service, Chaz's friend would advance a substantial sum to Mark, a proportion of which was a 'drink' for services rendered, and the remainder of it would be easily repayable thanks to the fact that Chaz's friend had no problem with Mark's taking advantage of the situation, by separately wagering some money of his own on the various tips which he received. Chaz had said that was the whole idea – he should look on it as his commission. After his own run of bad luck, Mark liked the idea of recouping his losses with a few certainties and he knew that he made an ideal front man, having already acquired a bit of a reputation as a high-stakes gambler. Serendipity. Or it would have been, if during the course of his third visit to a race meeting, armed with a large wad of cash belonging to Chaz's mysterious contact, he had not somehow misunderstood the instructions and backed the wrong horse, taking a big hit for himself, as well as for Chaz's unknown friend.

Mark had never seen this 'friend', and up until that moment had vaguely imagined him to be urbane and gentlemanly, as was Chaz himself, but after the mistake at Towcester, the mental image had begun to waver, with Chaz's friend gradually transforming into a big bloke, surrounded by heavies, straight out of *Get Carter*, or *Lock, Stock and Two Smoking Barrels*, who could inflict lasting – maybe even permanent – damage upon his person. When he had attempted to explain the Towcester mess-up to Chaz, Chaz had made it perfectly clear that his friend was unlikely to take the news of the loss well.

Mark had replayed the business of the mixed-up numbers again and again in his mind, and he still didn't understand how he had come to transpose them or to confuse the race time, or whatever the hell it was that he had done. Another commission had been forthcoming, but he was now extremely limited in the amount that he could personally raise to lay out, and factoring the stake money he had lost at Towcester into the picture meant that it was going to take much longer to clear the overall debt. What had looked like a lifeline, now appeared nothing more than another deadweight, dragging him further and further into the mire. Mark knew that the sooner he could draw a line under the relationship with Chaz and his friend, the better it would be. In his worst moments he had even begun to wonder whether he had made a mistake at all – whether it was possible that he had been deliberately fed the wrong information, in order to render him even more indebted than he already was. But no – that made no sense – you would have to be paranoid to think a thing like that.

He was so preoccupied by his recollections of the business with Chaz, that he almost drove right past the thick conifer hedge which screened Laurel Cottage from the road. There was only a modest sign to identify the house: an ankle-level wooden plaque on a post stuck in the grass verge, and easily missed. As he applied his foot to the brake, the thought occurred to him that either the place had been christened years before the planting of the leylandii, or else someone did not know their arboriculture very well.

Jude was safely in Spain again for a couple of days and anyway she had already told him that she never came here since the failed kidnap attempt, so he swung the car straight in between the wooden gateposts which marked either side of the entrance, confident in the knowledge that the place would be empty. The house and garden were completely invisible until he turned into the drive, where he was astonished to see that the lawn was littered with kids' toys. A little girl with her hair in bunches was bouncing on a circular trampoline, while a woman – presumably her mother – lay on a sun lounger nearby. The woman had been reading a magazine, but the arrival of Mark's car caused her to look up, curious, maybe even a little startled by the presence of an unexpected visitor.

His tyres skidded to a halt on the gravel. Shit. This wasn't in the script. For a second he considered reversing the car straight back into the lane and speeding away, but that wasn't a good idea at all. Far better to improvise something which would allay her suspicions.

He silenced the engine and climbed out of the driver's seat, attempting a reassuring smile. The woman stood up, as if in readiness to meet him and the child stopped bouncing to stare at him, falling forward onto her knees, as the trampoline continued to vibrate beneath her. Though she endeavoured to hide it, the woman's anxiety was plainly written on her face. Laurel Cottage, Elmley Green, was an infamous address, after all. A woman had been held captive here for several days, and the man who had clearly intended to murder her was still at large.

'Sorry to bother you.' He called out to her across the grass, making no attempt to approach. He knew how important it was not to arouse the slightest curiosity and above all to appear unthreatening. It would be all too easy for her to memorize his number plate and make a call to the police, after he had gone. 'I'm trying to find Green Hedges.' (Green Hedges? Where the heck had that come from? Wasn't it the name of the house where Enid Blyton used to live?) 'My Sat Nav's got me this far, but I can't find the house. I saw your big hedge and I thought this might be it.' (Clever touch. Green Hedges was coming in handy after all.)

'I'm afraid I don't know it. We haven't lived here very long. This is Laurel Cottage.' The woman had relaxed somewhat, apparently willing to accept the innocent nature of his errand and seemed further reassured by his immediately preparing to resume his position in the car. 'You could maybe try asking at White Gates – it's only a little way on down the lane. They've lived here forever, and know everything about everybody. You'll see it easily enough, because of the big white gates . . . obviously.' She gave a short, slightly nervous laugh.

It was precisely the opening he needed. 'Not much sign of the laurels now,' he said, cocking his head in the direction of the impenetrable wall of leylandii which stood between the large expanse of lawn and the lane. 'Will you change the name of your house to something more appropriate, do you think?'

'It's not ours to change. We're only renting, while my husband does some contract work locally.'

'Well, it looks like a lovely spot to spend the summer. Specially now the weather's perked up. I'll leave you to enjoy it while you can.'

He gave a cheery wave as he climbed back into the car, taking a final glance around which encompassed the woman, her little girl and the entirety of the 'lovely spot' as he did so. A sense of relief filtered back as he reversed carefully into the lane. Jude had put some temporary tenants in. Fine. No problem. He hadn't managed to get as much of a look at it as he would have liked, but it was a nice place, in a desirable location, and he was confident that the purchase price would more than meet his obligations to Chaz's invisible friend. It surely wouldn't take much to persuade Jude that she would be better off selling a house which could bring back nothing but unhappy memories. She needed to make a clean break from the past and if he became her husband, he could help her to do it, volunteering to look after the whole transaction, leaving her nothing to do but sign the papers. That way she wouldn't even have to approve any estate agents' pictures, see its name printed anywhere, or so much as give the place a second thought. All she had to do was trust him – and she was beginning to do that more and more with every day that passed.

Eight

'I'm going for coffee, do you want your usual?'
Joel stood poised above Peter Betts's desk. For
such a big man he moved remarkably quietly,
often appearing as if from nowhere and startling
his colleagues with the sound of the voice: a bass
rumble which had terrified the wits out of many
a miscreant when PC McPartland was still a beat
officer and had arrived unexpectedly on the scene
and found them up to no good.

'Cheers, mate, but I've only just finished one.'

'I'm good too.' Hannah McMahon had not been
so deeply engaged with the papers on her desk
that she had failed to spot Joel's arrival, and was
scarcely able to control her mirth at Bettsy's
startled reaction and swift recovery.

'They ought to make him wear a bell or something,' Peter grumbled, when his colleague had
moved on. 'He'll end up giving some poor bugger
a heart attack – and not necessarily someone on
the wrong side.'

'He's probably doing it on purpose. I reckon
he'd rather be reviewing the Thackeray case, than
mucking about with the CPS over the Rashid
brothers. The Rashid case is a mess.'

'We've all had our share of crap to deal with,'
Peter said cheerfully. 'Guess it's just Joel's
turn.'

'Nah – this isn't about taking turns. The boss

41

gave you this because he knows how much you care about Jude Thackeray.'

He couldn't help but notice her faintly provocative tone. 'The Old Man doesn't allocate work on that basis,' he said. 'You know and I know that if he thought there was the slightest possibility of emotional involvement between an officer and a victim, he'd pull them off the case faster than you can say, "It's my round".'

'Yeah, yeah, no need to bite.'

'Sorry – didn't realize that I was.'

'Is something up with you? I'm not getting personal or anything, but you seem a bit out there today.' Hannah's voice had lost its teasing note.

'I'm OK. I just got an email from a mate that's set me back a bit.'

'Bad news?'

Typical woman, he thought. The other guys in the team would have left it alone, but McMahon, though her normal persona was one of trying to out-bloke the blokes – insisting on being addressed by her surname, toughing everything out, expecting and receiving no concessions – had suddenly chosen the worst possible moment to reinvent herself as the concerned, motherly colleague, to whom you could take your problems. Well, no . . . that was not entirely fair. McMahon was capable of displaying as much kindness and compassion as the next person. Joel, or Jerry, or any one of the team might have asked as much. He knew that behind the sometimes abrasive exterior, there was a generous colleague, who any one of them would be happy to have covering their back, whatever the situation.

'Not at all. Just the opposite.' He could see that she was curious, but he didn't want to say more – not yet. Apart from anything else he knew that she wouldn't get it. McMahon might be sympathetic, but when it came to the job, she thought in straight lines. Like all of them, she had probably already made sacrifices to her career. Being a copper was an all or nothing proposition, and he knew without even discussing it, that to someone like her, the notion of giving it all up – just like that – for a life as an itinerant musician, would be the height of madness. A series of chords sounded somewhere in the far recesses of his mind. Hannah McMahon probably didn't even know 'Johnny Be Good'.

'So,' he said, as if the pause while she waited, presumably hoping that he was going to say something more about his mysterious email, had actually been him taking a moment to gather his thoughts about the Thackeray case. 'Ready to walk through what we know about Mr X?'

She nodded and began: 'He called himself Rod Stanley, but so far as we've been able to ascertain, there's no such person. He didn't go to much trouble over creating a false ID. Never had a driver's licence, never tried to open a bank account. Now there's something you might have thought would trigger suspicions straight away – someone who always pays for everything with cash. Why didn't Jude Thackeray pick up on that?'

'I don't suppose she particularly noticed. They went on a couple of dates together. He takes her to a classy restaurant and settles the bill in cash, leaving a generous tip. She's enjoying her night out, loves the way this guy is making her feel – I'm sure she said that once, in a statement – "I loved the way he made me feel." By the end of the evening she's had a few drinks and is anticipating a nice romantic interlude back at her place. She isn't putting together an evidential trail for kidnap and attempted murder, so why should she particularly notice, or care, whether the guy uses cash or plastic to pay the bill?'

'That's another thing. They always go back to her place.'

'Because he says his place is in Leeds.'

'Which of course it isn't.'

'Actually it could be,' Peter demurred. 'Given that we don't know who he is, or where he lives.'

'Well, I bet it jolly old well isn't in Leeds, because every single thing he told her seems to have been a complete lie – and I'm pretty sure she describes him as having no noticeable accent.'

'Not everyone from Yorkshire is an eee-by-gummer. And he may have really believed that only saddos followed Twitter.' Peter kept all but a tiny edge of mischief out of his voice. He suspected that McMahon was a closet social media addict.

'So . . .' She failed to rise to the bait. 'He must have been living somewhere within reasonable proximity to Elmley Green in the early stages of the relationship, but we never managed to find out where. He told Jude Thackeray that his firm was putting him up at the George and Dragon Hotel in Ipswich, but the hotel had never heard

44

of him and she couldn't pick him out from any of the guests on their CCTV.'

'Hardly surprising, since this guy generally avoided anywhere with CCTV cameras like the plague.'

'Except for the camera at the garage on the night when he had her in the back of the van,' Hannah put in.

'Except for that one time, yeah.' Peter shook his head, as if attempting to reorder the thoughts inside it. He was thinking of the hours and hours that had been spent, trailing around every hotel and guest house within a thirty-mile radius, trying to find an establishment which had played host to Mr Rod Stanley. 'So,' he continued, 'various possible men who matched the description identified at hotels and guest houses in the area, all of them eventually eliminated. No record of anyone renting a room, flat or house in the general vicinity to a Rod Stanley, or anyone who even resembled him. Or at least, there are plenty of blokes who look a bit like him, but none of them *are* him.'

'Then there's the car . . .'

Peter managed to suppress a groan at the mention of the car. Or rather cars – in the plural – which Graham Ling and his team had vainly attempted to track down.

'Or rather cars,' said Hannah, echoing his thoughts. 'Jude Thackeray reckons she saw him driving at least three different cars. He explains that by telling her that the firm is fixing him up with a series of hire cars. She can't even describe the first one.'

'She's not into cars.'

'I know. Basically this woman is a rubbish witness.'

Hannah's exasperated tone set him jumping to the victim's defence. 'Oh, come off it, McMahon, she did her best.'

'I always said you had a soft spot for her.'

'Look, she managed to give us a colour and make for the other two vehicles and the digits in the registration plate of one of them.'

'Yeah.' Hannah's sarcasm was blatant. 'That really narrowed the field.'

'So – no joy with hire companies or stolen vehicles. There's always the possibility that one of them was his own car.'

'If it was, then you can bet it was the first one – the one that she couldn't remember at all,' said Hannah grimly.

'Then there's the white van. A Vauxhall Movano, stolen seven weeks before Mr X first encounters Jude Thackeray, which proves that he'd planned the whole thing very carefully, well in advance. The van was taken from outside a small block of flats, where a self-employed electrician had turned his back for a few minutes, leaving his vehicle unlocked. Van then completely disappears until the night of the attempted murder, when the next definite sighting is on the drive of Laurel Cottage, when he frogmarches Jude Thackeray outside, bound and gagged, and she's confronted with the van, which he forces her to climb into the back of. He then drives the van to a garage to pick up fuel—'

'For which he of course pays in cash,' put in Hannah.

46

'One CCTV camera picks him up on the fore-court and another one captures him entering the shop to pay, but he's wearing a hoodie and never raises his head, so we don't get a proper look at him. He drives on to Foxden Woods, where he muffs what should have been the final act in the drama. The victim manages to get away and when he can't find her in the dark, he eventually gives up searching and drives to a secluded lay-by off the Little Fordesley to Benton Heath road, where he sets fire to the van, thereby buggering our chances of any helpful forensics from the one vehicle we can tie him to.'

'So – we then get to the only helpful witnesses in the entire case,' Hannah prompted.

'Right. Mr Smethurst and Mrs Adderley – old-fashioned adulterers, meeting at a normally deserted beauty spot, after dark, for a dose of extramarital passion.'

'I can't imagine doing it in a car, can you?'

'I think that would qualify as an unprofessional enquiry, Miss McMahon,' he said with a grin. 'Anyway . . . these two lovebirds arrive and they're surprised to find that there's a car already parked there. Adderley gets there first – she's obviously keen.'

'Just a better timekeeper, being a woman.'

'She thinks the strange car is empty, but it's dark and she isn't sure. It puts the wind up her and she decides to drive on to a lay-by further down the road, where she tries to ring Lover Boy, but he hasn't got a hands free – and being a generally good egg, in spite of cheating on his wife, he doesn't pick up until he reaches their usual place of assignation, where he stops to check who's just called him, sees that it's Adderley and returns her call. He has obviously seen the strange car too and like her, he assumes that there's no one inside, but he agrees with her that they need to find an alternative venue for their little tryst. It's too dark to be sure what colour the car is, but he is pretty sure that it's a dark-coloured BMW.'

'For me,' said Hannah, 'this car has always been the best thing we've got. Mr X clearly left it there, in readiness to make his getaway after he had set fire to the van. Either that or someone else left it there for him. It's an isolated place, a lonely spot, a long way from anywhere. Adderley and Smethurst had been using it for their extra-marital get-togethers for at least six months and it was the first time they had ever seen another vehicle parked there. Both of them were pretty sure that the car was empty. Whoever drove that car there, must have had a second vehicle to take them away – unless someone actually sat there in the dark, waiting to pick up Mr X, once he'd set fire to the van. Whichever scenario you pick, there's a second person involved in placing that getaway vehicle at the lay-by.'

'It would have been a long time for someone to sit and wait. Smethurst and Adderley saw the car several hours before the white van was picked up on the CCTV at the garage. That's assuming they actually saw the car on the right night. Remember that it took them three weeks to come forward. It was a regular meeting place for them, and they'd got no particular reason to recall the date.'

'I think you're wrong,' Hannah said firmly. 'They would remember, because they had to change their routine that night and they would have read about the Thackeray case within a couple of days. They would have known right away that the burned-out van had been found in their favourite lay-by, because it was reported in the press. It wasn't a case of them taking a long time to come forward because they're people who've half remembered something, then written themselves into the story, several weeks later. The reason they didn't come forward right away was because they're reluctant witnesses, with something to hide.' She paused for a moment, then continued: 'Besides which it's too much of a coincidence – Mr X had to get away from there somehow. Don't tell me that he'd planned everything else down to the last detail, but not worked out how and where he was going to get rid of the van and get back to wherever he was based. Let's face it – he covered the rest of his tracks so successfully, that we've never managed to link him to any other vehicle, or any other address.'

'Smethurst and Adderley were the only people he'd reckoned without,' Peter Betts said thoughtfully.

'Well, you can see why. The only people likely to find their way up there on a dark winter evening would self-evidently be up to no good. It was just his hard luck that more than one person had chosen that particular parking area for their not-so-good deeds that night – and he could hardly have anticipated that there were still people who were gagging to have sex in the back of a

Volkswagen Passat. I thought that had gone out forty years ago.'

'I don't think they had Volkswagen Passats, forty years ago.'

'You know perfectly well what I mean.'

'And you've been in this job long enough to know perfectly well that some people have tastes which the majority of the population would find somewhat outlandish. Including a lot of stuff that's a good deal weirder than making out in a Volkswagen Passat.'

'Talking of outlandish, did you know that Joel sometimes puts sachets of strawberry jam onto his hamburgers?'

'Is this a thinly veiled reference to your desire for a lunch break?'

'I wouldn't say "no" to a sandwich.'

'Come on then. Canteen it is.'

Nine

In spite of growing up in the north, Mark had never been to the racecourse at Thirsk before. It was not the first time that his errands for Chaz's friend had taken him into previously uncharted territory. The first of the bets had entailed him travelling down to Taunton, which while it was a bloody long trek from London, had been nothing like such a lengthy and tedious journey as this one. Next thing they would be demanding that he go to Ayr or Fairyhouse!

50

At Taunton he had been pleased to discover that from the top of the stands, Glastonbury Tor was visible through his binoculars. The famous tor was one of those places he had always meant to visit. At one time he had been really into myths and legends: that whole King Arthur and Holy Grail stuff. As a boy he'd been a big reader and loved watching those old black and white movies on the telly. *Ivanhoe*, *Robin Hood*, it was all good stuff. His older brothers had been into rugby, cricket, tennis and squash. Basically anything physical at which they could beat him. Loads of brothers seemed to spur one another on to be sportsmen – the Lloyds, the Nevilles, the Murrays – there was an endless list of them, whereas his brothers had achieved the absolute opposite, turning Mark into a sofa-bound spectator, inclined to be spotty and podgy, and favouring crisps and Coke over energy drinks. As an adult he had learned to keep an eye on the diet, but in spite of compulsory school sports and his father's extravagant praise when Monty and Michael had each in turn been selected for the county juniors, Mark had retained his preference for being a film buff, rather than a sportsman.

He did not particularly like putting himself out to travel to these far-flung venues, but when he had commented that it was a long drive to Thirsk, Chaz had only had to raise his eyebrows before Mark had immediately fallen into line, confirming that of course he would be more than happy to place a large bet on a horse running in the 4.15 at Thirsk, at the behest of Chaz's mystery employer.

It was essential to continue fulfilling these periodic commissions – inconvenient though they sometimes were – until he could access another source of finance with which to clear his debts. In the meantime, it was all about buying time. Time, he thought, was all that he needed. The relationship with Jude was coming along nicely, but it couldn't be rushed.

It augured well for the future that Jude enjoyed a day out at the races. It had been the good old gee gees which had originally brought them together. A chance fortuitous meeting, when he had literally bumped into her, initially just taking her for a particularly gorgeous specimen, then almost immediately recognizing that she was none other than Jude Thackeray, one-time kidnapped heiress, and now the answer to all his prayers. He had not, however, suggested that Jude accompany him to this meeting, not least because he couldn't think of a plausible explanation for coming so far, when there was a perfectly good fixture at Goodwood, which would only have entailed travelling a fraction of the distance. Furthermore he wasn't sure that his overdraft would bear a weekend in a sufficiently luxurious country house hotel, with the racing disguised as an afterthought.

Anyway, he preferred to take her to meetings where they were more likely to bump into mutual friends and acquaintances. Drifting around at racetracks like Billy No Mates wasn't really his scene. It made his gambling appear less social . . . more . . . well . . . compulsive . . . sort of. He didn't have a problem – not really. There had just been a lot of bad luck, followed by that terrible mix-up over the wrongly placed bet at Towcester. He still couldn't understand how that had come about. Surely . . . but he got no further, because his train of thought was shattered by the appearance of a familiar face among the crowds of racegoers who were milling in front of the on-course bookies, sizing up the odds for the next race.

'Chaz!' He all but yelped the name, such was his shock at seeing his contact approaching. It was unlikely that Mark's voice would have carried very far above the general hubbub, but it did not need to, for at the same moment in which he cried out, Chaz caught sight of him and immediately changed direction, making for Mark in a way which suggested that this was no accidental meeting. A sickening presentiment of unease slid upwards through Mark's alimentary canal. Chaz did not normally frequent the meetings at which Mark was commissioned to 'do his friend a little favour'.

Instead of a greeting, Chaz motioned him across towards the rail, close to the finishing post; an area which was currently deserted, with all the spectators seemingly gone to stand around the parade ring, or look at the betting on the next race.

'Chaz.' Mark extended a hand, ignoring the hollow sensation in his guts and summoning up a smile.

The other man ignored the proffered hand. He was wearing the immaculate suit and silk tie of a gentleman racegoer, but Mark knew that the costume was deceptive. Whoever Chaz worked for, it was no gentleman – and neither was he.

'Plans have changed. We want the stake money back,' Chaz announced without preamble. No 'please'. No messing about.

'What do you mean? How can I put the bet on, if I give you the money back?'

'Someone else is going to place the bet. Someone more reliable. We don't want you going anywhere near that bet – you are to going to pick another horse and put your money on that.'

'But then I'll lose. You want me to deliberately lose some money?' Mark's voice rose slightly as he regarded Chaz in disbelief, not bothering to disguise the fact that he thought the other man was out of his mind. 'Why would I deliberately set out to lose?'

'Because you've been told to – and keep your voice down.'

Mark glanced around. Chaz's caution appeared superfluous, since there was no one near enough to hear them. 'Can't I just not bet on the race at all?'

'No. You place a bet. Not betting would be suspicious.'

'To whom? And why are you putting your boss's bet on, instead of me, anyway?'

'I'm not. I'm passing the money on to someone else. In a minute or two, you're going to walk towards the Hambledon stand and I'm going to walk in the opposite direction and from then on, if you see me again, you're to keep well out of my way. At precisely 3.30 you enter the Gents closest to the Saddle Room Bistro, wait until the first cubicle is free, go in, stay in there with the door closed for precisely three minutes, then come out, leaving the money sitting on the cistern. Someone will be waiting to follow you in. Don't acknowledge him in any way, don't make eye contact, don't attempt to see where he goes after that.'

'Suppose the wrong person is waiting?'

'They won't be. Do you think I'm some kind of fucking amateur?' Chaz glowered at him.

'But why?' Mark asked again.

'Because you're no use to us anymore. You're being watched.'

'What?' Mark looked seriously alarmed.

'Someone's interested in you, Marky boy. Someone's been making enquiries.'

'Who? Why? How do you know?' A sickening sense of panic rose up alongside the words. He had known from the beginning that the little errands he had being fulfilling in line with Chaz's instructions were connected to something shady. When a man knows for a certainty that a rank outsider is going to come in at long odds, such knowledge is unlikely to have been gained via a legitimate tip on Channel Four. He had been around racing long enough to know that people involved in race fixing (he didn't like to qualify it with those words, but alas they were indisputably the words which came to mind) did not place their own bets, or even use the same people to place their bets every time, because telephone and internet accounts could be traced back, while on-course bookmakers remembered faces that cropped up too often behind unlikely winning tickets, which commanded unusually large pay-outs. He had not done anything dishonest, he reminded himself. He had put on the occasional bet for a friend – nothing more than that.

He realized that Chaz was reading his expression, weighing him up, and he experienced the sense of humiliation which comes from being assessed and found wanting. Chaz had rumbled him as a coward. Well, why not? No one wanted their features rearranged.

'Who's said something?' he asked again.

'One of your associates – Matt Blakemore – was approached out of the blue, by some chap at the evening meeting at Windsor. He'd seen Matt having a drink with you and claimed to be some sort of acquaintance.'

'So what? I have a lot of acquaintances.'

'It was a fishing expedition. Was it true that your family's firm was in a bit of trouble? Maybe your own finances weren't on too steady a footing? All that sort of thing. Wanted to know whether you'd said anything to Matt about this woman you're seeing – Judy Thackeray – and whether you'd mentioned anything about her having money. It wasn't exactly subtle, I can tell you.'

'I have no idea why anyone would be having that conversation. Anyway how did Matt Blakemore come to be telling you about this? I didn't know that you knew Matt Blakemore.'

'I know all sorts of people.'

Chaz sounded so pleased with himself that Mark, who normally avoided any kind of violence, was gripped by the urge to slug him. During the brief silence which followed, the cogs turned and he got it. There had been rumours a year or so back that Matty Blakemore was in a bit of trouble – an expensive divorce, a run of bad luck – no doubt the suave, persuasive Chaz had introduced himself into the picture with promises of temporary financial assistance to 'see him through a bad patch' in return for some 'little favours', one of which was presumably appraising Chaz of any potentially harmful gossip about his friends. The fact that Matt seemingly knew that he, Mark, was a person of interest to Chaz, merely served to increase his sense of humiliation all the more. He began to wonder how many other people in his circle were spying on one another, because they had somehow become indebted to Chaz's anonymous employer.

Though he was facing away from the track, the sound of approaching hooves, beating against the turf, told him that the runners for the next race had begun to gallop down the course towards the start.

'Better go and put your bet on,' Chaz instructed. 'And don't forget – 3.30.' He turned to go, but Mark impulsively grabbed his sleeve.

'Get your hand off my jacket.' Chaz's voice contained an unexpected note of menace, which demanded instant obedience. Though Mark immediately let go as instructed, his impulsive gesture had momentarily arrested Chaz's progress, and it gave Mark the chance to ask, 'Who was this guy who was asking about me? What was he like?'

'Matt said he'd never seen him before. Average

kind of bloke – average height, brown hair, brown eyes, sounded like an Essex boy attempting a Hollywood accent.'

'It's Jude's brother. I bet it was Jude's brother. There's nothing at all in that for you to worry about, Chaz.' The words were tumbling out, far too fast. 'It's got nothing at all to do with our business. Let me put the bet on for you.' He put pride aside, heard himself begin to plead. 'How can I put things right and repay the debt, if you won't let me put the bets on any more?'

'Not my problem, old chap. We'll be in touch . . . over the debt.'

'It's Robin Thackeray,' Mark called after Chaz's departing back, heedless of any listeners nearby. 'He's just asking around because he worries about who's seeing his sister . . .' He trailed into silence, as he realized that his words were making no impression on Chaz, who had continued to stride out of earshot.

'It's that fuckwit, Robin Thackeray,' Mark said more quietly, all but choking on the words. Jude Thackeray was supposed to be his Master Plan, but instead his involvement with her had just made things much, much worse.

Ten

Detectives Betts and McMahon had left off talking about the Thackeray kidnap over lunch. It was often better to take time out, have a proper break and come back to things afresh. Jerry Wilkins had joined them and the conversation had turned to his date with the latest 'incredibly fit girl' of his acquaintance. 'So I took her to that new place that's opened, where the Grapevine used to be. Big mistake.'

'Too expensive?'

'Bit on the pricey side, but that wasn't the real problem.'

'Which was?'

'Entire menu was in bloody cookery-ese. A tian of apple and Wensleydale. I mean what the fargo is a tian, when it's at home? Partridge in a game reduction. A game reduction! I ask you. It sounds like what happens when your team gets docked three points for fielding an ineligible player. Talking of which, I see your lot did all right against Crystal Palace at the weekend.' Jerry addressed this latter remark to Peter. The new season had just begun and it was well known that Bettsy followed the fortunes of Arsenal FC.

'What I don't get,' Hannah said, 'is how you can claim to support a team that you've hardly ever been to see in person. I mean, most turncoats who choose not to follow their local side join the Manchester United mob. Why the Arsenal, for goodness sake?'

It was a well-trodden conversational path, along which Peter always gave as good as he got. 'You have to admit that there's not much street-cred in supporting a team which has a carthorse on its badge and is known as the Tractor Boys,' he said.

'At least I'm loyal to my origins – and don't

59

forget that last time Ipswich won the cup, they beat Arsenal, one nil.'

'Ancient history,' Peter said. 'We've won it seven or eight times since then.'

'Not against Ipswich.'

'Yeah, right . . . and didn't Ipswich also win the title once, and even the UEFA Cup – also before either of us was born?'

'Real supporters stay true to their roots. They even go to games, shifts permitting.'

'Yeah,' Jerry put in with a grin. 'Mind you, I bet it's a bit easier to get tickets for a game at Portman Road, than it is to get them for the Emirates Stadium.'

'People who support a team known as Swindon Town Nil, have no business ganging up with an Arsenal supporter,' Hannah protested.

'I support Swindon because somebody has to,' Jerry said. 'Now then, children. Some of us have to get back to work.'

The point was acknowledged by all three pushing back their chairs in unison.

Graham Ling had set aside a small, first-floor room where his two chosen officers could concentrate on the Thackeray review without too many interruptions. As they climbed the stairs from the canteen, Hannah got back on topic, by raising the lamentable lack of forensic evidence at their disposal. 'Was he clever?' she asked, 'or just damned lucky?'

'A combination of both, I'd say. He was careful not to have sex with her for several days before the intended murder. During the kidnap he wore disposable gloves, which he duly disposed of.

He burned the van that he'd used to transport her to the woods, probably destroying the pay-as-you-go mobile at the same time. He appears to have washed the towels and bedding they'd been using, and thoroughly cleaned the house. There's no single sample of DNA which can definitely be said to belong to him. The bin men had been the day before he took her away from the house, taking away whatever food containers etc, had been used.'

'That's an amazing touch,' Hannah mused. 'Taking the wheelie bin up to the road, while you've got the owner of the house, tied up in a cupboard under the stairs.'

'He had an eye for detail,' Peter remarked drily.

'And he was lucky, because unlike a lot of houses, where hardly anyone but the occupiers had any cause to be in there, the Thackerays had let Laurel Cottage to holidaymakers in the recent past, leaving SOCO with traces of unidentified DNA all over the place – absolutely impossible to eliminate them all. We've got lots of DNA, but none of it necessarily even belonging to him. What's more, if we ever do put a name to him, you can bet your bottom dollar he'll run a defence that his DNA got into the place because he once visited some friend or relative who was holidaying there.'

Peter ignored the optimistic leap ahead towards an arrest and successful prosecution, saying instead, 'He also chose his victim well. She leads a fairly solitary life – doesn't have many really close friends or family. Relatively few people ever saw her out with his guy, which leaves us with hardly anyone who can describe him. How many on our list of witnesses?'

There was a pause, while Hannah located a document, before commenting wearily on the vagaries of identification evidence. 'It's the usual story. Everyone looks at the same person, but sees someone different. The staff who waited at the places where they went out for a couple of meals were useless. The one girl made the guy out to be a dead spit for Robin Thackeray – who she'd probably seen in the papers or on television after the case made the news – while the guy who served them in the Italian actually thought Mr X was blonde – which isn't how anyone else describes him at all. Later on, this chap, Guido – his English wasn't that great and I do wonder if something got lost in translation – said he thought the chap's hair might have been dyed, but that's obviously crazy, because Jude Thackeray would have noticed if her boyfriend suddenly decided to dye his hair for the evening.'

'Quite. Wasn't there also a sighting in the lane?'

'Yup. Some of Jude's neighbours were out walking their dog . . .'

Peter groaned. 'Of course, the dog people. I remember them now.'

'They saw Jude driving her car,' Hannah continued inexorably. 'They'd not long set out to walk their dogs, when Jude's car passed them in the lane. It would have been the same day that the new boyfriend suddenly turned nasty, decided to tie Jude up, forced her to give him her pin numbers, and started to systematically raid her bank account. They're sure of the day, because it was the same day that their grandchildren arrived to stay, and we're sure of the day, because the first cash withdrawals were made in the early hours of the next morning.'

'Which is good evidence in theory,' said Peter.

'But doesn't help us much in practice,' Hannah finished for him. 'According to Mr and Mrs Andrews, they stepped back onto the verge to let the car go by. Mrs Andrews said she was a bit surprised, because Jude didn't acknowledge them at all. Jude was driving the car and they were walking on her side of the lane, so they didn't get much of a look at the guy in the passenger seat. Mrs Andrews said she thought the man and Jude Thackeray both looked annoyed about something, but she admitted that it was only a passing glimpse. Mr Andrews said he was paying more attention to one of their dogs, because it was off the lead and he had to catch it by the collar when he saw the car coming, as the dog's a bit unreliable.'

'Didn't Mrs Andrews also say that the car was being driven rather fast?'

'She did. That all comes into her impression that Jude wasn't in too good a temper.'

'Hmm. Mrs Andrews constructing a little story for herself do you think?'

'Couple have a row and he beats her up and locks her in a cupboard? I see where you're going. I can't remember – what did Jude Thackeray have to say about meeting the Andrews in the lane?'

'Nothing much,' he responded promptly. 'Initially she said she thought the Andrews might have got the day wrong, because she didn't think that she and Mr X had been out in the car that day at all, but later on, she remembered that she'd popped out to buy some milk around midday, because they were running out, and she thought that Lover Boy had probably come in the car with her, though she couldn't be sure. She said she didn't recall meeting the Andrews in the lane, but that she was so used to seeing them out walking their dogs, it could easily have happened as they said, but she'd simply forgotten. It was such a commonplace thing that she wouldn't have taken any notice . . . Here it is . . .' He had been scrolling through a statement as he spoke. 'She said that she usually slowed down for people walking, but maybe she hadn't seen them until the last minute. She doesn't remember being annoyed or upset, but agreed that maybe she had been a bit irritated about forgetting to get any milk, when she'd only ordered a delivery of shopping, the day before.'

'I reckon the Andrews were probably right about him being in the car,' Hannah said, thoughtfully. 'He had everything planned by then. He wouldn't have wanted to let her out of his sight that last day before he took her captive.'

'Maybe. But the guy in the village shop is pretty sure that Lover Boy didn't come in with her for the milk – though of course he wouldn't, because he took care not to be seen by anyone, if he could avoid it.'

'Did the man in the shop actually confirm the trip for the milk?'

'He wasn't positive about it. It's another one of those routine things that he wouldn't have particularly noticed, because it happened all the time . . . and it would have been a cash transaction, so nothing specific to help us in the till records.'

'The Andrews ought to be really useful,' Hannah mused. 'They only live just along the lane but although they saw him in the car and they saw various cars parked on her drive a few times, there's never anything concrete. He's "ordinary looking" with short, light-brown hair, and "an angry face" according to Mrs Andrews. One of the cars is "a dark-blue one". It hardly narrows the field.'

'The drive is pretty much completely hidden from the road by that whacking great hedge. You can't see anything of the house until you look directly in through the gateway. If you're passing by on foot that takes no more than a couple of seconds – even less when you drive by in your car. He couldn't have been any luckier with that either. Talk about retaining your privacy.'

'Nil desperandum,' Hannah said, affecting a cheerfulness which neither of them felt. 'At least we've got two comprehensive descriptions of the guy – from Jude Thackeray and her brother Robin.'

Eleven

It was immediately obvious to Rob that Jude had been drinking. Quite aside from the fact that she had a half-empty wine glass in her hand when she admitted him to the flat (he had a key but she had double locked the door from inside), she also had a particular look on her face which only arrived there after the consumption of at least half a bottle of wine.

He didn't bother with a preamble. 'I've found out a bit more about the engineering firm. He's definitely not a director. It's run by his two older brothers.'

'Oh please, Rob. Not now. We already know that his grandfather left him shares in the business, and that his mother inherited a pile from *her* father. We've even read the probate of his father's will and know that he left assets of well over ten million.' She simulated a huge yawn. 'Will you please let it rest?'

'I managed to have another chat with that chap I saw him with at the races. Bloke called Matt Blake or something like that. I knew I would manage to bump into him again.'

'Is that really wise? I mean it sounds awfully like you're stalking his friends.' She had slumped full length on the sofa, but now she raised herself sufficiently to reach for her glass and take another gulp of her drink.

'It's wiser than leaving things to chance – and a hell of a lot wiser than lying around, getting pissed.'

'I have to deal with things in my own way,' she snapped. 'And I have a lot to deal with.'

'Sure you do. But burying your head in the sand isn't clever. Suppose he rings and you're drunk. Do you want to end up losing him, by saying something silly?'

She made a clicking noise with her tongue, before responding. 'Sometimes I don't know where you're coming from. On the one hand you don't want me to commit myself, in case this guy turns out to be not what he seems, on the other you're worried that I might lose him.'

'Oh well, I'm sure you wouldn't want to do that.'

The sarcasm in his voice sobered her somewhat. She turned to see the look on his face. 'Why Rob,' she cooed. 'I believe you're jealous.'

'Don't be stupid.'

'Attention everyone—' she waved her glass to encompass an imaginary crowd – 'the green-eyed monster is in the building.'

'Sometimes you just go too far.' He stalked across to the kitchen door, pausing when he reached it to ask, 'Is there anything for dinner?'

'Not unless you brought sandwiches. Ring for a takeaway, if you're starving.'

'Have you had anything?'

'A packet of crisps. Didn't want to drink on an empty stomach.'

He tried not to be irritated by the flippant tone. 'I'm ordering pizza. For both of us. Sometimes I don't know what to do with you – 'specially when you're in this half-crazy mood.'

'I'll be OK in the morning.'

'If you carry on drinking, you'll have a stinking hangover in the morning.'

'I never get hangovers.'

'Oh really? Since when?'

He went into the kitchen to find the phone number of the pizza place. In spite of her repeated assurances to the contrary, he was afraid that she had become so enamoured of Mark Medlicott as to be no longer entirely rational about him.

He, on the other hand, retained a healthy scepticism. Surely Jude of all people hadn't lost sight of the fact that it wasn't hard to affect fictional wealth for a short period, in order to snare an unsuspecting partner. Medlicott appeared to have the right kind of background, but there was always the possibility that he was putting on a front. Jude's kidnap had made all the papers. In the aftermath of the publicity, she had received numerous letters from would-be suitors, some professing undying love to this rich young woman whom they had never met, all of them promising to look after her. (There had been some vile letters too, saying that she was a tart, a trollop, and worse, who had got what she deserved for sleeping with a man outside of matrimony, while others went into graphic descriptions of what they would like to do to her, in the event that they ever happened to have her tied up in an isolated property for two or three days. All of these communications had been passed on to the police.)

Mark Medlicott did not, of course, belong to this lunatic fringe and she had met him in a public place, in a seemingly ordinary way, without his apparently being aware of who she was. In the initial stages of the relationship with Medlicott, Jude herself had been as careful and wary as Rob, but lately he had sensed a growing recklessness in her. Medlicott's apparent enthusiasm and now his hurry to cement their relationship, made Rob's suspicious hackles rise. Medlicott's friend at the races had been worryingly non-committal in the face of his gentle probing. There had definitely been something in his manner which had made Rob feel uneasy. Of course, it might just be a bloke protecting the privacy of his mate – refusing to share gossip with an unknown stranger.

If only we could be sure, he thought. But you never could be – not one hundred per cent, because it was so easy to construct a false front, if you were absolutely intent on deception.

Twelve

'So . . .' Hannah paused to stretch out her arms to their fullest extent, flexing her long slim fingers, then bringing her hands back onto the table in front of her, before continuing. 'The brother reckoned that our Mr X was a wrong 'un from the start.'

'Benefit of hindsight,' Peter Betts said.

'That's a bit dismissive.'

'And also wrong,' Peter conceded a few seconds later, 'because it says here that he and his sister had a bit of a row about her seeing so much of the bloke. Robin Thackeray thought it was all going a bit fast, whereas his sister could see no wrong in the guy.'

'He's a bit possessive, isn't he – the brother?' Hannah said. 'Do you think that came about because of what happened with Mr X, or do you reckon he's always been like that? Their father's dead, right? That might have encouraged the brother to think that he had to take on the head of the family role. If the brother was forever stepping in – interfering – that could have made things worse.'

'How do you mean?'

'She's a grown woman and big brother tries to come the heavy and suggests she sees less of the new bloke? I mean, that's just calculated to have her saying, "You're not the boss of me", and going all out to defy him.'

'Quite likely. There's no real indication of why the brother didn't like him.'

Hannah referred to her pile of notes: 'The exact phrase appears to be, "there was just something about him that I didn't take to".'

'Well, it's always helpful – when a witness can be so specific.'

'So . . . the slightly possessive brother – who maybe doesn't take to *anyone* who dates his sister – notices something which may or may not be discernible to anyone else, and which he is unable to explain. Apart from that his description is very much like the victim's. He thinks the guy is about the same height, or slightly taller than he is himself, whereas his sister definitely puts the guy a fraction taller. He never clocked the eye colour; Jude says the guy's eyes were brown. Both agree on short, light-brown hair, medium build, no particular accent. Jude says he has a small, dark mole on one buttock; brother is understandably never in a position to notice it. They can't provide an address, but understood him to be staying at the hotel in Ipswich, paid for by his company. He evidently drives a series of different cars, allegedly hire cars, which are also supposedly provided by his company. The company is called Odec, or Adec, or Amec, or something similar and supposedly specializes in some kind of revolutionary heating system for offices and showrooms – though all efforts have so far failed to trace any such company, or anyone attempting to sell or install this marvellous system – whatever it may have been – in the immediate area.'

'I think we can be fairly confident that it doesn't actually exist. The point is that it sounds plausible.'

'He told the victim that he had worked abroad, including spells in Holland and Belgium and demonstrated his ability to speak the language when she asked him to say something in Dutch for her.'

'Which is also inconclusive,' said Peter. 'Given that she doesn't speak Dutch, and he presumably knew that, so he could have been speaking any language and she would have been none the wiser.'

'He's one hell of a blagger, isn't he?'

'It just seems to have been an incredibly detailed set-up, for relatively little reward . . .'

'Right. He's apparently planned and executed everything to perfection, right up to the moment when he lets her get away. Let's have another look at that, shall we . . .'

Peter frowned, waiting while Hannah turned up the relevant passages from among Jude Thackeray's screeds and screeds of witness statements.

'OK – here we are. "He stopped the van and

came round to the back. When he opened the door, a light came on in the back of the van, so I could see him and see that the door was open. I would have known anyway, because I heard the door and felt a rush of colder air. He was standing outside the back of the van, wearing the same clothes that he'd worn earlier in the house, except that he'd put a ski mask over his face and he was wearing a hood. It looked like he was all in black. I remember wondering why he'd done that, because I knew who he was – or anyway, who I thought he was – and also what he looked like. After he opened the door, he sort of hesitated. I'm not sure if he actually said any proper words. I think he might have said something to himself that I didn't catch, or maybe he just sort of grunted, and then he moved out of sight – it sounded as if he was going round to the front of the van and I guessed that he'd forgotten something. I knew it was my only chance, so I sort of rolled – I'm not exactly sure how I did it – I was on my knees at one point . . . Anyway, I sort of fell out of the back of the van, scrambled up and ran." Not so easy, with her hands tied behind her back,' Hannah interrupted herself to say.

'It's amazing what you can do when you're desperate,' Peter said. 'Go on.'

'"It was really dark,"' Hannah resumed reading. '"I couldn't see anything, but I just ran. I didn't know where I was, or what direction to go in, but I thought that if I ran in a straight line, away from the back of the van, I'd be on a road, and someone might be driving along, who would stop and help me."'

'Sounds reasonable enough.'

'"But I realized that I wasn't on the road, because the ground was bumpy and I could hear my feet on leaves and twigs and things. I realized that the noise was going to help him follow me, so I stopped. I think it was as soon as I stopped that I heard a banging noise behind me. It might have been one of the van doors. I seemed to be surrounded by bushes and little trees and I'd been running through all these scratchy branches. After the big bang, I tiptoed really quietly for a few feet, then I crouched down, by the side of some sort of bush and I listened. It was pretty quiet and I knew he would be hunting for me. I heard him come quite close, but he didn't see me. Then after a few minutes had gone by, he must have gone back to the van for a torch, because I saw this light flashing around among the trees. I could feel myself starting to cry, because I thought he would find me for sure, but then I realized that he was going the wrong way. I thought about trying to run again, but I decided that the worst possible thing would be to make a noise, because that would lead him straight to me, so I tried to keep absolutely still. He turned back and the light came nearer and nearer . . ."'

Though Hannah was doing the reading, Peter could almost hear Jude Thackeray's voice. He remembered the mounting tension in it, when she had reached this part of the story, and the tears which had spontaneously appeared in her eyes.

'". . . although I knew that I mustn't make a sound, I swear that having the gag in my mouth saved me just then, because it reminded me

73

not to scream. I thought for sure that he was going to get me, but when he was within about six or eight feet, he turned away again. He kept on searching for ages – well it seemed like ages to me – and I kept thinking that any minute, he would turn back and shine his light on me and that would be it, and all the time, I was freezing cold, and the scratches on my bare arms were stinging, and I knew that I was shaking . . . It all seemed to go on forever . . . He'd get further away and then come nearer again, and I kept thinking that it was only a matter of time until he found me. And then . . . well, I realized that he was gone. One minute he was searching and the next I couldn't see the light of the torch anymore. I heard the engine of the van start up, its lights came on, and then I heard him driving away."'

Peter took up the tale from memory. 'And she stayed there until it got light, then made her way out onto the road, where she was seen by the AA man, who was heading back to base after attending an early-morning breakdown. I wonder why he gave up?'

'The AA man?'

'The attacker. He must have known that she could identify him.'

'Except that as it turns out, she couldn't.'

Peter shook his head. 'He was clearly motivated to murder her, when they originally left the house. Why give up, when he had her in the woods? Surely he realized that she couldn't have got very far, with her hands tied behind her – and he'd got a torch?'

74

'Perhaps the battery gave out.' Hannah sounded almost bored. 'Don't forget that he probably didn't see her actually getting out of the van. From the way she remembers it, he was busy doing something in the front when she got out of the back, so he wouldn't have seen which direction she'd initially gone in. On the face of it, it sounds as if he had the upper hand, but there are woods on either side of the road just there. It wouldn't be easy to track her in the dark, providing she stayed still and didn't make a noise.'

There was a brief silence while they considered this. A muffled burst of laughter bounced along the corridor outside, the faint precursor of voices which grew momentarily louder and then fainter again, as they passed by on the other side of the door. Hannah picked up a pen and flicked it against the edge of her desk two or three times, before musing, 'It's almost as if he let her go on purpose.'

'What?'

'The way he left the van door open, then let her get away into the woods. And if he'd always intended to finish the thing by killing her, why bother with a false identity at all?'

'Pay attention, McMahon,' he said. 'He needed the false identity for everyone else. He couldn't have her knowing who he really was, then sharing that information with all and sundry in the run up to the crime.'

'True. But in that case, why did he stop looking for her? He must have known that she couldn't get far. Bound, gagged, and barefoot? He'd got every advantage, including a torch.'

75

Peter noticed that she had just contradicted herself, but he also knew that she was not really arguing the position, just thinking aloud, trying to prompt something useful.

'Maybe he had a deadline to work to,' he suggested. 'There's the hypothetical other person, remember. The one we think may have driven the car to the lay-by, so that he could get away, once he'd torched the van. While he's at Foxden Woods, supposedly finishing off his victim and dumping her body, he's out of communication with this accomplice, because as we know, he doesn't want to risk making use of a mobile phone. Meantime, perhaps the accomplice is expecting him to rendezvous somewhere? Does a Plan B kick in, if he doesn't show up on time? Or maybe there's another reason that he couldn't afford to stick around. Having disposed of her, what does he need to do next? Does he have a ticket for a cross-Channel ferry? Maybe he's proposing to fence some of the jewellery abroad?'

'That's an interesting one,' Hannah said. 'He told Jude Thackeray that he'd got some previous connections with Holland. Harwich is not a million miles away. We should be able to get records of the vehicles which took the ferries that day from the early hours onwards.'

'It would take some following up. Better talk to the boss about it.'

'Meantime, it won't cost anything to drive home via Jude Thackeray's lay-by in Foxden Woods. I know it's all been looked at before, but you never know: going back there, one more time, something might just come up.'

Thirteen

As he jumped from the dinghy and splashed ashore through the shallows, dragging the boat behind him, Stefan could not help but feel pleased with the way it had gone. He had navigated his way to the place – Anonymous Bay, as he had taken to thinking of it – easily enough, and encountered no difficulties in bringing his craft into the beach. Better yet, from out on the water, he not only commanded a view of the entire beach, but also of significant lengths of the path which ran along the top of the cliffs, and this, he thought, would enable him to choose a time to come ashore when there were no troublesome hikers around to ask questions. He calculated that by early evening most of them would be well out of the way, stuffing their faces with pasties or locally caught shellfish, at some hostelry or other. In any case, if the boat – or rather boats – because he would need to tow a second one in for the actual operation itself, were well pulled up, they wouldn't be easy to see from the top of the cliffs, and from all of his observations so far, it did seem as if visitors to the beach itself were extremely rare.

The place would have been even better with the addition of some kind of cave, where he could leave a few essentials in advance (in particular the grappling hook – he had decided that a large stone from the beach was not going to suffice) but you could not have everything and in every other way the location was looking better and better. The weather was the one unpredictable factor. Tides he could handle, but the weather had to be right. Not just for bringing the boats in and launching them again, albeit that this was a vital part of the plan, but also to render it likely that someone with relatively little experience would have attempted to take a boat out, before meeting with an accident.

Not, he thought, that it would take too much believing. The south-west coast of England was a positive magnet for idiots who assumed that they were safe to attempt to sail, or surf, or pootle out to sea using their newly acquired boats and boards, at all states of the tide and in all kinds of weathers. Stefan had grown up close to the sea and he knew better. A plan involving the sea was going to serve him much better than the previously flawed operation on land had done.

He nodded to himself without realizing it, and set about re-launching the dinghy. Once the outboard came to life, he reached the deeper water in less than a minute. Five minutes and the detail of the beach was lost, becoming a line of colour which he could barely differentiate from the cliffs. The lines of waves making their way ashore had merged into a single lacy thread, which marked the division between the land and the water.

It would be dark, of course, when he actually had to do it, but with luck there would be some moonlight and if not, then a torch would have to suffice. It was a clever idea, he thought. A well-thought-out scheme, much better than the last one. This time it was going to work.

Fourteen

Though Peter had been surprised by Hannah's suggestion of a call at the lay-by where Jude Thackeray had escaped her would-be killer, he had been perfectly willing to go along with it. Sometimes an off-the-wall suggestion unexpectedly led somewhere useful and it had certainly never occurred to him that his colleague might have been entertaining some sort of ulterior motive, entirely unrelated to the Thackeray enquiry.

It was not until they had arrived on the edge of Foxden Woods and been sitting in his parked car for about five minutes that the situation took an abrupt diversion from its expected course, with Hannah returning the conversation to the lovers who had observed a parked car in that other lay-by, where they normally played out their extramarital fixtures. Though he had initially failed to see where this was leading, Peter abruptly flagged an amber danger signal, when his colleague mused, in an odd tone of voice that she had never attempted to have sex in the back of a car. The amber signal turned red a moment later, when he unexpectedly found McMahon's hand resting on his thigh.

The gesture generated a sensation which ran from his hairline to the soles of his feet. It would have been ridiculous to pretend to himself that he didn't find her attractive, but he also knew that becoming embroiled in a relationship with a colleague was the dumbest thing he could do right now, with major decisions to be made about the future, so he attempted a light-hearted tone and asked if she wasn't the person who had said that sex in the back of a car was distinctly passé, a diversionary tactic which failed dismally, when Hannah responded by agreeing that it would be far better if they both went back to her place.

At this point Peter Betts did a mental double take. He hadn't been sure whether to take her initial remark, and even the follow-up hand on his leg, as a joke, but her persistence suggested that she was serious. He was completely wrong-footed. His dealings with McMahon had always been maintained on a strictly professional level. In spite of her undoubted attributes, he had never allowed himself to think of her as a potential date. She was one of the team in a way which made a proposition from her as unexpected as would have been a proposition from the determinedly heterosexual Jerry. It was an awkward situation and not one for which they prepared you in basic training.

He hesitated, then said carefully, 'Look, Hannah' – he usually addressed her as McMahon, but that didn't feel altogether appropriate under the circumstances – 'it isn't that I don't find you attractive, because I do, but relationships with work colleagues – specially in our job – well,

I've always thought they're just too full of complications. In fact . . .' he hesitated, then continued, 'I seem to remember you once saying something similar, after that business when Timpson had to ask for a transfer. I know some people make it work—'

'Who said we need to have a relationship?'

She was looking him straight in the eye, but he fancied that he detected an element of false bravado in her voice. While he was still trying to think of something else to say, she added, 'Don't you want to get laid? Without any complications, I promise.'

That's what they all say, he thought, but none of them ever mean it . . . except maybe for Ginny, which reminded him again of the still unanswered email.

Hannah almost read his thoughts, as she said, 'And there was me, thinking that you had a wild streak, Bettsy. Haven't you always tried to let on that you have this secret, parallel existence? Sex and drugs and rock 'n' roll, and all that.' She attempted a laugh, but did not quite manage to bring it off.

'I'm a part-time guitarist, not a fully paid-up member of the Rolling Stones.' He tried to keep it light, but the trouble is, he thought, that even though nothing had happened, her suggestion and his rejection would become a future source of awkwardness. He might as well have taken advantage of the offer and slept with her. It came as a surprise that she even found him attractive. He had never for a moment suspected it – or maybe she didn't and she really was just desperate

81

for some plain, uncomplicated sex. It was sometimes hard to have normal relationships. Not for nothing did many of the older hands talk of being married to the job.

'I think we'd better get back,' he said. 'There's nothing to see here.'

Her car was still parked at headquarters and the drive back was conducted amid an air of false heartiness, with each of them trying and failing to pretend that what had happened in the lay-by didn't matter. In the underground car park she thanked him for the lift, then unexpectedly leaned across from the passenger seat and very deliberately kissed him on the mouth. 'Just to let you know what you're missing.' Afterwards he told himself that it had only happened because he hadn't been quick enough to anticipate what she was going to do and take evasive action.

She got out of his car and walked over to her own without looking back, head held high, heels elevating her to just over six feet tall. Giving him the full benefit of her swinging hips and neat backside. He knew exactly what she was up to and for a moment he was tempted. What did it matter anyway, if he intended to take up Ginny's offer and join the band? In his head, Steppenwolf roared out the chorus of 'Born to be Wild'. He hummed it as he drove away.

He hadn't made a decision on Ginny's offer yet, but Hannah was helping to push him the wrong way – or was it the right way? Having sex with a colleague in the back of a car was somehow such a cliché, and rendered all the more sordid by the idea of congress taking place at a crime scene. That wasn't how he wanted his life to be.

Though he knew next to nothing of McMahon's private life, he didn't think it was how she wanted her life to be either. The episode left him uncharacteristically bewildered. McMahon never came on to colleagues. (If it had ever happened with anyone before, he was confident that he would have heard about it. There were no secrets in CID.) If anything, she had encircled herself with an invisible barbed wire fence, which said, 'Don't even think about it.' She was always professional, never flirted, and no one (not even Jerry) messed with McMahon. Her behaviour was all the more unsettling because it had come from nowhere.

It was also unresolved. What had that parting kiss been all about? McMahon regaining some dignity? Having the last word? How would they be together, when they had to work one-to-one again tomorrow? At least there would be a brief, enforced cooling-off period, because in the morning he had to temporarily abandon work on the Thackeray case, in order to make a court appearance in connection with a juvenile accused of armed robbery.

It was an unusual business. A bullied youth, goaded into robbing an elderly shopkeeper at knifepoint, in order to impress his tormentors. The kid was a wimp and would never have actually used the knife, but the shopkeeper wasn't to know that, had been traumatized at the time and had lost his confidence since. There were no winners in a case like that. It was lose-lose whichever way you looked at it. Many of the people against whom he had helped to gather evidence, were inadequate in some way. A significant proportion needed treatment as much as they needed punishment. Sometimes, as in the Jude Thackeray case, there was no one to bring to court at all, because in spite of their best endeavours, he and his colleagues failed to find the perpetrators, or failed to make a case which would stick.

Those unsolved cases were the worst. Getting a result was not just about the personal satisfaction which came from gaining a conviction, not just about being on the winning team. Failing to put the perpetrators of a particularly vicious crime behind bars was almost akin to breaking a promise, betraying the trust invested in you by the victim.

In some way that he couldn't quite explain to himself, having sex with McMahon at a crime scene associated with the Thackeray case would have been to let the victim down in a particularly bad way. He did not want to spend a lifetime letting people down. As he drove back to his flat, the standing ovation he had received with Shuffle 'n' Deal all those months ago replayed itself in his head, like some sort of in-vehicle entertainment system. There was another life out there, and maybe it belonged to him.

Fifteen

Mark had gone to a lot of trouble to set the scene. It had taken him very little time to realize that Jude was extremely susceptible to romantic gestures – a bunch of red roses, a thoughtful little non-Valentine's Day card – but creating just the right atmosphere tonight had assumed gargantuan importance, because it was vital to gee her up before making his pitch. 'We love one another . . . we're so right together . . . when you're sure you've found the right person, why wait . . . I just can't live without you . . .' He had practiced his lines until they were stale in his mouth. All clichés of course, but what woman didn't want to be told that she was the most beautiful, most desirable, most special person in all the world?

He liked to think that he was good with women. He had a track record. He was both gentle and gentlemanly, and women liked that enough to overlook things like the extra few pounds that he carried around his middle. Otherwise it would have been mad to contemplate a scheme like this, however desperate he was. It wasn't as if he was doing anything illegal – in fact it was a lot more legit than placing all those dodgy bets on behalf of Chaz's friend, and hey, once they were married, she would be entitled to share whatever he had. There was his flat (even if it was mortgaged to the hilt and the service

85

charge was crippling him, property in London would inevitably escalate in value, making it a good investment in the long term). Once he had everything back on an even keel, he would be able to build up another portfolio of real estate. He had done it before; he could do it again.

It wasn't as if he would stop being kind to her, once they were safely hitched. Keeping her happy had not proved so very difficult up until now, and once he had access to her funds it would be easier still. Fair point, it wasn't the way he had ever imagined that he would end up marrying someone. (Truth be told, he'd never really given much thought to getting married until now.) But they were both in need of different kinds of security and there were far worse reasons than that for tying the knot.

He took another look around the kitchen (gleaming, thanks to the attentions of Agnieska – his cash-in-hand cleaner) mentally ticking everything off. It was in his favour that Jude didn't much enjoy eating out. She claimed that ever since all the publicity surrounding the kidnap, she always felt as though people were looking at her: recognizing her face from the television and the newspapers, remembering the case and imagining how it had been for her, and what had been done to her. Personally he'd always thought she made too much of it: most people's memories were short and the case had been out of the papers for months now. Even so, she was definitely paranoid about being recognized, and though he had reservations about the likelihood of that, he could understand how she hated the thought of it happening: this private person, entirely unknown to the general public, until she had achieved unwanted celebrity as the victim of a violent conman, who had first robbed, then attempted to murder her.

Initially he had tried to reassure her that she was nothing like as recognizable as she thought. Personally he thought it more likely that people took a second glance because she was jolly attractive, or else because they vaguely recognized her face, and assumed that she must be an actress or something. This was borne out by the occasions when complete strangers had found an excuse to accost her, in an attempt (always thwarted by Jude) to ascertain who she was. Worse still were the insensitive idiots, who having realized exactly who she was, enquired with syrupy solicitude, whether she was 'better now', or 'over it all', as if being reminded of a terrifying ordeal by a complete stranger was likely to assist in the healing process. The intrusive nature and crass stupidity of a celebrity fixated public, never ceased to amaze him.

Anyway, he had soon stopped trying to persuade her that she was completely safe from recognition and curiosity, because her reluctance to be seen out and about in public places represented a useful saving on restaurant bills and tickets for events, and was particularly handy right now, as it provided the perfect excuse for another romantic night in together.

He supposed that a true romantic might have arranged to propose on a weekend in Paris, which was all very well, if you didn't have to draw down money on yet another new credit card, just in order to pay the cleaning woman. Mark was risking a shortcut, with dinner à deux, against a backdrop of the London skyline. He was a pretty decent cook – it was another thing that women liked about him – but tonight of all nights, he didn't want to risk any unexpected culinary cock-ups, or fail to focus his attention completely on her, so he had bought the lobster ready prepared, put together a crisp, colourful salad to accompany the very best steaks that he had been able to obtain (any fool could manage to keep half an eye on a steak) and to follow all this he had obtained as the pièce de résistance a fabulous concoction of delicate sponge, topped with peaches soused in liqueur, meringues and whipped cream, (Jude shared his love for desserts) which had been provided – after not inconsiderable negotiation and a quite ridiculous amount of money changing hands – by the chef of his favourite local restaurant. Even Mark, who was more of a bread and butter pudding man, had to admit that these confections looked so pretty, perched on individual glass plates in his fridge, that it really would be a pity to dismantle and eat them.

He was just lining up the ingredients to make her favourite Bellinis when his mobile rang. He had to retrieve it from the other side of the room and when he reached it, he recognized Chaz's number on the display. For a moment he was tempted to ignore the call and let the recorded message cut in, but then it occurred to him that Chaz might ring again, while Jude was there. Suppose he switched off his mobile and unplugged the house phone? But then Chaz might realize that he was avoiding him. He might even take it into his head to come to the flat – 'pay him a visit' – as Chaz himself was wont to describe it. On balance, perhaps it wasn't all that likely that Chaz would turn up on his doorstep, but now that the idea had occurred to him, Mark knew that the thought would prey on his mind, a spectre to haunt his evening, completely putting him off his stroke, so he decided that on balance it would be better to answer the phone.

Chaz had left him to stew for about a week after the Thirsk fiasco, before initiating contact again and instructing him to show up at a South Bank café, where over coffee and pastries (for which Mark had been expected to pay) Chaz had made it very clear that there would be no more commissions involving race meetings, informing Mark that he would have to find some other way of coming up with the money, and suggesting that unless a good proportion of the debt to his 'friend' was forthcoming soon, some other 'friends' of his friend would soon be 'paying Mark a visit'.

Naturally Mark had begged for more time – he was so close now, so very close to getting his hands on a sizeable amount of money, he told Chaz. (He had calculated that even if the tenants could not be evicted from Laurel Cottage and the property put on the market at once, there would be no problem about raising some money against a prime piece of real estate like that, and as well as Laurel Cottage, he knew that there must be plenty of other assets, which might convert even more easily into the ready cash that he needed.)

Up until that point in the conversation, he had reckoned Chaz to be merely the purveyor of threats, who neither knew nor cared what his plans for raising the necessary monies might entail, but this illusion was rudely shattered when after he had intimated that his finances would be drastically improved in the near future, Chaz had laughingly referred to the 'Thackeray bint', saying that under the circumstances, it might be possible to persuade his friend to wait just a little longer, in order to allow Mark a chance to 'milk the cow'. It had been unnerving to discover that his private intentions were so transparent – even if Chaz's knowledge of them was the thing which had won him a little more time.

That meeting had taken place only two days ago and the implications of it were running through Mark's mind in the seconds before he hit the green button on his phone and greeted Chaz with less than good grace. 'Hello. What do you want?'

'Someone has gone and told my friend that the girl in your life is the Thackeray bitch.'

Mark experienced the familiar wave of nausea which now tended to accompany any mention of Chaz's friend. He decided not to ask who, if not Chaz himself, could possibly have been conversing with Chaz's friend regarding his private life. 'What if they have?'

'My friend considers it absolutely laughable that anyone could come up with – still less rely on – such a crazy scheme. He asks me if you can possibly be serious. His reasoning is that someone has already tried to get their hands on Miss Thackeray's little stock of goodies, which means that she will now be completely wised up to people like you, *mon ami*. The big man laughed his socks off, when he found out where you think your salvation is coming from. He says you haven't got an ice cube's chance in hell of getting your hands on her money – even if she's letting you put your hands just about everywhere else. Time's up, I'm afraid. No more extensions.'

'Chaz, look – wait – as it happens, Jude Thackeray is absolutely mad about me.' He was babbling, he could hear himself babbling. 'The very worst possible thing I could do right now would be to directly ask her for money, whereas in a couple of weeks' time—'

'You'll be in Easy Street,' Chaz interrupted, sarcastically. 'Come off it, man. My friend's right. You're not going to get a penny out of her. Meantime other people are starting to get interested. Word gets around. Some people want to know why the Big Fellow is letting you off so lightly. Can't have people speculating that he's gone soft, or everybody will start to think that they can give him the run around.'

'I'm not giving anybody the run around, I promise you – and who else knows that I owe him money anyway? I haven't breathed a word. Chaz, you have to listen to me—'

'Yeah, yeah, give me another week or three and everything will be fine,' Chaz mimicked a whiney, unconvincing tone. 'What makes you think that it will be any easier to get anything out of Little Miss Moneybags in two weeks' time?'

'Because in two weeks' time we'll be engaged, or even married.'

Chaz responded with such a huge guffaw of laughter that Mark had to shift the phone away from his ear. 'Got the church booked and the cake ordered, have you? You're a fucking fantasist.'

'Just give me two weeks.'

'Time's up. We'll be in touch again shortly.'

'No – wait, Chaz, surely you can give me another few days? Just another couple of days . . .'

Chaz cut off the call without making any reply.

Mark replaced the phone in its former position, then stood in the kitchen, leaning both hands on the cool, granite worktops and breathing hard, as if he was recovering from running a marathon. Chaz had not made any specific threats as to what was going to happen next, and at least that was something. Or maybe not. Maybe Chaz considered that the final warning had been issued, time was up and that was the end of it. He might at this very moment be on his phone to someone else, arranging for a couple of heavies to 'pay him a call', with the intention of extracting either money, or revenge.

Chaz had been introduced as a friend of a friend. A mate of a bloke who had been at school with one of the guys who formed part of Matty Blakemore's set. He hadn't initially come across to Mark as the sort of chap who knew the kind of men who were liable to burst in through your front door, taking maybe as little as five or ten minutes (if you were lucky) to render you in need of the ambulance service. Yet even without seeing any actual evidence of it, Mark did not doubt for a moment that Chaz had exactly those kinds of contacts and was exactly that kind of man.

The cold of the worktops failed to stem the clamminess of his palms. He wanted to move across to a chair, but his legs refused to obey him and his guts had begun to dissolve in such a way that he felt incapable of doing anything other than sinking to the kitchen floor and sobbing – an instinct to which he must not succumb, with Jude expected any minute.

When the doorbell startled him a moment later, his first instinct was to somehow barricade himself into the kitchen, before dialling 999. Then he remembered that it would be Jude. Deep breaths. Think and act calmly. Smile. Could he find an excuse to change his shirt, which he suddenly realized was sticking to his back?

The bell rang again. 'Coming,' he shouted, his voice sounding unnaturally high.

Calm down. Walk normally. Open the door with a flourish, big smile, huge hug, welcoming kiss. 'My darling, how lovely you look.' Kiss her again. Time is running out. Have to make this work tonight. Got to make it work.

Sixteen

'I haven't given up, you know.'

The words startled Peter, coming at him unexpectedly, breathed low, close to his ear, as Hannah passed behind him on her way to fetch the coffees, when they took their first break of the afternoon, after resuming work on the Thackeray case.

She didn't wait for a response, just glided out of the room, shutting the door behind her; leaving him to stare at the familiar quartet of greenish-grey dots on the dark blue paintwork, caused when someone had removed a notice stuck on with Blu-tack, goodness knows how long before.

To his relief she had not bothered to look back and check on his reaction, because he felt the colour rise in his cheeks, though he told himself that his first instinct was not to be embarrassed, but appalled. What had gone wrong here? How had a normal, professional relationship shifted so radically in the space of twenty-four hours? They had spent the whole of the previous day working together, without him picking up so much as a hint that McMahon was remotely interested in him. Since then he had run their interactions through his mind several times, without being able to identify any warning signals from her at all. He had not picked up a single vibe, until the moment when having lured him out on a fool's errand, she had propositioned him.

He had continued to ponder the situation while he waited to give his evidence at Crown Court that morning, wondering what, if any, reference would be made to the episode when they next saw one another on his return to headquarters, but that afternoon he and McMahon had resumed work together as if nothing had happened. She had behaved perfectly properly, for at least an hour, giving no sign that she even remembered what had happened – or for the most part had not happened – in the lay-by the evening before, though he had felt acutely aware of it, as embarrassed as a guilty school boy, caught out in a crush on his teacher. Which was ridiculous, he thought, as he hadn't been the instigator. Was she aware of his discomfiture? Was that why she had all but whispered in his ear, on leaving the room?

Was it a joke? A wind-up? Maybe the whole team were in on it – though somehow he did not think so. It was sexual harassment. Not that he would ever report her. He liked McMahon and anyway he'd be laughed to kingdom come if it ever came out. (Which of course it would – there were no secrets in CID.) Maybe if he ignored it – just made it politely clear that he wasn't interested? (It would have been so easy to *be* interested – that kiss in the car park was enough to get anyone warmed up). She might be winding him up. She had never come across as the scary, bunny boiler type. If he didn't rise to the bait (hmm, maybe not the best of expressions in the circumstances) perhaps she would lose interest.

Of course, he could always ask to be transferred. He could tell the boss that he and

McMahon were not getting along. That might lead to awkward questions, and besides which, he didn't want to move. If anyone ought to move, it was her, damn it, because she was the one who had made the pitch, and thereby made things awkward.

Of course, if he was going to resign from the force anyway . . . Ginny's email still sat unanswered in his inbox. She had told him to take his time to think about it and he *was* thinking about it. It wasn't as if he had responsibilities or ties. A policeman's lot, as Gilbert and Sullivan had memorably pointed out, was not a happy one – and they had written that years before all the cutbacks and efficiency drives and the management initiatives which, far from resolving anything, just set up arguments about whose responsibility it was to do which bits of the job. Endless protocols and new initiatives; 'Policing by tick-box,' as Lingo had disparagingly referred to it. All the older hands claimed that they would not want to join up today – but maybe everyone approaching the end of their career, in whatever walk of life, said that things were not what they used to be. The job still had a lot to offer. No two days ever the same – it wasn't a case of running through the same repertoire, time after time. Job security against complete uncertainty. Music versus the Thackeray case. Not just the Thackeray case. There were lots of cases: always had been, always would be, though the Thackeray case featured high in his imaginary list of priorities. The key to unlocking that case lay somewhere in the evidence; he felt it and he suspected that Lingo felt it too. Why else spare two officers for a week-long mini-review? There was a previously unexplored clue somewhere in those files and he badly wanted to find it.

If he was absolutely honest with himself, when it came to Jude Thackeray, it wasn't just the good copper's desire to bring the crime home to the culprit. Yes, of course he shared the team's collective frustration at being beaten by this nasty little bastard, whoever he was, but there was also Jude Thackeray herself. He was forced to admit to himself that McMahon had been right when she had asserted that he found Jude Thackeray attractive.

Jude Thackeray was not only pretty, but had a quality about her which appealed to all his protective instincts. Sitting by, while she had relived her ordeal at the hands of a man she had initially trusted, he'd had to make a conscious effort to remain objective and uninvolved. At times, he had lived it with her, almost had to fight the urge to enfold her in his arms and comfort her. These were thoughts which he could never afford to share. Maintain a professional distance – that was the mantra. Unprofessional or not, he knew that he had come dangerously close to falling for Jude Thackeray.

He was still picturing her, bravely attempting to answer their questions, when Hannah breezed back into the room, a paper cup of coffee in each hand. 'Right then,' she said, 'let's get back down to business, shall we?'

Seventeen

As Mark passed the oval mirror in his hall, he caught himself grinning. 'Victory in sight,' as Errol Flynn might have said in one of those classic black and white adventure movies, which he had watched again and again as a boy. (When a secondary image of Michael Caine and Steve Martin in *Dirty Rotten Scoundrels* popped into his head, he banished it at once.)

In the end it had been surprisingly easy. When he had eventually popped the question (as his late grandmother would so quaintly have put it), Jude had collapsed into his arms, seeming to laugh and cry at the same time, and when he had prompted, 'You haven't answered my question, yet,' she had gasped out, 'Yes, oh yes, of course yes.' It was pretty much as emphatic as you could get.

In many ways, he could scarcely believe it himself. Chaz's friend was right, inasmuch that it had been a risky scheme, unlikely to succeed: so crazy that he would never have dreamed of attempting anything like it, if he had not been so desperate. Well, 'Who dares, wins,' as that eighties film would have it. He hadn't been able to disguise the triumph in his voice when telephoning Chaz the next morning to inform him that Jude Thackeray had not only accepted his proposal, but had even agreed to his suggestion that they get a special licence and do the deed quickly, before the papers got hold of the story. She had been so totally on-board about this, that he had scarcely needed to remind her that delay increased the chances of word getting out and of course all the papers would want to report that 'tragic kidnap victim Jude' or however they chose to describe her, 'finds happiness with new man'.

For some unknown reason, Chaz hadn't taken the news of the engagement particularly well. If anything, Mark thought that he had sounded downright disappointed, almost as if he would have preferred the idea of letting loose a couple of heavies, instead of being able to convey to his friend the information that repayment in full was now assured. After hearing Mark out, Chaz had offered no congratulations or comments, beyond saying that he would have to take the information back to 'the big man' and would 'be in touch', a phrase which he invariably managed to invest with a distinct level of menace.

In spite of Chaz's chilly reception to the news, Mark's success with Jude had imbued him with a newfound confidence and he refused to be rattled. He knew that he wasn't out of the woods yet, but her surprising willingness to marry him immediately had filled him with a sense that he had triumphed against all the odds. It was the equivalent of ignoring all the pundits, putting your house on a thousand to one long shot, then seeing it romp home, twenty lengths ahead of the field. Chaz's attitude was bizarre, because surely his boss would prefer to receive his money in full? What was the point of dishing out some sort of violent reprisal for non-payment? That wasn't going to restore any cash to his bank account.

Aside from Chaz, the only other fly in the ointment was Jude's brother. The brother had already been making awkward enquiries and news of an engagement would probably send him into overdrive. Whereas at one time, Mark had believed it was possible to keep his financial situation under wraps, some of the things which Chaz had said suggested otherwise. Who knew what people were saying behind his back and how easily that sort of gossip might reach Rob Thackeray's ears? With this in mind, he had proposed that their engagement remain a closely guarded secret, and in the initial euphoria, Jude had been completely in agreement. As well as having the advantage of avoiding the media's gaze, she had described the secrecy as 'romantic'. (Mark, while relieved, could not help thinking her something of a rarity, since so far as he could gauge from the experiences of friends and relations, most women's idea of 'romantic' in the context of a wedding seemed to involve a country church, a pantechnicon load of flowers, big frocks, bigger bills and a marquee full of friends and relatives, all quaffing gallons of free drink.) However, in the cold light of morning, it had soon become clear that while she was quite happy to keep their nuptial arrangements a secret from family (both her parents were dead anyway) and friends – she wanted to make an exception when it came to her brother.

'We're so close,' she had said. 'I can't not tell Rob. He would be devastated. I know how upset

I would feel, if he went off and got married and only told me about it afterwards.'

Mark had tried her with: 'I won't be telling my brothers until afterwards,' but it did no good, because as she rightly pointed out, he wasn't exactly close to them.

'It's different with Rob and me,' she said. 'With both our parents gone, we've always looked out for each other.'

It ran through Mark's mind when she said this, that Rob hadn't been looking out for her very well when some sadistic imbecile had kept her tied up for several days and tortured her into revealing her pin numbers and the combination to the safe where she kept her jewellery, but he didn't say so. Instead he decided that he would have to swallow her determination to share their 'romantic' intentions with her brother, because a) everything else had gone so jolly well and b) let's face it, he couldn't really stop her.

Part of the trouble was that he had never liked the brother and he knew that whatever Jude might say to the contrary, the brother didn't like him, either. There was a watchfulness about Robin Thackeray, which had always made him feel uncomfortable. It was partly guilty conscience, he supposed. When you've deliberately made someone the target of your affections, for less than straightforward, honourable reasons, it's only natural to wonder whether the big brother can see right through you. In Robin Thackeray's case, though, it went a bit further than that. Mark had sometimes caught Robin Thackeray looking at his sister with an air of possession which went above and beyond a comfortable norm. He would go so far as to describe it as faintly creepy. So much so, in fact, that if Mark had not needed Jude Thackeray as much as he did, the brother's manner might have actively put him off. OK, the guy must have felt that he had let his sister down, in failing to protect her from the bloke who had almost gone on to murder her, but even so, the way Robin watched Jude, the way he seemed to be forever hanging around – the whole thing was a bit heavy.

He was also worried that the brother exerted a dangerous level of influence on her. Mark had a nasty suspicion that Rob might advise his sister about financial matters. She trusted her brother implicitly and probably ran any big decisions by him. Then again, the brother wouldn't be with them on their honeymoon and that was when he, Mark, was going to hit her with the story he had ready prepared, for why he needed an immediate, short-term loan.

He had been particularly worried about financing an appropriate kind of honeymoon, but even this potential problem had been unexpectedly resolved, when she had spontaneously suggested that they go to her place in Cornwall. Up until then, he hadn't been aware that she had a place in Cornwall (some days things just got better and better) but when he tried to find out a bit more about it, she had revealed very little, saying that it was 'only a cottage' and 'miles from anywhere'. He had noticed in the past how dismissive the wealthy often were about their pads in the country, down-playing their spacious seaside retreats, Victorian rectories and premises little short of a stately home, as if they were taking you to spend a weekend in a mere shack.

'We can laze around and be completely on our own,' she had added and he had made a mental note to ensure that there was plenty of champagne, since he didn't want to have to rely on her making the right decisions, while intoxicated with happiness alone.

It was all working out far, far more easily than he could have expected. He felt exuberant enough to shout or sing. The face in the mirror grinned back at him. 'It's all but in the bag,' he told his reflection out loud.

Just then his mobile went into its distinctive combination of a train whistle, accompanied by galloping horses' hooves. He took it from his pocket and saw that it was Chaz. Good. Chaz calling back so soon after receiving news of the engagement must mean that he was about to climb down a bit.

'Hi.' Mark was conscious of a cheerful note in his voice; a quality which was normally absent when he knew that it was Chaz on the line.

'I've spoken with my friend.' There was something in Chaz's voice that chilled Mark immediately. 'When I appraised him of your forthcoming nuptials, he asked me to pass on his congratulations and to tell you that the sum owing has now doubled.'

'What?'

'I should imagine you will be well able to pay – once you become Mr Jude Thackeray.'

'But why? Why has it doubled? A fair rate of interest – that's what you told me.'

103

Chaz gave a contemptuous laugh. '"From each according to his ability to pay, to each according to his needs." Karl Marx, old boy. You're going to have access to considerable means, if what the papers have said about Ms Thackeray is correct.'

For a moment Mark couldn't summon up any words at all. Eventually he spluttered out, 'But that's not fair.'

'Since when did that alter anything?'

'I won't pay it. No more than what we agreed.'

'Oh, I think you will, Marky, my lad. Because you've handed the Big Fellow a prime bargaining chip, don't you see? If you fail to come up with what my friend asks for, *when* he asks for it, he'll be having a word with Ms Thackeray's brother. He's very interested in you. Remember he's been asking questions. We don't want him hearing any wrong answers, before you've got a ring on her finger – or afterwards, if it comes to that – do we now?'

Eighteen

'How's it going?'

The two detectives simultaneously looked up from their deliberations to find Graham Ling framed in the doorway.

'Nothing new so far, I'm afraid.' Peter Betts tried not to sound as downhearted as he felt. At the outset he had genuinely believed that something might come out of all these hours spent poring over the files, but so far nothing much had emerged apart from an inappropriate proposition, which he was trying to forget about.

By contrast, Hannah seemed positively perky. 'We're building up a good overall picture,' she said. 'There's still a fair chance that something will shake loose. I thought you were going to be tied up with the Bradley case all week.'

'So did I,' Ling said rather grimly. 'But old Badger Bradley's got a good barrister – Hickson,' he added, in response to an enquiring look from his colleagues. 'Bugger's got the trial stopped on a technicality. Don't worry,' he added as Betts swore expressively, 'we'll get him at the retrial. Softly, softly and all that.'

'I was wondering,' Peter said, 'whether it would be worth going back to Jude Thackeray, one more time. To see if she remembers anything else.'

'If she thought of something, surely she would let us know,' Hannah demurred.

'Maybe we're not asking her the right questions.'

Graham Ling sounded irritated as he said, 'We asked her every bloody question under the sun. She talked for hours and hours, but we essentially never got anything more from her than the bare bones she'd given us in the first twenty-four hours after it happened.'

Peter could picture the scene clearly. Jude Thackeray in a hospital bed. (Private nursing home, of course.) She had suffered no major physical injuries, but the doctor wanted to keep her in as a precaution, so the interviewing officers had stationed themselves at the bedside, and Jude had been only too willing to talk; her story spilling out, with her sometimes becoming tearful, sometimes physically trembling, sometimes just shaking her head at 'how gullible' she had been.

'One idea we've come up with,' Hannah said. 'Maybe we should get the low-down on all the vehicles which travelled on the ferries sailing out of Harwich in the twenty-four hours or so after our man torched the van.'

Ling shook his head. 'That would encompass hundreds of vehicles. If you can show me something definite that says he left the country on one of those ferries, or better still provide a vehicle reg to check against their records, I'll give the go-ahead. Otherwise it's a definite negative on speculative wild goose chases. You've got a couple more days. After that, I want you back to normal duties. I'm not sanctioning a trip out of area to question the victim again either, unless you can offer me something better than a hunch that she might have something else to say. It's strictly a desk-based review. No jollies and no field trips.' He laughed as the younger man's head shot up.

Peter felt himself redden as the boss caught his eye. Dear God, did everyone know everything?

When he was sure that Ling was out of earshot, he hissed at his colleague, 'Did you tell anyone about going out to the scene?'

'Of course not. Why?'

'The Old Man seems to know about it. You heard him just now.'

'Saying what? I don't know what you're on about.'

106

'When he made that crack about field trips. He looked straight at me and laughed.'

'So? He thinks you're after having a nice little away day to wherever Jude Thackeray is currently residing, with petrol claimed and lunch on expenses.'

'Look me in the eye and swear to me that you didn't tell anyone about what happened the other night.'

'Point one, *nothing* happened. Point two, I am hardly going to broadcast to everyone that I threw myself at you and you turned me down. Point three, if I ever get wind of the slightest hint that *you* have shared the circumstances of this humiliating rejection with anyone, I will retaliate with a story from which your reputation as a stud will never recover. Point Four, I am still free tonight, in the event that you want to reconsider your original answer.'

He couldn't help laughing. 'You're not serious.'

'Deadly. I need to check out the rumours.'

'What rumours?'

'Didn't you know that your sexual prowess is the talk of the constabulary?'

'No, it isn't.' He grew abruptly serious again. 'Pack it in, McMahon.' He knew that he didn't have a reputation. He couldn't decide how far the joke went and how much she was in earnest about wanting to sleep with him, but whichever way round, they should stop talking about it. It was his own fault for bringing it up, because when he stopped to think about it properly, there was no doubt that she was right about the cause of Ling's remark – not least because he knew that the boss would not be in the least bit amused by the idea of his officers propositioning one another in local lay-bys, or snogging in the underground car park. However much the modern police force went along with personal relationships between its employees, so far as Old Lingo was concerned, it got in the way of work and nothing should ever be allowed to do that.

'Do I take it then, that I'm washing my hair tonight – alone?'

'I mean it, McMahon. Pack it in.'

There was a long pause. He had spoken far more sharply than was normally acceptable when addressing a colleague.

When she spoke again, she sounded strained, as if she might be fighting back tears. He pretended not to notice. It was her own fault for taking a bad joke too far. Another couple of days, as the Old Man had said. After that they could return to working with the rest of the team and with a bit of luck he could swing things to avoid being one-to-one with her again.

'He's obviously very plausible, our man.' Hannah had begun to straighten a paperclip, keeping her eyes focussed on the slender strand of metal in her fingers, while speaking slowly and carefully, as if weighing every word. 'He was with Jude Thackeray the whole of that last day before he attacked her, and yet she claims that she never noticed anything out of the ordinary about him at all. That means he didn't get obviously strung up, or nervous, even though he must have known what he was going to do.'

'Exactly.' Peter seized on her words, grateful

that they were back to concentrating on the case. 'He'd laid his plans, gained her confidence. It wasn't some random, unpremeditated attack. This was what he'd been planning all along.'

'Of course, we have to allow for the possibility that she's particularly bad at picking up danger signals.'

'She didn't strike me as being dumb.'

'Nor me. So let's go through it, step by step. It's fairly late when things eventually kick off. At least eleven o'clock, she thought, by the time they were getting undressed, ready for bed.'

Peter nodded. 'She reckons they'd drunk at least one bottle of wine between them, that evening, but of course he was smart enough to be sure that everything went out with the recycling and the bin-men next day. That's attention to detail – planning your attack to coincide with a fortnightly refuse collection.'

'So they're getting undressed, maybe helping each other out of their clothes . . .'

Peter glanced up suspiciously, but Hannah – who had discarded her redundant paperclip – was shuffling through various items of paperwork which were spread around her laptop and continued without pause, 'She's down to her bra and knickers, when he comes up behind her, grabs her hands and secures them with a cable tie. Standard white plastic – easily obtained via hundreds of retail and online outlets. Apparently she's too surprised to put up much resistance, and says she doesn't realize what he's doing until it's too late.' She hesitated, then asked, 'Do you reckon that she didn't want to own up to a bit of bondage?'

'No. She was asked and she said they'd never gone in for anything like that.'

'But she also said that initially she thought he was playing some kind of a game with her.'

'OK, maybe they'd played around before. I don't see that it really matters. What she says here . . .' He paused to check. '. . . Is that she was startled and a bit uneasy, but not actually scared. She thought it was some sort of joke, and for the first moment or two she didn't take it seriously, not even when he initially made her lie down on the bed, and asked her for her pin numbers.'

'Because during dirty sex, boyfriends ask you for your pin numbers all the time,' Hannah commented sarcastically.

'She never even saw where he got the cable tie from,' Peter went on. 'She thinks it must have been in his jeans pocket, but she wasn't really sure.'

'Then he asks her for the pin numbers again and she gets scared and tells him to untie her, which of course he doesn't. Instead he starts to threaten her, saying that he's going to hurt her if she doesn't co-operate. At this point, she's face down on the bed, but in the mirror, she can see him dragging the belt out of his trousers – the irony being that it's a leather one which she herself had brought him back from Spain, as a present, a few days before. Does that indicate anything?' Hannah paused, assuming a thoughtful expression.

'Only that he's an evil bastard.'

'Right. So she decides that he means business

110

and tells him the pin number, which is the same for all three of her cards. He repeats it, she confirms it. Then he asks for the combination of the safe at the family house in Colchester, at which point she panics, because she can't remember it. She tries to tell him that she doesn't know it. She says that only Robin knows it, but Laddo isn't convinced. He tells her that he remembers her opening it once, while they were at the house without Robin, and she realizes that she did and therefore that he knows she's lying.'

'It's then that he yells at her and starts to strike her with the belt.' Peter paused again, while he checked for confirmation of the details. 'Evidence of at least seven or eight blows still apparent three days later, according to the medical report.'

'That's not really very many.'

'Jesus, Hannah. How many times do you want him to have hit her? I should think it would feel like more than enough.'

'That's not what I'm getting at. Our man is dangerous, but he's not into violence for violence's sake. Yes, he clobbers her with a leather belt, hard enough to leave bruises, but he's doing it as a means to an end. He stops when she gives him the combination of the safe. If he was into it, he wouldn't have stopped. Compared with a lot of victims, she actually got off quite lightly. Think of all the people we've seen who've been put through the mincer, with their faces black and blue, broken ribs. He hardly touched her face, didn't actually break any bones. Yes, he's hurt her pretty badly in this initial attack, and there's

111

another one still to come, but he doesn't torture her. He's not getting off on it. He beats her because it's a way of making her give up information, that's all.'

'Well, so long as that's all, we can afford to be dismissive about it.'

'I'm not being dismissive, I'm being objective. It's a pity you never have been – entirely objective – where Jude Thackeray's concerned. I bet you wouldn't have turned *her* down.'

The comment found its mark. 'DS McMahon, I swear if you make just one more reference to what you suggested to me the other evening, I *will* make a formal complaint to Ling. Stop messing with me and get on with the case.'

Hannah flashed him an angry look, but he stared her out. A couple more days he thought. Only a couple more days and after that I'll manage to find a reason for not working closely with her again. Ever.

When it became obvious that she wasn't going to break the silence, he said, 'Let's pick up where we left off, shall we? He's struck her, at least half a dozen times . . .'

Hannah accepted the prompt. 'She says she was screaming her head off, although she knew that there was absolutely no chance of anyone hearing her.'

'And she was panicking, because she couldn't remember the combination of the safe, and couldn't remember where she'd put a note of the number.'

'Right. So she made up a number – yelled it out, just to stop him from hurting her.'

'Which works, though it's obviously a risky game to play in the long run.'

'He writes the number down, drags her off the bed and makes her go downstairs, where he forces her into the cupboard off the kitchen, which was once some sort of larder. You know,' Hannah broke off, 'it has always surprised me that the cupboard was empty, ready and waiting for her. Who has an empty cupboard in their house? My cupboards are all stuffed to capacity. Open any of them and something is liable to fall out on top of you.'

'The place was very tidy,' Peter said. 'I guess there was no need for a larder, in a fully fitted kitchen, with a big fridge freezer. She only used it as a weekend place, so they didn't keep much in, I suppose.'

'Right. Not like those of us who have to manage with just one property to keep all our stuff in. Anyway . . . he also gags her, before putting her in there. He shuts the door and somehow jams it shut. She isn't sure how and after a while she tries to push against the door, and even shoulder charges it, but she can't make it budge.'

'Some of the bruises on her upper arms are consistent with this.' Peter was again consulting the medical report.

'She doesn't actually hear him drive away, but she guesses that he must have gone to withdraw money on her cards . . .'

'Which is exactly what he did do, as confirmed by her bank statements. Maximum cash withdrawals of three hundred pounds from each account, just before midnight at the cashpoint in front of Endersley Village Stores – no witnesses and no CCTV.'

'She also assumes – rightly – that he has taken her keys and gone to the house at Colchester, to try out the combination of the safe, and of course she's out of her mind with terror, wondering what he's liable to do to her, when he finds out that she's given him the wrong numbers.'

'Not a nice situation to be in. Locked in that cupboard, in the dark, just waiting for him to come back.'

Nineteen

'Matty, my boy, how's tricks?'

Matt Blakemore didn't even bother to twist his features into the semblance of a smile. 'What do you want, Chaz? I've told you before not to call me out of work like this. I've done your latest "little errand" – now what do you want?'

Although he knew it was never a good idea to antagonize Chaz, Matt found it increasingly difficult to disguise his loathing of the man. He hated those peculiar greetings, halfway between the public schoolboy which Chaz undoubtedly was, and the East End gangster, for whom he presumably provided a front. Although Chaz gave the impression of being very much a part of the 'Big Man's' organization, Matt assumed the reality to be that Chaz was as much a captive to debts as he was himself. Or maybe Chaz had always been the type to team up with the bullies, the sort who got a buzz out of kicking the other chap, when he was down. Most of all, of course, Matt, hated the hold Chaz – or his shadowy employer – had over him. A bad run at blackjack was all it had taken. That and the reckless notion that a short-term loan from a dubious source would see him out of trouble.

The suggestion that he approach Chaz had come from Dominic Phillips-Warde, whose reputation for being more than a bit wild had never encompassed being downright crooked, though probably poor old Dom had been working to Chaz's instructions too. He could imagine Chaz telling him to: 'Find me another mug, and I'll knock a few thou off what you owe.' Well, he doubted that Chaz and his boss had ever recouped much from Dom Phillips-Warde, who had been dead within six months of embroiling Matt in Chaz's various schemes. A drug overdose had always been on the cards with Dom. The inquest resulted in an open verdict – could have been an accident, might have been suicide. Matt shuddered to think of a third possibility, though he knew that such a thing *was* a possibility, and made all the more likely, given Chaz's comments that Dominic was 'a loose cannon, with a big mouth' and 'a bloody great liability'.

Whatever the truth of the matter, it was hard not to associate Chaz with Dom's death, and seeing Chaz, awaiting him at the bar, dressed in the typical gentleman about town tailored suit, striped shirt, and silk tie, looking as pleased with himself as ever, was like a red rag.

'It's that very thing I wanted to talk to you about,' Chaz said. 'I was passing the end of your street and I thought I'd just check in with you and see how it went.'

'It went the way you wanted it to.' Matt glared at the other man. 'I met this bloke, as you asked, the one who'd been asking me questions about Mark Medlicott at Windsor. I walked up to him at the bar, and said, "Haven't we met before?" also as you asked me to. He said he didn't think so, then I said, "Wasn't it at the races, about a week ago", and didn't we have a mutual acquaintance in Mark Medlicott? He remembered me then and seemed quite keen to talk, so we had a drink together.'

'And,' Chaz prompted.

'I did what you told me to. I bigged up Medders's supposed fortune. I don't know why you wanted me to and I suspect that it's actually quite the opposite; that Mark's in trouble with the guy you work for, and that's why you're involved with him in some way. You'd better not be using me to stitch him up. I didn't like the look of that bloke. There was something about him that didn't seem quite kosher to me. *Are* you setting Mark up?'

'Really, old chap. As if I would.'

Matt glared openly at his tormentor, provoked still further by the Burlington Bertie expression. 'I don't want to be involved with anything criminal,' he said.

Chaz laughed. 'Are you suggesting that *I* would be involved in anything criminal? Dear Boy, I'm cut to the quick.'

'If that's all you wanted, you could have phoned me, preferably out of office hours.' Matt turned to leave. 'I've told you before not to bother me when I'm at work.'

'Never know who might be listening in at your end,' Chaz said. 'I won't offer to buy you a drink as I know you're bursting to get back to the office.'

Twenty

'You know what? It doesn't matter how long I do this job, I will never get used to seeing photographs like these.'

Peter noticed that Hannah sounded extremely weary. They had agreed at the beginning of the week that while it would be impossible to cover every detail of the Thackeray case, in order to get through as much material as possible, they would work an extra hour or two each evening. This had made for very long days, shut up together in the stuffy little office, with its quartet of Blu-tack spots on the door and its carpet repaired with a line of Do Not Cross tape (at least someone still had a sense of humour).

She was leafing through the pictures as she spoke. Images which showed in detail the welts and bruises which had decorated Jude Thackeray's body, when she initially arrived at the hospital. 'Imagine how humiliating it must be, having to strip off for the camera and show your battle scars. Horrible.'

'Don't look at them, then. Concentrate on the verbal descriptions. Unless you've had enough and want to call it a day?'

'No.' Hannah sighed audibly. 'Let's get through this part of it.'

'OK. So Jude Thackeray is locked in the cupboard, knowing that she's given this thug the wrong combination to the safe and therefore that before too long, he's going to come back, asking her for the right one.'

'Right.' Hannah resumed the role of narrator. 'She's absolutely hysterical with fear, but then she manages to calm herself down enough to think about the combination. She knows it's based on birthdays and anniversaries and she reckons that it's her parents' birthdays, thirteen and twenty three, coupled with the year they got married, which she thinks is seventy-four, but then she also recalls where the slip of paper with the combination can be found.'

'I wonder why she or her brother never changed the combination to something easier, after both parents had died.'

'I suppose they never saw any need to. Anyway, the next thing she remembers is him flinging open the cupboard door, and attacking her. She remembers him grabbing her by the hair, slapping her head and face, and landing a couple of kicks as well. Obviously he's furious, because he assumes that she gave him the wrong combination on purpose.' Hannah swallowed hard.

You weren't supposed to let this sort of stuff get to you, Peter thought. The Thackeray case was by no means the worst violence either of them had seen inflicted on a fellow human being, yet for some reason McMahon seemed to be finding the bald facts particularly difficult to handle. He had never known her go soft on them before.

'We should stop and take a break,' he said.

'No.' Hannah spoke fiercely, almost angrily. 'We have to get through this part before we go home tonight.'

He raised his hands in a gesture of surrender and she began again, recounting Jude Thackeray's story, while he tried not to let her see that he had noticed her unmistakable efforts to stave off distress.

'She tried to tell him about the combination and where he could find the piece of paper so that he could check it, but he carried on hitting her – slapping her, she says here – and even when she'd told him the combination at least three or four times, he then says that he's going to test her and see if she's telling him the truth and that's when he heats up the sharpening steel and places it against her bare skin, a few times.'

'Where does that sit with your ideas about him not being particularly sadistic?'

He had spoken quietly, not challenging her so much as prompting debate, and she answered in an equally measured way, 'I still think it isn't violence for violence sake. Some of these scum-bags – remember the Butcher robbery – go mad, give half a chance to lay into someone. Teeth knocked out, broken bones . . . This guy isn't into that. It's all incredibly controlled. He puts on disposable gloves before rifling around in the kitchen to find something suitable for his purpose, chooses the steel, which he calmly heats up, using the gas ring. He intends to hurt her enough to make her tell him what he needs to know, but he doesn't go absolutely over the top, even though he ultimately intends to kill her.'

'Mmm . . .' It was his turn to be thoughtful again. He did remember the Butcher case only too well: a hapless, middle-aged couple, subjected to a hideous amount of violence, by a couple of armed thugs – now happily detained at HM's pleasure – all for a relatively small amount of cash and a couple of mediocre antique figurines. 'I don't think we should mistake this for kindness,' he said at last. 'The plan entails walking her out to the van and then probably walking her some way into the woods at the other end of the van ride. He doesn't want to have to carry her, so there's nothing to be gained from any excessive violence, above and beyond what he sees as absolutely necessary.'

'Fair point. And of course he may be saving himself up for the last act of the play, when they get into the woods.'

'Right. Is there anything in the way he uses things that are to hand in the kitchen, rather than coming equipped?'

Hannah considered for a moment, before answering. 'He may not have anticipated the need to do anything to her in the kitchen. Presumably his original idea was that she would give him all the information he needed, when he first gave her a going over in the bedroom, for which he had come equipped, with a hefty leather belt that she had provided for him.'

'Which has never been found.'

'Probably still hanging in his wardrobe . . . wherever that is.'

'Could be useful when we track him down.'

'If.'

'When,' he responded firmly.

'So, after threatening that if she sends him off on another wild goose chase, he will come back and kill her, he eventually accepts that she's told him the truth about the combination, and he shuts her back in the cupboard. She tries to get her hands free, but she can't and only succeeds in chafing her wrists against the cable ties. In the meantime we know that he was quite busy that day. He gives everywhere a thorough clean and does the laundry, if you please.' She gave a laugh, but it was a bitter, half-formed thing, which hung uncomfortably in the air.

'Neat touch that. You can't fault a man who strips the bed and puts everything through the washer-drier after he sleeps with you. That's got to be a step up from promising to call but never bothering.' Peter hadn't intended to get anywhere near topics like that, but Hannah suddenly seemed so low that he badly wanted to make her laugh properly, which she did.

'So far as we know, the only person to call at the house that day is the postman,' she continued. 'He drops a couple of circulars through the door, sees no one, doesn't remember anything unusual and can't remember what vehicles, if any, were parked on the drive.'

'Another in a long line of helpful, productive witness statements, in fact.'

'There are no visitors, no telephone calls. Local people passing the end of the drive don't notice anything either. There are absolutely no sightings of the white van, though we know it must have arrived at some point during the twenty-four to forty-eight hours prior to him using it to drive her to the lay-by.'

'My gut feeling is that our man exchanges his own car for the white van during the trip back to the house at Colchester, when he helps himself to the contents of the safe and pays his second visit to the village cashpoint, in order to withdraw another £900 from the three accounts that he's now got access to.'

'Another late-night operation, when he manages to avoid being seen by anyone. It's like chasing the Invisible Man. Even the jewellery is pretty much impossible to follow up since the Thackeray family have never bothered to get it valued, photographed, or individually listed on their insurance policy, so all we have to go on are their verbal descriptions, plus one or two photos from the family album, showing Jude dressed up in a necklace, plus her grandmother sporting what appears to be a diamond brooch against her fur coat, circa 1950.'

'Again, he's very disciplined,' Peter noted. 'He enters the house, letting himself in with a key. He goes for the safe, doesn't appear to touch anything else or do any damage. The other thing that has struck me time and again, is that he put in a lot of work for relatively little return in the end. We don't know the exact worth of the family jewellery, but having to fence it will reduce its value considerably, and he settled for the £1800 he was able to withdraw from the cashpoints across the time period while he held Jude Thackeray captive. That's not a hell of a lot, for what amounts to several weeks work – all that time spent gaining her confidence.'

'Perhaps he's not all that clever, after all,' Hannah said. 'He could probably have done just as well by forcing his way into the house one night, wearing a Mickey Mouse mask, so that she never got to see his face. He could still have forced her to give up the pin numbers and the combination to the safe, and as she'd never got any sort of look at him, he would have saved himself the trouble of having to murder her – or trying to.'

'It's not a lot for such a carefully constructed plan. And we know that he didn't come up with the idea once he'd got to know her, because he was laying a false trail from the very start. There's definitely something that we're missing here. Maybe he didn't get as much as he'd hoped for? Maybe there was another part of the scheme which went wrong? Perhaps he'd over-estimated the amount of assets that she would have readily available?'

'All possibilities, but presently unknowable.'

'I bet he didn't get anything like as much as he'd hoped for. It's hardly enough to retire on, is it? Some antique jewellery and a couple of grand? Maybe this was some kind of trial run. I think he'll wait awhile, then try it again, targeting some other wealthy woman.'

'Which he may be doing right now – he's a

dangerous guy.' Hannah waited to see if her colleague had anything more to say, but when he remained silent, she continued, 'At some point, either before or after the initial attack, he changes vehicles, because when he takes Jude from the house, she is absolutely clear that the only cars on the drive are hers and the white van, whereas his car had been there the day before.'

'We also know that he wasn't picked up by the CCTV on the main road, so he must have driven to both the cashpoint and the house at Colchester via the back lanes – but then our man's such a careful planner that I wouldn't have expected anything less of him. No doubt he had all his routes sussed out, weeks before.'

Hannah nodded. 'We don't know which way he went, or have any times except for the cash withdrawals, but at some stage he arrives back at Laurel Cottage in the van. That van must have been garaged somewhere reasonably close to his route between Elmley Green and Colchester. He gets back to the house, lets himself in again with her door key, and eventually he opens up the cupboard, orders her out, then marches her straight through the kitchen, out of the back door and round the side of the house. This activates the security lights, so she sees the van standing there, with the back doors open, and he makes her get inside.'

'And she was sure that there was no one else around.'

'Right. No question of an accomplice at the scene, unless there was someone else in the cab of the van, but there's nothing to indicate that.

Jude has absolutely no idea of the time by this stage, only that she's been locked up for what feels like an age – but we have the timings of the withdrawals from the cashpoints, so we know that it must have been well after midnight by the time he went back to collect her. She gets into the van and before he shuts the door, she sees a loop of wire or string, which she has described as a garrotte, lying on the floor of the van. When he shuts the door, the back of the van is in darkness – she thinks it was screened off from the front seats somehow.'

'This garrotte, or whatever it was, has evidently been brought in from the outside. No clues as to what happened to it and no sign of it in what was left of the van, though it may have been completely destroyed by the fire. Wasn't Joel in charge of pursuing possible leads on the van?'

'Yeah. No definite sightings from when it was pinched from outside the flats, until it was found burned out. Hundreds of lock-ups identified without establishing any definite links. Miles of CCTV footage checked, but it's another complete non-event, evidentially, except for the one sighting when Mr X and Jude Thackeray were on their way between Laurel Cottage and Foxden Woods, when he stops to top up with a tenner's worth of diesel, at the all-night garage.'

'That's the part I really don't get,' Peter interrupted. 'He's been so incredibly careful, then he rocks up at a garage and gets captured on CCTV. You said "on their way", but actually the garage isn't on their way. He had to go out of his way to visit it.'

'That's probably because it's the only twenty-four-hour garage for miles around. Someone's noted here, "shows local knowledge".'

'For me this is the part that really doesn't fit. You don't plan everything so meticulously, then notice that you need to stop for petrol.'

'Except that everyone makes at least one mistake.'

'Which for him, turns out not to be a mistake, since we can't see his face at all on the footage, and get nothing concrete from it, except that he has the height and build of Mr Average, which is no more than we knew already. It's as if he's bloody taunting us – "look, look, here I am, captured on camera and you're still no wiser".'

'And of course the cashier on duty takes absolutely no notice of him,' Hannah said with a sigh as she read: 'Cannot recall any kind of conversation apart from asking him if he wanted a VAT receipt, to which our man allegedly said, "no thanks". Witness wouldn't know the man again if he saw him and wouldn't recognize his voice which was apparently "ordinary" – whatever that might mean.'

'One slightly interesting thing emerged in a later statement,' Peter said. 'Here it is – the cashier thought that he didn't take any particular notice of the man, because he might have seen him before.'

'I don't remember hearing about that. Was the cashier asked to look through mug shots and previous CCTV?'

'Apparently not. What the garage guy seems to be saying is that he wouldn't actually be able to recognize the man again, but he had a feeling that he'd seen him come into the garage before, which was why he didn't take any particular notice of him.'

'Gotcha. So in the unlikely event that our suspect ever pops in there to top up his tank on some future occasion, the cashier might instinctively recognize him – though probably not, if he was in the middle of some really exciting game of *Call of Duty* at the time?'

'Exactly.'

'Do you ever wonder why we do this job?' Hannah asked, in a tone which Peter suspected was not entirely rhetorical. 'Is it just so that we can amass the maximum amount of frustration that it's possible to take in any one lifetime?'

'I reckon we've had enough frustration for one day. Come on, it's time to pack it in for the night.'

'Home time.' Hannah's affected a cheery, School's Out tone, then abruptly crumpled and started to sob.

'McMahon? Hannah? Hannah? Come on now . . . what's the matter?' He stood awkwardly a foot or two from her desk, wondering what he should do.

'I'm sorry,' she mumbled between tears. 'Please, take no notice. You should go.'

'If the case is getting to you . . .'

'It's not the case.'

'Hannah . . . it's not because . . .?'

She turned her head away but he could see that she was frantically applying a tissue to her eyes and trying to regain control. 'No, no, nothing to do with that. It was stupid of me anyway. I shouldn't have embarrassed you or myself. I'm sorry.'

'No harm in suggesting it.' Magnanimity seemed to be the order of the day in the face of this unprecedented display of emotion. 'I was flattered – honestly. But I don't want to mix work and pleasure, and—'

'Oh, forget about the sodding sex!' she exclaimed.

'Then what? Why?'

She took a deep breath, seeming to struggle with her better judgement, before she blurted out, 'My sister's terminally ill. It's cancer. She's only thirty-four. She has two little kids. I'm not dealing with it very well.'

Half a step closed the gap between them. He put his arms around her and she sobbed into his shirt.

'Why didn't you say something before?' he asked, after a decent interval had passed and Hannah was again applying a tissue to her face.

'It seemed easier not to.'

'What do you mean?'

'"How's your sister doing, McMahon?" "Oh, not so well." "Sorry to hear that." This isn't a story which is going to have a happy ending, you know? There isn't ever going to come a day when I can say, "Yeah, my sister's doing great today and she's nearly all better." The more people who know, the more people I'm going to have answer one day with the words, "Actually my sister died." It's bad enough with my family and I definitely can't handle bringing it into work with me every day. Work is a Clare-free zone. Except that it isn't, because when your sister is only thirty-four and approaching the end of the road, it's very hard not to think about it all the time.'

'What are you doing to cope?'

'Mostly going home alone, and crying – or occasionally, by way of a variation, going home alone, getting drunk first and then crying.' She gave a sad little laugh. 'Pretty pathetic, eh?'

'Come on,' he said, assuming command, in a tone which he knew she would have resented in normal circumstances. 'Dry your eyes and get your coat on, I'm taking you out for a drink.'

Twenty-One

When Jude leaned over the back of the sofa to rumple Rob's hair, he immediately lunged backwards and made a grab for her, but she had anticipated it, and a nimble movement took her out of his reach.

'Amazing slice of luck,' he said. 'Bumping into that bloke again.'

'And at last you've accepted what I've been telling you for weeks. The guy is loaded. I told you right from the off, that this was our man.' She laughed and shook her head. 'I showed you his father's obituary and the piece in the paper, saying how much he'd left in his will, but you still had to go sniffing around.'

'Trust you to claim all the credit. Anyway, you didn't hit on him straight away.' He laughed, as he picked up his glass for another slug of Bacardi. 'You had that Dimitros bloke at the top of the list to start with.'

'How was I supposed to know that he was on the verge of announcing his engagement? And it wasn't Dimitros anyway – it was Dimchek. You're getting mixed up with that tennis player.'

'Well, who cares? We've got our man and we've almost made it.'

She had to pass him on her way back from refilling her glass and this time he had no difficulty in catching hold of her, swinging her into his lap and giving her a lingering kiss.

'You shouldn't drink so much,' she reproved, as they disengaged.

'Look who's talking!'

'Seriously,' she said. 'I know it feels like we're nearly home and dry, but tomorrow you have to drive down and make sure that everything at the cottage is ready. We can't afford to make any slip-ups now.'

'Have there been any slip-ups so far?' He took another gulp of his drink, just to wind her up.

'It's all gone perfectly – so far. In fact I can't believe how easy it was in the end, getting him to propose.'

'Look at you.' With his free hand, Rob reached out to stroke her cheek, letting his fingers continue downwards, progressing from her chin to her navel. 'Who wouldn't want to marry you?'

'Flattery will get you absolutely everywhere.'

'Is that the kind of corny line you employed on him?'

'Never mind what kind of lines I employ on him.'

She knew that he had drunk too much, which always had the potential for trouble. It took no more than a couple of large Bacardis to position him at the edge of a dangerous mood, but she was still surprised when he abruptly jerked her off his lap. 'That's the part I can't stand,' he said.

'Hey,' she protested. 'Do you think I like making up to him all the time, or shagging him?'

'Shut up about that. We agreed not to talk about it.'

'Rob, please . . . You know I'm only doing it because—'

'Shut up, I said,' he shouted.

She instantly switched her expression from pleading to anger. 'Do you think any of it has been easy for me? What do you think has been my favourite part, Rob? Maybe keeping my hands tied behind my back for over twenty-four hours, to make sure the damage looked authentic by the time they got me to the hospital? Or maybe some of those other things you did to me, so that the police would be convinced?'

He faced her out. 'You know I didn't do anything without you telling me to,' he said angrily. 'You know that I thought we were going too far.'

'I'm sorry.' She managed to sound genuinely contrite. 'I know you hated doing that stuff.'

His mood changed just as abruptly. 'It wasn't easy, you know. Beating up my wife.'

'I know.'

He put down his glass and took her back into

131

his arms. 'I wanted to stop. You had to make me keep going.'

She held onto him, saying nothing. It was true. When it had finally come to the point and he was still hesitating, she had yelled at him to get started, and when he had hit her so hard that she'd screamed, he had initially refused to go on. She remembered how she had sworn at him and instructed between sobs, that he had to get on and finish the job. Later on he'd had to release her hands long enough for her to inflict the burns herself. Not that there had been anything brave or stoical about it, she thought. She had merely done what they had agreed to do. The things which had been necessary to generate the right amount of proof. She told herself now that it had not been so very bad. It couldn't possibly equate with being beaten up by a stranger, not knowing what was going to come next, thinking that you might be tortured or raped or killed. They had worked to a pre-ordained script. She had always been in control.

'So you're going with him to make the arrangements tomorrow and then you'll call me. I wish now that we'd decided that you would get married without me being there. I don't want to stand there and watch you marrying someone else.'

'We stick with the agreed plan,' she said, firmly. 'No last-minute changes, because that's how slip-ups are made. Comfort yourself with the thought that it isn't really legal.'

'That worries me as well.'

'It needn't. The only record of any wedding involving Judith Thackeray in this country will be to Mark Medlicott. There's no record of *our* wedding in this country. There's no way anyone is going to catch on.'

'Come to bed.'

'Not yet. Noooo . . . Pack it in, Rob.'

'But you said flattery—'

'Let go.' Her tone was affectionate but firm. 'We'll do whatever you want, once we've gone through this once more, to make sure that we're both absolutely up to speed on what happens next. Finishing with him is the most important part. We can't afford to let anything go wrong. Don't have any more to drink,' she exhorted, as he released her and reached for the Bacardi bottle.

'Finish with him,' he said in a thoughtful voice, as he ignored her request and poured another generous measure. 'That's such a neat way of putting it.'

He was drinking far too much, she thought. She would have to keep an eye on that.

'That's what you do with old unwanted boyfriends, isn't it?' he continued. 'You finish with them.'

Twenty-Two

Peter was uncertain whether or not Hannah had fallen asleep, but he continued to stroke her hair, which looked darker than usual, alongside the pale skin of his chest. (He was too blond and too busy to ever spend any significant amount of time

133

lying out in the sun.) He knew that sleeping with her was probably a very bad idea in the long run, but at the pub he had encouraged her to unburden herself about her sister, and this had led to another slightly tearful interlude, during which he had found himself holding her hand in a way which felt perfectly natural and right.

He had chosen a pub where neither of them were known and stuck to tonic water himself, while encouraging her to drink a couple of large glasses of Pinot Grigot, on a promise that he would drive her home later. It had gradually emerged that she felt unable to talk to her family about her feelings, because they were already weighed down with their own grief in the face of this cruellest of circumstances. As the hands on the fake Victorian pub clock had circled its oversize face, making a second round and then starting on a third, she had apologized several times for 'going on' and 'getting upset', but he kept on encouraging her to talk, offering a third drink, which she had declined. On their way out of the pub, she had apologized for propositioning him. 'It was just that I was so desperately down. I needed something to distract me from it all.'

She had stopped then, exclaiming, 'Oh no! That sounds really bad – as if I don't even fancy you. Now I've compounded the felony by insulting you as well.'

'It's OK. I'm not insulted.'

At that moment she had caught sight of herself in the ornately framed mirror which hung on the wall, next to the main entrance. 'God! What a mess I look. Eyes all red and face all blotchy.'

'You look fine. Never lovelier, in fact.' And that was when he had kissed her. After that he had driven her back to her house, where he had very competently distracted her for the next hour, without any lack of enthusiasm on either side, apart from the one moment when she had paused in the act of unbuttoning his shirt, to say, 'You don't have to do this, you know,' to which his only reply had been to press his lips onto hers again.

It was the most unusual – and enjoyable – favour he had ever done for a friend. Odd he thought, while continuing the gentle, repetitive motion of his hand across her head, how much more attractive he had found the semi-distraught, crumbling McMahon, to the competent, efficient McMahon. Did he prefer women who were needy? And was that OK? It probably made him some kind of Neanderthal, where sexual relationships were concerned. As far as he could guess (and who knew what really went on inside women's heads) most women were looking for an equal partnership, not a protector. He had never consciously noticed this protective side of his nature before, but maybe that was what had attracted him to Jude Thackeray too? Someone he had first encountered as a victim, brutalized by the man who had made free with her affections, then hurt and robbed her?

It was some weeks since anyone from the investigation had been in direct contact with her. After the assault she had gone to live elsewhere, being understandably less than enthusiastic about a return to Laurel Cottage. She was lucky like that, he supposed. Most people had nowhere else to go, and often no alternative but to return to a home where their confidence had been destroyed and their personal security violated, but the Thackerays enjoyed the luxury of several alternative addresses.

Hannah stirred and half opened her eyes to look up at him. 'You're lovely,' she whispered, in a voice slurred with satisfaction and drowsiness.

But would she still think so in the morning? From where an outsider sat, he thought, it looked horribly like taking advantage of a colleague who's drunk too much Pinot Grigot on an empty stomach. Not that he could exactly count himself as an outsider, while he was lying here under her lime green duvet (whoever would have imagined that McMahon had such outlandish taste in home furnishings?) He could see however, how it would look to a third party.

To a copper who had professionally encountered his fair share of date rape allegations, the fact that McMahon had all but begged him earlier in the week, or acquiesced readily enough after an evening which began in the pub, was no guarantee that she would perceive him in the same rosy light, tomorrow morning.

The thought of the morning brought up another big question. In the words immortalized by The Clash, 'Should I stay or should I go?' She had not invited him to stay. She had not even specifically invited him in, come to that. On the other hand, sliding out of bed and leaving while she slept seemed callous and more than a bit uncaring.

He decided to stay – a decision which he

assumed that McMahon was fully on board with, when they made love again, before rising for breakfast together.

Twenty-Three

'I promise it will feel more romantic on the day itself.' Mark was doing his best to strike a note of optimism.

To his relief, Jude smiled back at him, her crestfallen expression erased. 'I know it will. I suppose I hadn't expected anything so clinical. I mean, I understand that they needed to see ID and everything, but it felt a bit too much like trying to open a bank account.'

Mark squeezed her hand. He felt in serious need of cheering up himself, because the news that the wedding could only take place after twenty-eight days had elapsed was a bit of a body blow. It meant more juggling with credit cards, more outstanding interest payments and another appeal for extra time via Chaz. It simply hadn't occurred to him that the law required couples to wait that long. His original idea had been that they could get some sort of special licence and tie the knot the next day, but when he queried it with the registrar, she had laughed and said that while it might have been the case in the past, these days the formalities gave you time to change your mind. She had said it like it was some kind of joke. Jesus! Jude hadn't better change her mind or he was completely basted and barbequed, make no mistake.

Fortunately Jude hadn't appeared in the least surprised at the delay; merely a bit miffed because it was all so civil service and bland. He reminded himself that maxed-out credit cards or not, the day itself needed to be roses and champagne all the way, with a surprise vintage white Rolls Royce to collect them from the door. (There was low-key and low-key, after all.)

'The other question is who to have as our second witness,' he said.

'I don't know who to ask. I thought one of the staff would be allowed to do it.'

'Apparently not. Honestly, I can't believe all these rules and regulations. Whatever happened to spontaneity and true romance?'

'We still have that. It's just that government bureaucrats enjoy making things more difficult.'

'I could ask my eldest niece.' He had a light-bulb moment. 'Monty's daughter, Katrina. She's in her first year at University College. I bet she'd love to do it. She's a nice kid too.'

'Can she keep a secret?'

'Of course.' (He wasn't altogether confident on the point, but he would have to bribe her. Every woman has her price, he thought, and it might be no more than enough for a new handbag or a fancy pair of shoes, in the case of a student.) 'I bet she'd love to do it,' he repeated. 'It would make her feel grown up – she's still only in her teens, so I bet she's never been a witness at a wedding before.'

'So it will be just you and me, Rob and your niece – what's her name again?'

138

'Katrina.'

'Katrina . . . right.'

'I wish we could have got married today,' he said. 'Just the two of us, like we first imagined.'

'Never mind.' She appeared to be completely sanguine. 'It will be just as romantic when we do it in four weeks' time.'

'And you'll have time to plan what to wear. Have a dress made or something.'

He sensed right away that he had hit a wrong note.

'Oh . . . yes. I suppose so.' She appeared to hesitate, then pulled herself together and said, 'Do you want another coffee?'

He didn't get it. All the women he knew would have been already planning what they were going to wear. Talking dressmakers or designer labels. It was the most important day of her life, after all. Something going on there that he didn't understand, he thought. It surely couldn't be about the kidnap? What on earth would that have to do with getting a wedding outfit? Or maybe it was her parents being dead? That was another ever so slightly touchy subject. Maybe it had to do with her father not being there to give her away, or her mother not seeing her in her wedding dress or something? That would be it – a sentimental, family thing. Just make a mental note not to mention her outfit again. It was nothing to worry about.

Twenty-Four

Graham Ling was not altogether satisfied with the outcome of the Thackeray case review. Fair enough, you couldn't expect anyone to conjure new leads out of thin air, but he entertained a strong suspicion that instead of bringing his entire focus to the case, Bettsy had used some of the time to effect closer personal relations with DS McMahon, or vice versa, and this made him privately question whether either officer had been as fully and effectively engaged in the task as he would have expected them to be. You couldn't keep secrets in CID – they were supposed to be detectives, after all – and it had therefore been all round the building by lunchtime on the day in question, that McMahon and Bettsy had arrived at work together that morning, having left her car at the Horse and Jockey car park all night. The pair of them never said a dickey bird and thought they were being clever about it, but Snouty Bramham in Fast Response had it on good authority that ever since then, Bettsy had been spending the night at McMahon's place, then going home next morning for a shower and a change, so that they still arrived separately at work.

Ling metaphorically shook his head over the pair of them. In his heart he identified with an earlier era, when relationships between serving officers had been frowned upon and he still believed that in the long run, a romance between two coppers on the same team and the same shift got in the way of the job. He had known more than a few inter-officer romances and affairs in his time, and while some had worked out, a significant number had fallen apart eventually. (Once with the spectacular consequence that a long career had ended in the imprisonment of a sergeant who had attempted to run down a fellow officer, with whom he'd had an affair, after she had threatened to tell his wife.) The team was too close, the job too much of a pressure cooker, to allow for sexual relationships – they simply got in the way – that at least was DCI Ling's personal take on the matter.

As a direct consequence, once he had called time on the Thackeray review (McMahon and Betts had asked for more time, but he told them that he didn't have it to give) he had teamed Hannah McMahon up with Joel McPartland and sent them out to take statements on the Pitcairn Estate, in connection with Operation Farthing, issuing parting instructions that they were not to get diverted by any Bounty Hunters: a remark which was met with puzzled looks from both officers, leading Ling to wonder inwardly at what the hell they were teaching the kids in school, these days. As for Peter Betts, he put him back onto the stabbing at the Three Horseshoes, which since it involved attempting to extract information from their substantial Eastern European community, was generally regarded as a sort of punishment. Serve the little bugger right, Ling said to himself, for messing around on the job.

In fact neither of the objects of their boss's covert wrath had the slightest objection to being kept apart at work. 'It's not as if we're madly in love and inseparable,' Hannah said, while she stirred pesto into a pasta sauce and Peter laid out the place mats and cutlery on her kitchen table. 'We don't need to spend every minute together. It isn't like that.'

The not being in love part had been absolutely clear right from the start. 'Just friends,' Hannah had said. 'Supporting one another through a difficult time. Not even good friends,' and she had laughed.

In spite of not being particularly good friends, Peter went back to her house pretty much every night. They ate together, watched TV, and chewed over the events of their respective days, with an ease which would have been the envy of many a married couple. They shared her bed every night (he had discovered that she had another lot of bedding in sunshine yellow, vibrant purple and silver grey, which was almost as lively as the lime green set which had formed part of his original introduction to what constituted McMahon's idea of homely interior decor).

Their long conversations were not confined to work. She sometimes talked about her family. He found it unexpectedly easy to tell her about Ginny and the band. (He had sent Ginny a reply, telling her that he was thinking the offer over and asking how much time he actually had to make up his mind.) To his surprise, Hannah had not decried the idea of chucking up his career in the police for a life on the road, saying instead that she'd had no idea he was *that* good a musician. 'If you've got a talent that will take you all round the world, maybe you should use it.'

By now Ginny had responded to say that he still had plenty of time to make up his mind, because the new contract didn't start for several months yet, but he knew that wasn't really true. Ginny needed an answer, because if he said 'no', she would need time to line up someone else and furthermore he would have to give at least four weeks' notice if he decided to leave the police force. He hadn't checked the precise procedure, because he didn't want to start the rumour mills grinding.

It had also occurred to him that like Hannah, Ginny was happy to sleep with him without any commitment, or even any significant level of affection on either side. He supposed that some blokes would be pretty pleased about that, but he found it oddly unsatisfactory. Maybe I'm an incurable romantic, he thought, then laughed at himself for thinking it.

He wasn't at all sure what was going on between himself and McMahon. They led ostensibly separate lives which had never the less converged. Contrary to what she had initially told him, she spent relatively few nights at home alone, because hardly an evening went by without her either visiting the hospital, or else taking a turn at babysitting her nieces, which enabled her brother-in-law to go in and see his wife. The first time she arranged to attend the hospital straight from work, she had given him a door key, doing it in such a way that it was obviously a mere convenience for them both and no big deal. When she returned home that night he had dinner in the oven and a bottle of Sauvignon chilling in the fridge. 'Bless you,' she had said, giving him a quick kiss, before kicking off her shoes and sinking into a chair.

Though Hannah had said they were: 'Not actually living together', but, 'just friends, staying over', it had already become simpler to bring some clothes and toiletries across to 'make things easier'. However, given that they were 'just friends, staying over', he had not informed the police that he wished to register a 'change of abode' as it was still quaintly termed in the constabulary. In similar vein, because Hannah was not 'his girlfriend', he had never offered to accompany her to the hospital, and nor had he invited her to go with him, when he made one of his regular visits to see his grandmother. In any case, as well as the fact that arriving with a young woman in tow would have put entirely the wrong sort of ideas into Granny Mina's head, Hannah was otherwise engaged, taking a rare Saturday afternoon off from both work and hospital visiting, to go shopping with friends.

Though he was close to Granny Mina and visited often, he had decided not to mention Hannah (who was not really his girlfriend after all). He would have found the relationship with Hannah difficult to describe. He knew that if he mentioned her as a friend, his grandmother's eyebrows would rise and she would fix him with the look which had never enabled him to get away with anything. His carefully cultivated policeman's poker face just didn't seem to work on his grandmother.

Technically speaking, she wasn't actually his grandmother, but the second wife of his paternal grandfather, who had married Mina after his first wife died. Mina was barely more than a decade older than his own mother had been and the two women had fortuitously got on well, remaining friends long after Grandfather Betts had died. When his own father had 'done a runner', as his mother so eloquently put it, it had been Granny Mina who had stepped up, minding Peter after school and in the holidays, while his mother was at work. When kidney failure had claimed his mother at a prematurely early age, it had naturally fallen to Peter to keep up the connection, which had never been a hardship, since Granny Mina could always be relied upon to provide a hearty meal, and unqualified support for his every achievement and endeavour. He knew that if he told Granny Mina about the chance to travel the world, playing guitar, she would encourage him to do whatever would make him happiest – the problem being that he couldn't decide what that would actually be.

He had phoned in advance to let her know that he was popping in on Saturday afternoon, and turned up not long after three, letting himself in at the unlocked front door (Granny Mina didn't do security) and calling a greeting down the hall.

Her house was comfortable, shabby and full of happy memories. His step-grandmother had taught him his first card trick, how to make paper boats which really floated in the old-fashioned

145

pink bathtub, and allowed him to win at Cluedo and Monopoly, playing with ancient sets which had belonged to her own parents. However she had never let him win at card games, of which she seemed to know innumerable varieties. The Tuppeny Halfpenny Game, Crazy Eights, Whiz. Granny Mina was an expert at every one, which meant that actually beating her was a real achievement. One of their favourites – he could no longer recall its name – had involved gambling for plastic cocktail sticks. It might have been some variation on poker, he thought. Certainly it had involved deciding whether to stick with the hand you had, or whether to take a fresh card from the dealer, having discarded one of your own, a process known as 'stick or twist'. He would have to ask her one of these days to refresh his memory on the rules.

'It's me, Granny Mina,' he called, as he advanced down the hall, passing the familiar views of sheep grazing in pale green pastures while storms gathered above the dramatic moorland in the background. (Granny Mina was originally from the north and still referred to Yorkshire as God's Own Country.)

'In here, Peter, love.'

The first thing he observed on entering the crowded living room was a table groaning with home-made cake, (some of which he knew she would later pack into Tupperware boxes and insist that he take home with him). The latest football scores were scrolling in the background as usual, but the television set had been muted, because there was already another visitor in situ.

146

'Peter, how are you?' His grandmother rose and planted a kiss on his cheek, while he bent forward for the purpose. 'Do you remember Louise Salt?'

He made polite, non-committal noises, while Granny Mina reminded him that Miss Salt was a retired teacher, who had at one time taught at the same establishment where she herself had worked as School Secretary. At this Miss Salt of course dredged up a recollection of some previous occasion in the long distant past, when she had allegedly encountered him, while he was still in short trousers.

'How you've changed,' Miss Salt said. 'I wouldn't have known you now.'

Peter was tempted to say that it was just as well, because the police didn't accept snotty-nosed midgets, but instead, while Mina disappeared into the kitchen to make a fresh pot of tea, he attempted some polite conversation, asking Miss Salt which school she had moved on to after leaving the comprehensive where Mina had spent the last decade of her pre-retirement life.

'It's funny you should ask, because your gran and I were just talking about that, before you arrived. She was telling me that you're a detective now,' – Miss Salt's voice rose into a little trill of excitement, investing the job with that element of astronaut-meets-film-star-type glamour, which was generally absent in real life – 'and I was wondering whether you'd investigated a case involving an ex-pupil of mine. Oh, don't worry,' she cut him off before he could open his mouth, 'I know you're not allowed to talk about your work. We were just speculating. Your granny didn't give away any secrets.'

Peter smiled, not bothering to point out that when it came to his work, Mina was not in possession of any secrets to give away. 'What pupil was that then?' A polite interest never came amiss, and anyway, you were never entirely off duty. It was amazing sometimes, what you could pick up, just from a casual acquaintance or coincidental meeting. He gave her at least ninety per cent of his attention, while casting a covert look at the television screen, to check on the Arsenal score.

'You will definitely have heard about it, even if you didn't work on the case. Young Judy Thackeray.'

'I think everyone's heard of Judy Thackeray,' he said with studied casualness. 'What school was this again?'

He had always assumed that Jude Thackeray was a private school type, so he was surprised when the establishment Miss Salt named turned out to be a very ordinary comprehensive, about forty miles away. He had trained himself never to betray anything, however unexpected the information with which he was confronted, but he decided that in this case a modest expression of surprise would be in order. After all, everyone who had taken any interest in the case would have heard Jude Thackeray's voice on TV, and the money in the background was common knowledge. 'Is that right?' he said. 'I would have had her down as going to somewhere much posher than that.'

'Oh no. The Thackerays were a very ordinary

148

family. Her father drove a delivery van, or a taxi or something like that. I can only think that they must have come into a lot of money later on, after Judy left school. She wanted to be an actress, I remember. I've got a vague idea that she went on to study drama at college. I'm sure she would have been warned that it was a very overcrowded profession . . .' Miss Salt sighed, in the manner of one long accustomed to offering wise counsel, only to have it rejected by those still possessed of impetuous youth. 'She was very good in the school plays. I remember she played Abigail Williams in *The Crucible* one year. A most ambitious choice of production I always thought, but David Davis – he was Head of Drama at the time – was convinced that he could pull it off. He was very fortunate to have had several quite talented students coming up through the school at the time . . .'

Miss Salt continued with her reminiscence, naming various other ex-pupils who had played major roles in this and other productions, until Granny Mina came back, carrying a loaded tray, which Peter instinctively stood to help her with, while considering what he had just learned. At that moment, he wanted nothing more than to drive to police HQ, and check on something, but then he considered the possibility of misidentification, and decided to fish a little more.

'Did you teach her brother, as well?' he enquired of Miss Salt, while Granny Mina clattered about with cups and saucers. (Peter knew that this was for her other visitor's benefit – left to themselves, they would have had their usual mugs.)

149

'Sorry dear, what was that?'

Granny Mina had moved between them, handing Miss Salt a dainty china plate topped by a folded paper napkin. The napkin had holly on it and was presumably left over from some past Christmas.

'Jude-ee's brother, Robin,' he persisted. 'Robin Thackeray. Did you have him in your class too?'

'I don't remember anything about a brother. In fact I think she was an only child.'

'You're probably right,' Peter conceded easily. 'I thought I remembered there being a brother, supporting her at a press conference, or something like that. It was probably some other relative, or maybe a friend.'

Twenty-Five

Jude fidgeted with the tassel on the corner of a sofa cushion, while she waited for Rob to finish his run-through of preparations down at the cottage. For goodness sake, it wasn't rocket science. When he had finished, she said, 'I'm thinking of arranging another little trip. I need to get away from him for a few days.'

'What do you mean? Where to?'

'I thought Spain, to look at some more property.'

'Another fictitious trip, you mean? It's too dangerous. He might offer to see you off at the airport.'

'So?'

'Then he would know that you weren't actually going anywhere.'

'Maybe I should actually go.'

'Don't be ridiculous. You don't need to go anywhere. You said yourself that the beauty of calling him on his mobile is that his phone tells him it's you, without telling him where you're calling from. Anyway, I don't see why you need to pretend to be going anywhere. You need to be here, keeping an eye on him.'

'What for? He's not going to run off with someone else in the next couple of weeks. I told you. I need to get away. I need . . . some breathing space. It's getting harder and harder to fend off awkward questions.'

'Fine – so ask him about his own stuff. You still don't know a thing about his business or his investments.'

'I told you,' she said impatiently, 'it's absolutely impossible, because whenever I fish for any specifics, he sort of comes back at me with another thinly veiled enquiry. It's like "I'll show you mine, if you show me yours." He isn't suspicious, but he's curious. I've vaguely talked about property in Florida and Spain, but I daren't say too much, in case he starts looking stuff up on the internet.'

'You never said before that he was checking up on you. What makes you think that he's getting suspicious?'

'I don't. But it would be natural for him to be curious. That's why I think that the less chance he has to spend time with me between now and the wedding, the better it will be.' She did not add that it would save her from having to mount a virtuoso performance every time they went to bed together. It was one thing to be good at faking and another . . . well . . . it would be impossible to explain it to Rob, but as they got closer and closer to the end game, the thought that she was making out with someone fast approaching his death was becoming kind of creepy. No one could train you for a role like that.

Twenty-Six

'Possible case of mistaken identity?' Hannah's words were somewhat muffled by the fact that her mouth was full of Granny Mina's Victoria Sandwich, which was none the worse for the very faint taste of plastic which it had acquired on the journey home.

'Could be. We're talking about someone who's been retired for the best part of ten years, and must have taught hundreds, maybe even thousands, of kids in her time. Alternatively she might have remembered Jude, but forgotten the brother.'

'He might not have gone to the same school. Siblings don't always end up at the same places.'

'Fair point.'

'At the same time, we didn't bother looking at the background checks on the victim's family. Presumably that was all checked in the initial stages of the enquiry. Surely we didn't just take

152

it on trust that her parents were dead and that she had inherited a lot of money?'

'And also that she had a brother. Though I don't see anything to be gained from *pretending* to have a brother.'

Hannah was sitting on the sofa, virtually surrounded by carrier bags. She glanced around the purchases from her afternoon shopping expedition, rather as if she was hoping that inspiration would unexpectedly jump out of a shoe box. When it didn't, she finished her mouthful of cake, before saying, 'I'm not sure where you're going with this? She may have trained to be an actress – *if* your granny's friend has even got the right person – but the best actress in the world couldn't fake those injuries. It wasn't Twentieth Century Fox make-up department who convinced the doctor. The violence in the case was real enough.'

'Though, as you pointed out, it differed in several respects from the sort of violence we'd normally expect to see, when a person who is going to be murdered anyway, gets beaten up in advance of a final attack – no facial marks to speak of, no broken bones.'

'You're right, I did say that . . . For goodness sake, put the lid on this sponge cake before I'm tempted to have another piece. Your granny could market this stuff and make a fortune. It isn't just Mr Kipling who makes exceedingly good cakes.'

'We should put this to Lingo and ask him for the time to have another quick look – just to be on the safe side.'

'Right. First thing on Monday.' She licked the residual cream and crumbs from her fingers. 'You know,' she went on, 'not only does the brother, Robin, not look like her, but he doesn't sound like her either. That's unusual in siblings who were brought up together. Have you ever noticed the way his accent occasionally slips? Maybe your old retired teacher buddy woman is right and Jude Thackeray and her brother are just ordinary common-or-garden guttersnipes, like you and me. Maybe she picked up that posh little accent at drama school?'

'Guttersnipe? Cheeky devil. Speak for yourself.'

'All right then – a guttersnipe just like me.'

'If this is true, why are we only just noticing it all now?' Peter sounded doubtful again. What had initially seemed like an intriguing anomaly, was beginning to look more like an irrelevant dead end. For his own part, he had never liked the brother. Was that personal prejudice, or copper's instinct for a wrong 'un? Maybe he was latching on to these imagined differences *because* he had never liked the brother?

'Sometimes,' Hannah said, 'it takes time for ideas to crystalize. If the Thackerays are not quite what they seem, that could change everything about this case.'

Peter shook his head abruptly. 'We're losing the plot,' he said. 'It's no good going to Ling with some half-baked tale from a retired teacher. Teachers can't be expected to remember everything about everyone they ever taught. Even if this woman's got the right Jude Thackeray – she called her Judy, by the way – why would she remember whether or not this particular pupil had a brother? And secondary school isn't like primary. Bigger school, more pupils, more staff, far more chance that a sibling might never take your subject, be in your class, or cross your path at all.'

'Mmm.' Hannah nodded, preoccupied by the discovery of another smear of jam which needed to be licked off a finger. 'Anyway, I expect someone checked all this as a matter of routine, right at the start. We concentrated on what actually happened. I suppose the background stuff is all in the system.'

Twenty-Seven

When his phone rang, Stefan grabbed it immediately, but he did not recognize the number on the display, so he answered warily, then all but slammed the phone on the table when he realized that it was some stupid message about a mis-sold pension that he had never taken out. The trouble was that it was never the call he was waiting for and the waiting was making him twitchy.

He wasn't a superstitious kind of guy, but lately he had been troubled by a recurring dream, which always started with him building a sandcastle on a beach. The beach sometimes looked a lot like Anonymous Bay right from the outset, though sometimes it was a different beach, which was fringed with palm trees, had yachts bobbing at anchor and a distant bar, all of which would eventually vanish as the beach gradually became Anonymous Bay.

He would never notice exactly when and how the location changed, because his concentration was entirely absorbed by the construction of the castle. It was an incredibly elaborate affair. He made turrets, which he decorated all over with sea shells, and it was surrounded by a deep moat, crossed by a drawbridge, made from wooden lolly sticks, which he discovered in the sand. There was a central courtyard, paved in tiny, pale grey pebbles, also collected from the surrounding beach and a series of larger stones were embedded in its walls, to represent doors and windows. It took him ages, particularly the intricate laying of the courtyard, and from time to time he would become aware of a shadow falling over his masterpiece, as if someone had stopped to watch. In his mind, this person presented some kind of threat to what he was doing, but whenever he looked up, there was no one there.

The dream always ended the same way, with the shadow finally coalescing into the outline of a man, which grew larger and larger until it loomed over everything, blocking out the sun, and this time, when Stefan looked up, preparing to tell the man to piss off, he would hear the man laugh and in the same instant a great wave would come swirling out of nowhere, swamping the castle and as he scrabbled to save it, Stefan would slide into the moat and start sinking into the morass of sand and water, so that when a second wave rolled in, it engulfed him too. At which point, he always woke up.

It was a stupid dream, he told himself. Just a stupid, pointless dream. Dreams didn't mean anything. It was the waiting. Weeks of waiting. It was driving him crazy. He had learned to be patient, but patience only took you so far.

He scrolled through the pictures on his phone, until he found his favourite. Waiting made you obsessive. She hadn't realized that he had taken the picture. He had caught her just as she turned her head, and was not even looking directly at him. Her lips were parted, the way they were before a kiss. In the dream, he thought he was making the castle for her. That was why it had to be perfect.

He had to be very careful with that picture. He never looked at it unless he was alone, never lent his phone to anyone. No one must know that he had a picture of her on his phone. No one must be able to make a connection between them until well after the killings had been done.

Twenty-Eight

Peter Betts's phone went off while he was in the dentist's waiting room. He was supposed to have bagged the first appointment for his check-up, but on arrival he discovered that there had been some sort of mix-up, which meant that he would have to wait for half an hour. It was going to make him late getting in, which though not a big deal, was a nuisance. He had settled down to read a copy of yesterday's *Daily Mail*, presumably abandoned by some other patient the day before, and was a couple of pages in when he had to silence the phone, ignoring the looks of irritation from the two other occupants of the room.

'It's me, McMahon. Are you on your way?'

'No. There's been a mess-up. I'm still waiting. Have you managed to ask Lingo about some extra time?'

'No point. Two bodies found in a garage, back of Desray Street, first thing this morning. Boss wants everybody on it.'

'Should I come right away?' He kept any vestige of urgency out of his voice. He knew the other occupants of the waiting room would be listening. It was natural human instinct. He also knew that it was never advisable to attract unnecessary attention to yourself, by creating a drama. For all the concern in his voice, the caller might have been alerting him to a minor leak under the washing machine.

'Unless you want your arse kicked that would definitely be a "yes".'

'OK. Will do.'

He cut the call and swung himself up from the chair, approaching the receptionist's desk and saying quietly, 'I'm afraid I've been called in to work urgently. I'll have to ring and re-make the appointment for another time. Sorry.'

Although his movements were apparently unhurried, he was out of the door before the receptionist had a chance to reply.

Part Two

Twenty-Nine

'You're very quiet,' Mark said. 'You are happy aren't you?'

'I'm fine,' she said. 'I was just relaxing, enjoying the scenery.'

'I love this part of the world, don't you?' He aimed for a note of enthusiasm. 'I can't wait to see this cottage of yours.'

'It's only an ordinary little place. Please don't get your expectations too high, or you'll be disappointed.'

'I'm about to spend our honeymoon in a secluded love nest, with you – how could I possibly be disappointed? And as for the cottage, I have absolutely no expectations, because up until a short while ago, I didn't even know that you had a cottage in Cornwall, and ever since you told me about it, you've absolutely refused to show me any pictures, or tell me anything about it at all. You do play your cards very close to your chest, in all kinds of ways, my darling. I hope that now we're married, we can be a bit more open with one another. What's the name of the cottage, by the way?'

It hit her like a blow between the eyes that she couldn't remember its name. It was one of those weird, local names, which began with 'Pen', but she couldn't bring the rest of it to mind. She had only been down to see it a couple of times, having left most of the arrangements to Rob. It had been an expensive undertaking, renting a place for the entire summer, but it would have been too big a gamble not to have it reserved well in advance. Very few properties combined the special features which they required. The name of it though, what was the name?

'Why don't you wait and see?' She tried to sound playful. It was exhausting, she thought, being constantly on her toes, ready to fend off these awkward questions which came at her out of the blue, or to engage in lavish displays of affection with a bloke she didn't particularly rate. In the early days, she had sometimes needed to keep herself awake for hours after they had gone to bed, just in order to fake the nightmares which had to come in the early hours of the morning in order to be convincing. All that trouble and effort. Acquiring the photograph of an unknown woman in a fur coat and diamond brooch, in order to back the idea that her original attacker had stolen family heirlooms from the safe. Leasing the place in Elmley Green, the house in Colchester and now the cottage in Cornwall. Renting the fancy cars, pretending to fly out to Spain and New York. Calling him from their flat while affecting to be in Barcelona. It had taken months of planning and a lot of seed money.

She sometimes wondered if they had gone too far, in their quest for authenticity, but she had invariably come back to a favourite phrase, *the devil is in the detail*. And it had all paid off, she told herself, because they were almost there. Step by step she had guided Mark to the right place,

162

and very soon now everything would come together, just as they had planned it.

The next scene in the drama had been prepared with the same meticulous care as every other. It would look like an accident, and as the curtain rose on the last act, she would transform herself into the grief-stricken widow, just long enough to mop up every possible asset, before she slipped away to live abroad. She could visualize the headlines in her mind's eye – 'Tragic Jude', or 'Tragedy Strikes Again for Brave Kidnap Victim'. The inevitable publicity was a nuisance of course, but it would probably be a nine-day wonder. She already had an outfit for the funeral, bagged months ago in a sale. Very important to make the right sort of impression on the in-laws she had never met. She had mentally rehearsed the story for them – how much she wished now, that she and Mark had had a proper wedding, with everyone invited – how their keeping the wedding quiet had made no difference in the end, because poor, poor Mark's tragic death had put her right back into the headlines, so that they might just as well have done the thing properly, the big frock, the bridesmaids, the attendant photographers . . .

Mark's voice jolted her back to the present. She must not look too far ahead. It was vital to concentrate on the moment, because it would be so easy to make a slip, even at this late stage. 'Sorry, sweetheart,' she said. 'I think I must have been dozing off. Say that again.'

'I said that I'd better stop at this garage.' He was already slowing the car, in readiness to pull onto the forecourt. 'Not a good idea to let the tank run low, out in the wilds.'

'We certainly don't want to run out of petrol, while we're crossing Bodmin Moor,' she agreed.

'Be an angel. Nip across and join the queue to pay, while I fill up.'

'What for? There's no hurry.'

'But I hate standing in a queue, and *I* am in a hurry. It's all right for you. You know where you're going whereas it's all new for me and I can't wait to get there and start our honeymoon properly.'

She considered a playful protest to the effect that *she* didn't want to stand in the queue any more than he did, or better still, to come up with a quick fire excuse for asking to use his credit card instead of her own, but she decided against it. She didn't want to pay for the petrol, because their initial capital had pretty much gone, and finances were getting tight, but she reminded herself that it was only a little while longer. Probate might take a while, but very soon now, he would be paying for everything.

Thirty

Raindrops began to hit the windscreen, just as Peter Betts reached the turn for Benton Heath. It was only then that he realized his route would take him past the lay-by where the van used in the Thackeray kidnap had been dumped. The last three or four weeks had been too hectic to allow any further time on that particular enquiry. As well as the Desray Street murders, there had been another attempted indecent assault in the Albert Park area and a nasty domestic murder on the Fairfield Estate. The fact that all the perpetrators had been quickly identified and rounded up did not – as the general public often seemed to imagine – signal the end of the work required to bring in a successful prosecution.

Small wonder then, that when Peter had approached the boss about the encounter with Miss Salt, Graham Ling had made it abundantly clear that he wasn't listening to any nonsense about putting someone back onto the Thackeray case for yet another look. 'I can't spare people on the basis that some old bird who once reckoned to have taught the victim, has developed a bee in her bonnet. Besides which,' he had added, 'I've always been able to smell an ulterior motive a mile off. You must think I was born yesterday.'

Peter had not bothered to protest that he did not understand what his superior meant.

Hannah had not taken the news particularly well.

'What did the gaffer say?' she'd asked, when Peter saw her in the canteen, later the same day.

'Discovering that a victim may have attended a comprehensive school where your mother once worked as the school secretary hardly constitutes a new lead,' Peter parroted mechanically, as he dragged a chair out from under the table, so that he could sit facing her.

'That isn't what you told him.' Hannah had not

165

attempted to conceal her irritation. 'He wasn't even listening.'

'Nope. He thinks we're trying to get it reopened so that we can work one-to-one again.'

'Did he say that?'

'He didn't need to.'

'We don't need to work together. We're sleeping together.'

'I'd say that a bit louder, if I were you. There might be someone down in the cells who didn't quite catch it.'

It had been one of her stipulations, that they keep their relationship quiet. That way there would be no awkwardness when they went their separate ways, she had said. No suggestion of anyone throwing anyone else over, or being heart-broken, or any of that kind of stuff. He had gone along with it, much as he had gone along with everything else: partly because he had no wish to argue with her over it and partly because he remained bemused.

'Do you mind?' she asked unexpectedly. 'If people do catch on to us?'

The words came out before he could stop them. 'McMahon, this is the police force. There's no "if" about it. Everyone from Grigor, the canteen kitchen porter, to Danny Burridge, doziest police dog handler in history, will already know all about it.'

To his surprise she didn't appear to mind. 'Then it doesn't matter how loudly I say it in the canteen. Anyway, I say we carry on in the evenings – when we're off duty.'

'Well, I wasn't about to throw you across a desk and ravish you in the middle of a briefing.'

'I'm referring to the Thackeray case. Lingo can't stop us thinking about it, on our own time.'

Instead of pursuing the conversation any further, he had given his full attention to removing the paper case from a double chocolate chip muffin. He didn't want to say anything more on the subject to Hannah, because he was uncertain about how things really stood between them, and didn't want to give himself away. There were a lot of competing, confusing factors. He had always thought that the ideal home life was one where you could get away from the job. It was all-consuming at the best of times and he had tended to the opinion that the best girlfriend to have was the kind who didn't ask questions about what you were working on, or what you had done that day. His music had always ensured that he didn't completely eat, sleep and live the job, but now here was Hannah, suggesting that they look into the Thackeray case in their spare time.

That was another thing – what spare time? Outside work, most of her time was spent offering her family support, while a great deal of what was left over was spent in bed, and while he had no problem with that at all, he drew the line at any suggestion of post-coital discussions regarding Jude Thackeray, or indeed any other investigation. He had always feared that a relationship with a fellow detective would make it even harder to leave the job at the door and this conversation represented the living proof of it.

Of course, he thought, Hannah would argue that we aren't actually having a relationship. According to her, he was no more than being a good mate, but for him it was becoming a bigger and bigger lie. Inch by inch he was getting drawn further into her life, bringing in groceries, driving her to visit her dying sister in hospital. He had even grown accustomed to the lime green bed linen . . . and as for the softness of her body, the smell of her hair, the way her eyes lit up when she smiled. Her sister only had a matter of weeks now, the doctors said. Soon there would be no dying sister and no reason for him to stay.

Thirty-One

'This is it . . . see where there's a parking place on the left-hand side?'

Initially Mark could not see anything other than the single track lane itself, but then he spotted the place she was indicating: a level rectangle of gravel at the side of the tarmac, with just enough space for two cars side by side. The hedge which had hemmed the lane up to this point gave way to a rustic wooden fence, which separated the parking spaces from an uncut field of swaying grass. A board had been nailed to the fence, which read PRIVATE PARKING FOR PENMENDHU COTTAGE ONLY.

'We have to walk from here,' Jude announced, as he executed the turn, bringing the bonnet up to the fence in order to clear the lane. 'You'll need to pull back out and get in closer on this side.'

'Why?' He was feeling tired and bolshie. The journey had taken hours longer than he had anticipated, the sky had turned overcast, and now it seemed that you couldn't park anywhere near the cottage itself, so before you could have a much needed drink, you would have to hump the luggage through a bloody field, heaven only knew how far, to a house which wasn't even in sight.

'Because if you leave the car like this, right across the centre of the parking area, you can only get one car in. We always leave room for a second vehicle.'

'Why? We're not expecting anyone, are we?'

'Of course not . . . It's just that we always do.'

'We?' Though he remembered just in time how important it was to keep her sweet, he felt obstinate. I'm not being told how to park the blasted car, he decided. Adopting a lighter tone he said, 'It's you and I, now darling. We're the "we" – and we don't want any interruptions, or any visitors, so if I leave the car here, we won't need to rely on that notice to prevent people from parking here, when they're not wanted.'

He turned off the engine with a decisive gesture. 'Right then. How far do we have to walk?'

'Oh – it's not very far.'

She sounded a bit vague and he sensed that for some reason she was still preoccupied by his refusal to shift the car. Maybe she was just unaccustomed to his not instantly giving way. Up until now he had tolerated every trivial whim and fancy, and on reflection, perhaps he should have gone along with her about this too – it was such a little thing after all – but it was too late now.

169

In fact it would make more of a thing of it, if he re-started and manoeuvred the car. He decided that she would soon realize that it wasn't important and forget all about it.

As he got out of the car, he glanced around hopefully, but there was no sign of any habitation nearby: not so much as a chimney pot or a rooftop in sight. He took the case and the largest bag, while Jude carried a Kool box containing their champagne and smoked salmon supper, together with a much smaller bag, which still left a rucksack and a box of groceries for a second journey.

'What on earth made you choose a place this far off the beaten track?' Struggling slightly under the load, he tried not to allow his breathing to get in the way of the question.

'I didn't choose it. I inherited it. Me and Robin, equally, from our parents. We used to come for family holidays.'

The mention of Robin unnerved him. It hadn't occurred to him that any of the properties – the London flat, the Essex cottage, the Cornish retreat, or the place in Spain – might be jointly owned with the knuckle-dragging brother. Had she wanted to leave that free parking space . . .? No. Stupid thought. The guy knew they were on their honeymoon. Surely it was only mere force of habit that had made her comment about the second space being normally left open.

She led the way as he panted the length of one field and then embarked across another. The path was beaten earth, and ran between the massed stems of tall, unidentified grasses on one side, and a weedy margin which ran alongside a waist-high, barbed-wire fence to the other.

'Did your parents never think of putting in a proper drive?'

'They don't own this land.'

'Couldn't they have bought it?'

There was a brief silence. Shit, he thought. I've hit a wrong note there, but when Jude spoke again, she sounded perfectly unruffled. 'The farmer wouldn't sell. You know what farmers are like. We've got right of way across the field, providing we stick to the path. There . . . you can see the cottage from here.'

She paused to point ahead. He looked beyond where she was standing and saw that they were now within sight of the upper storey of a small cottage, its walls unpainted grey pebble dash, its roof slate. Expectations of a grand summer retreat, the sort of house with diamond pattern windows, topped with sun-faded awnings which could be lowered to protect the furniture from harmful rays; a patio with furniture for lounging away the long summer days, maybe a loggia, or a wrought-iron balcony accessed by French windows from the master bedroom, overlooking a swimming pool, all instantly evaporated in the face of this small, mean-looking building.

'I know it doesn't look much from here.' Jude must have sensed his disappointment. 'But it's got one massive advantage that you're going to love.'

With the suitcase and the large bag trying to drag his arms out of their sockets, he couldn't summon up the protestations of enthusiasm which she was no doubt anticipating, so he said nothing and continued to trudge towards their objective, stealing another glance ahead every so often. The building's appearance did not improve on closer proximity. If anything it appeared to squat in the landscape like a malevolent toad, filling him with an unaccountable sense of foreboding.

When they reached the front door, Jude initially had trouble with the keys, and once they got inside, he realized that the place was even smaller than he had first thought. There was just one living room downstairs, furnished with a trio of two-seater sofas which formed three sides of a square around a wood burning stove at one end of the room, and a table with six dining chairs at the opposite end of the room, next to a hatch into the kitchen. She didn't give him the opportunity to take more than a cursory glance around, insisting that he walk straight across to the ugly modern patio doors which had been installed at the rear of the property. These looked out onto a paved area which was nothing like the glamorously appointed recreational space of his optimistic imaginings, comprising as it did of just a rectangle of cheap, concrete slabs, in alternate off-white and dirty pink, which had a few tubs of neglected pansies in one corner, and a wooden picnic table in the centre. It was the kind of picnic table found in public parks, where the table and benches were fixed into a single, uncomfortable element, with a hole at the table's centre, ready for a sun umbrella.

Jude seemed unaware of his disappointment. 'Look,' she said, pointing out of the window. He followed the gesture with his eyes, taking in the wide scrubby area of gorse and grass beyond the garden fence, which eventually met the sky without offering an intervening view of the sea. 'You see where the grass stops?' she continued. 'That's the cliff edge – and over the top is our own private beach. It's a bit of a climb down, but no one ever comes there except us. I told you the place had something pretty special going for it. We'll get the rest of the luggage across and then maybe later on, when we've had a drink and some supper . . . or probably tomorrow morning, after breakfast, I'll show you the beach.'

'Hey, yeah, great.' He made the words come out without thinking about them, then turned back to the spartan living room. 'Can't we have a cup of tea, before we fetch the rest of the stuff from the car?'

It wasn't just his disappointment that the place was so much less nice than he had expected. True, it was not a bit like the houses in Colchester and at Elmley Green, but that wasn't the whole story. There was something wrong with the whole set-up, he thought. Something which made him feel vaguely queasy.

Thirty-Two

'I had another quick look at the Thackeray stuff this afternoon,' Hannah said. 'Joel had to go to that meeting with Lingo, and I figured that even if the Old Man found out what I was up to, he wouldn't go ballistic over a half-hour excursion off piste.'

She had already called in at the hospital en-route home from work, and now they were sitting side by side on her sofa, enjoying a 'cheeky one', as she referred to a pre-dinner gin and tonic. Between the crazy workload in CID and Hannah's commitments to her family, her suggestion that they attempt to pursue the Thackeray investigation 'on their own time', had so far gone no further.

'And . . . ?' Peter prompted.

'It's a bit irregular – a bit odd.' She paused for another sip of her drink. 'Normally we'd have checked out antecedents, associates, contacts – because obviously a kidnapper may have found out stuff from a friend or a relative, even though the victim doesn't realize that there's a connection – but in this case we've got very little on file about the victim's antecedents or background.'

'Someone's messed up?'

'Not exactly. I mean . . . well no, not really. The Thackeray parents are both dead. According to Jude and Robin, their mother was an only child, whose parents are also dead. Father has two half-sisters in Liverpool, from whom he'd been estranged for years. Jude Thackeray reckoned she wouldn't know these people if they walked up to her in the street. She gave us the names, we made contact with colleagues in Liverpool and the story checked out. Usual thing – first wife dies, so Granddad Thackeray marries again, first family never got along with second family, all meaningful contact lost years ago – they don't even do Christmas cards.'

'Might have a motive there, if the Liverpool lot thought they'd been done out of their share of the family loot.'

'True enough, but no indication of it – and anyway it was the brother who stood to gain, if anything happened to Jude. The Liverpool rellys got nuttin,' Hannah concluded in her best impersonation of Scouse.

'The brother was always a person of interest, though we never managed to get anything on him.'

'Right. Brother Robin certainly has a motive, because for all that devoted brother and sister thing they've got going, if someone had succeeded in putting Jude Thackeray permanently out of the picture, little brother inherits the lot – according to Jude anyway, and it's safe to assume that she knows the terms of her own will. So setting him aside, the family angle is a complete non-starter. Which brings me to friends and associates.'

'Previous boyfriend before the nutter was some bloke who plays the flute in an orchestra, wasn't it?'

'Right first time. He was easily traced and easily eliminated. He'd only been out with her on a couple of dates. Relationship started when they met in a London pub and got into conversation. He was off on tour a lot of the time, and anyway they quickly decided that they hadn't got a lot in common. He seemed unaware that there was money in the background – and he didn't come across as remotely likely to be involved in anything dodgy.'

'Brother Robin also had a short-lived romance around the same time, if I recall.'

'You recall correctly. Girl called Letitia. Twenty-one, very pretty, but never going to get onto *University Challenge*. Quite volatile and quickly fell out with Robin Thackeray, though neither of them could remember exactly why. She apparently had no idea about the Thackeray wealth either and on learning that her ex-boyfriend had been a millionaire, referred to him as a "tight bastard".'

'Sounds like a charming example of womanhood.'

'Absolutely. But hardly the criminal mastermind. Same deal with the girlfriends that Jude sometimes hung out with. There were only two of them: both had only known her a short time and seem to have been little more than casual acquaintances. She met one of them when she joined an art class, and got to know the other woman because she's a mate of the first one. They were out having a drink with Jude when she met the flute player in the pub – but not when she met the kidnapper. They were aware of him though, because Jude once blew them off to go out on a date with him. Of course, they never actually met him.'

'It's pretty odd, when you come to consider it. If I remember rightly, there were no really old friends, or old flames in the UK.'

'No. But we accepted that because they hadn't long returned to the UK after living abroad.'

'So we've got nothing on record to confirm which school Jude and her brother actually attended?'

'No. We focussed on their adult life, which has been mostly spent overseas. They both provided plenty of names of people living in the States and the Caribbean, with whom they'd had friendships and relationships of one sort or another.'

'All of whom checked out?' It was more of a statement than a question. The list of previous contacts was not an area they had focussed on in their previous trawl through the files.

'Actually, none of them checked out.'

'Come again?' Peter was so surprised that he jerked forward, almost spilling his gin.

'When we reviewed the case, we skimmed through it on the assumption that there was nothing useful in their past history. Unfortunately it appears to have been – ahem – overlooked first time around as well.'

'But surely . . .' Peter shifted again in his seat. 'Surely someone was assigned to go through past contacts.'

'Jerry Wilkins and his sub-team were – and they did – up to a point.'

'Meaning?'

'It was complicated. Virtually nothing was local. The only way to check out all these overseas people was to ask for co-operation with other police forces. They then had to follow up the various names and addresses, which of course all took time. You know how it is. The information came in dribs and drabs, and it was always negative. On the face of it, none of the people the Thackerays had mentioned as friends, ex-employees, business contacts, or anything else you care to mention, had any kind of criminal record, or any suspected criminal contacts, or any known UK connections.'

'On the face of it?'

'What I mean is that nothing obviously suspicious turned up. But get this. One ex-boyfriend of Jude's had died in a car accident, a couple of others couldn't be traced at all. One of the women Robin Thackeray named as an ex-girlfriend had married and moved to Australia – the last note on the file suggests trying to find out her married name, but that didn't go any further. Basically someone who has lost touch with the Thackerays and moved to Australia several years ago doesn't flag up as especially likely to be worth pursuing. Some of the long-term neighbours they mentioned in Florida had gone into an old folks' home and it was decided not to pursue that any further either. Some other long-time friend was last heard of travelling in Thailand, and so it goes on. On the face of it, all these enquiries produced nothing of interest or relevance to the case, but . . .'

She left the word hanging long enough for Peter to interject. 'Are you saying what I think you're saying? Did Jerry and co. actually manage to make contact with anyone who is supposed to have known Jude or Robin Thackeray while they were living abroad?'

'The short answer is "no". The trouble is that this really only emerges when you look at the whole picture. Jerry's annual leave fell part way into all this and his second in command was Nina, who was heading for her maternity leave, and his other team member was Jack Drysdale, and he went off sick a couple of months into the enquiry – got some sort of virus. For some of the time it seems like Jerry only had the services of brand new PC Bostock, who was logging the information as it came back in, but of course it was a very slow process, with Jerry working on other things and only wanting to be alerted if anything significant cropped up.'

'And whenever anything new came in, it was always a negative?'

'Exactly. The sort of result to be noted on file as unsuspicious. Every time Jerry checked in, as it were, there was nothing of interest to report. Eventually Jack came back, but by then it must have appeared as if all these people had been followed up and nothing had emerged to be concerned about. At first glance, taken separately, it looks like a lot of irrelevant dead ends . . .'

'But in reality the whole picture taken together is dodgy, because what it really means is that *no one* checked out.'

'Exactly. In this case a lot of apparently innocent negatives could add up to something. On the one hand, all these people may exist and be perfectly legit. They may have all led exemplary lives, have had nothing at all to do with the Thackeray kidnapping, and be able to vouch for Jude and her brother having lived just where they said they did, hung out with just who they said they did, and cetera and cetera.'

'On the other hand, they may be people who've been chosen to provide a backstory, precisely because they're all untraceable.'

'A combination of people who're known to have died, or have moved away, mixed in with one or two people that you've completely made up, who will therefore be absolutely impossible to trace.'

'Would they gamble on us giving up when we couldn't trace these people?'

'If you turn that on its head,' Hannah said, 'if you were part of some kind of set-up where you wanted to cover your tracks, then you would have to take that gamble – because the other alternative is to give genuine contacts and risk them telling the police all sorts of things that you don't want them to know.'

'But what would they be hiding?' Peter shook his head.

They both raised their glasses and took another drink, unconscious that they were moving in perfect unison.

'This is dumb speculation,' he said after a moment. 'Yes, the brother is a potential suspect, because he stands to gain a lot if his sister meets with an unfortunate accident that ends in a one-way ticket in the back of a hearse – but what does Jude Thackeray stand to gain? There was no insurance pay out, or anything like that. They didn't sell their story to the papers. What possible motive would she have for faking a kidnap? If it was only the information from the brother that didn't check out . . . but lots of these names and addresses came from her.'

'I know. I don't pretend to get it. But what we've got is two people whose background information couldn't be verified, and I think there has to be a reason for that. There's always a reason for everything.'

'Might be nothing at all to do with the kidnap,' Peter mused, peering into his glass, before upending the last of his drink into his mouth. 'You might just be unlucky inasmuch that everyone you have ever dated or had any dealings with, just happens to emigrate or die.'

'No one is that unlucky. Let's have another drink – that was only a tintsy one.'

'Coincidences happen,' he mused doubtfully.

Hannah raised an expressive eyebrow in response, before taking the glass from his hand and heading back to the kitchen. He heard the freezer door open and a moment later, the sound of ice cubes falling into glasses.

'You know,' Hannah called though from the kitchen, 'I was thinking about something else too.' Her words were punctuated by the distinctive shumph of the freezer door closing, then by the screw cap, gurgle, screw cap routine that meant gin plinking over the ice cubes, followed by the hiss as she opened the tonic bottle. 'There's the Thackeray money.' She emerged from the kitchen with a glass in each hand, but before she had time to pass one over, her mobile began to ring.

Thirty-Three

'Listen,' Jude said, waving her half empty champagne glass in the direction of the window. 'The wind must have changed direction. I told you

181

that you could hear the sea from the house, if the wind was blowing the right way.'

Mark tried to look enthusiastic, though he couldn't help thinking that the sound of the sea was small compensation for a particularly uncomfortable sofa. So what if you could hear the sea? He'd heard it loads of times. In fact when he was a kid, he'd had one of those shells which gave off the sound of the sea, when you put it up close to your ear. How did that work, he wondered? Aloud he said, 'It's a real hideaway. Pity there's no phone signal.'

'That's the beauty of it,' she said. 'You can't be disturbed. No one can find you down here.'

'But it's a bit of a pain when you need to make a call.'

'You can get a signal back at the road, if you need to.'

'I can't believe your parents never had a landline installed.'

'I told you – they wanted to keep the place simple and unspoilt.'

He didn't answer immediately. Something had chimed wrong about the cottage from the moment of their arrival. His own family had never gone in for second homes. His father's preference had been for first-rate hotels, and in later years for luxury cruise ships, but as a boy at boarding school, Mark had sometimes been invited to the holiday homes of friends and these had generally fallen into one of two categories. There were the all-singing, all-dancing, jazzed-up properties of the arrivistes, with a cocktail cabinet springing at you out of every bookcase, and a kitchen so high-tech that it looked like something straight off the space shuttle; and then there were the much-loved summer homes out in the country, places which had been in the family for years – sometimes generations – where nothing ever changed, the stain on the dining-room wallpaper still bearing sun-faded witness to an accident with a bottle of wine a decade and a half ago, a long dead grandfather's walking stick propped in the hallstand, alongside a selection of forgotten umbrellas, and a child's shrimping net. There were dog-eared playing cards and an amalgam of assorted games and jigsaws stacked in the sideboard for rainy days and everything looked slightly battered after suffering the vagaries of several generations of holidaying kids. This place didn't have the right ambience to belong in either category.

It wasn't just the house that was wrong, he thought. Jude too seemed different since their arrival. Not like she should be, if she were completely at home in this familiar environment. He tried to push the sense of unease away. It was probably him, projecting nervousness onto her, because the time was fast approaching when he would have to broach the subject of money, which was in its way an even harder subject than a proposal of marriage.

'Oh well.' He attempted a tone of cheerful resignation. 'I'll just have to walk across the fields again later on, because there's a call I've got to make this evening.'

'Oh no.' She spoke so quickly that she almost startled him. 'You can't – not on the first night of our honeymoon. It's not romantic. Who can you possibly need to call tonight?'

'It's business – and important. It won't take me a minute. Or it wouldn't, if I didn't have to walk half a mile to make a call.'

'Don't go out again tonight. Stay with me.' It was her needy voice, which had always conveyed an undercurrent of something sexy. For the first time he wondered whether she was conscious of the effect, and able to manufacture it deliberately.

'I'll only be gone a few minutes. It's not a big thing.' (It isn't a big thing. Why is she so dead set against it?)

To his surprise she put her glass down and advanced on him, embarking on a prolonged kiss. He kissed her back, uncomfortably aware that he was being deliberately distracted, manipulated into not making his call. He had never known her to behave like this before. There was definitely something different about her tonight. He was tempted to disengage, but he needed to keep her sweeter than ever because the question of some readily available cash was becoming urgent. Chaz had called him only yesterday and given him an ultimatum. His friend was expecting to receive a down payment. Time was running out. Mark had only got Chaz off the line by promising that he'd call back with some news, within twenty-four hours, not that he had anything to offer yet, but he'd thought of another ploy to buy time. He intended to explain to Chaz that he and Jude had gone off to Cornwall for a few days but that he would have the money – some of it anyway – in Chaz's hands by the following weekend. He figured that Chaz would understand the desirability of keeping Jude happy for a few days in order to ensure a steady stream of finance in the future, and he also assumed that Chaz and his heavies wouldn't want to trek down to bloody Cornwall, just for the sake of another couple of days before they got a payment. However, being able to speak with Chaz again today was an important part of the plan, because he knew from past experience that Chaz didn't like it if you went quiet on him.

While responding to Jude's enthusiastic endeavours on the kissing front, he considered his situation. If necessary he would have to make prolonged, passionate love to Jude, before shoving on a pair of jeans and hoofing back to the lane to make his call before it got dark. It was still relatively early in the evening and would be light for a good hour or so yet. Even if she managed to delay him until after dusk, there was sure to be a torch somewhere.

To his surprise however, Jude left off kissing him almost as abruptly as she had begun. 'Let's go for a walk,' she said. 'I want to show you the beach.'

'But we've only just sat down with a drink.'

'We've got all night to drink and I want to show you the beach now. Come on . . .' She stood up and held out her hand.

He remembered in the nick of time that he was still being Mr Amenable. God, but this was going to take some keeping up in the long run. How long did you need to stay married to someone

185

before you were able to claim half their assets? Fortunately she hadn't so much as considered drawing up a prenup, and maybe he didn't even need half. Once he had everything sorted with Chaz's friends and had got himself back on the straight and narrow . . .

It was a funny sort of time to take it into your head to go for a walk, he thought, as he shrugged on a jacket. The weather had turned grey and overcast, with massing clouds in the south west which suggested that there might be rain before too long. In spite of this, Jude appeared to be in the brightest of spirits. She took his hand as they left the cottage – assuring him that there was no need to lock the door behind them, as 'no one ever comes'.

They had hardly gone more than half a dozen steps when she started eulogizing about how beautiful it was and how much she had always loved it there. Mark responded with some vaguely enthusiastic noises, while mentally wondering what on earth she was going on about. There was nothing to see except for an expanse of windswept grass which sloped away from them, ending abruptly against the dark grey sky, and it was not until they had been going for a couple of hundred yards that he glimpsed the sea. It was not the bluey-green of his beloved Mediterranean, sparkling in the sunshine and dappled by rainbow spray; the sort of view which might have tempted him to reach for a pair of trunks and a towel. It was not even an awe-inspiring stretch of ocean, capped with dramatic rolling waves, but merely the grey-green water he associated with freezing on the margins of an East Coast beach, while older brothers goaded him for being a wimp.

'It's so romantic here, isn't it,' she said. 'I always dreamed of walking hand in hand along these cliffs, with the man I loved.'

'And now you can.' Be grateful for small mercies he told himself. It could have been a lot worse. Imagine if she had demanded a honeymoon at the Hotel Danieli in Venice, or Sandy Lane in Barbados. Cornwall – with her providing the accommodation – was a let-off and no mistake. He slowed and drew her in for another long drawn-out kiss, but the wind spoiled it, whipping her hair around the side of his face, with the tendrils eventually working their way into his mouth, so that he was forced to stop and remove the strands in a singularly unromantic way.

'I suppose there isn't a phone signal out here,' he mused, as they continued their walk.

'No. Not until you get back to the road. Forget the phone. You're on your honeymoon.'

'Right. Sorry.'

They were heading across increasingly uneven ground as their route came nearer and nearer to the cliff edge, and though he still couldn't see the water actually breaking against the shore, he could hear it clearly now: the unmistakeable sound of waves whispering up a shingle beach, growing steadily louder. They were heading towards a couple of raised outcrops of rock, which protruded from the grass like a pair of crooked molars, right at the cliff edge, and when they reached the place he saw that it marked the top of a route down the side of the cliff, which comprised of a steeply sloping path, alternating with a series of rough steps and at one point a wooden stair, running between a couple of dodgy looking platforms, built into the side of the cliff.

As they stood contemplating what lay below, Mark noticed several things simultaneously: first that this initial glimpse of the waves which were breaking on the beach suggested a drop of at least sixty feet or more to the shore; second that the beach – in spite of Jude's requesting his confirmation of its loveliness – looked rocky and singularly uninviting; and thirdly that the way down looked almost as treacherous as an SAS assault course.

'You don't want to go down there now, do you?'

'Oh no,' she said. 'I just wanted to share it with you. We'll have plenty of time to spend on the beach in the next few days, and if it warms up a bit we can go for a swim.'

He was tempted to retort that it would take several more years of global warming before that was likely to happen, but he settled for nodding and squeezing her hand instead.

Having shown him the way to the beach, she seemed content for them to turn back. The wind had been on their backs, but now it was in their faces and he found it hard to swallow his irritation at her insistence on such a pointless errand. If he pushed her over the cliff edge, he thought crossly, he wouldn't have to worry about keeping her purring, or negotiating any future divorce settlement.

Thirty-Four

Stefan was extremely familiar with the crack which ran across his bedroom ceiling. He reckoned that if he had to close his eyes and draw it, he would be able to reproduce every nuance, every single minute fissure which branched out from the main stem. Sometimes he imagined it as a growing, living thing. The slender grey stem of an exotic plant, creeping steadily across the room, instead of a titchy crack in the plaster.

Soon he wouldn't have to see it ever again. He could leave the room, the crack, the crappy job selling Cornish pasties to greedy tourists (talk about seagulls, you should see the way some of those whale-fat bastards golloped through a fistful of minced lamb and turnips). The high life awaited and then it would be him buying the pasties, except that he wouldn't – *ever* – want to see a pasty again. Caviar and champagne, mate, that was what he would be buying. No mistakes this time. No mess ups.

Lying flat out on the bed, with his hands behind his head, he stared at the crack in the ceiling until it opened up like the lid of a treasure chest, onto visions of palm trees, sun-soaked beaches, swimming pools – hell yes, even a yacht. He was good with boats, so why not?

He turned away from these visions of the glittering life that lay ahead to spare a glance at his

189

phone, which lay silent on the white chipboard cabinet which passed for a bedside table. Not long now. He wasn't nervous. If he had cold feet, he told himself with an unconscious smile, it was purely because of the permanent chill in this dingy room. He would have complained to the landlord about the damp, but it didn't do to draw undue attention to yourself. Turn up at the crappy job, pay your rent on time, and keep yourself to yourself – but not so much so that you get marked up as the lone weirdo. He wasn't an amateur. He knew what he was doing. Once the business was done, he would have to come back here and carry on as normal, for three or four weeks at least. After that it would be heigh-ho for the bright lights and a brand new start for Stefan.

Heigh-ho? What sort of weird expression was that? Isn't it what the seven dwarves used to say to Snow White? No, come again, that was High-ho. Oh well, never mind. In Snow White didn't the bad old crone give pretty little Snow White a poisoned apple? The bad girls were all ugly ducklings in Disney. Poor old Cruella de Vil, with her funny hair, all of that lot. Yeah, well, sucks to Disney, because in real life, it was the pretty ones you had to watch.

He shifted on the bed, and noticed that a sliver of sunlight had appeared next to the window frame. The room only got the sun for about an hour at the end of the day (not even that much in the winter) and it never penetrated more than a foot or so into the room. He considered standing up and crossing to the window, so that he could feel the warmth of the dying rays, but he couldn't be bothered. It wasn't worth the effort, and anyway, he ought to save his energy for what was to come later.

On the other hand, he didn't want to drop off to sleep. Not much risk of that really. He extracted one hand from behind his head and held it out in front of his face. Steady as a rock. It was only his subconscious which betrayed him. Bloody stupid dreams about collapsing sandcastles. Well, after tonight, he was sure that there would be no more of those.

Thirty-Five

Mark could feel his heart thumping as he headed away from the cottage and hurried across the field which led back to the lane; not exactly jogging, but moving well in excess of his normal walking pace. If Jude took a long time over unpacking her stuff, he might easily get the call over and done with and be back to the cottage with her none the wiser. He had decided that it would be better to take the opportunity to slip away while she was otherwise engaged, because for some reason she had been pretty miffed about the whole idea of him going out to make a phone call, and there was really no point in antagonizing her over nothing, and plus he didn't want her getting curious about the nature of a call which was important enough to interrupt their first evening of marriage.

Every few seconds he glanced down at the phone again, to see if he had managed to get within range of a signal. The screen glowed in his hand, emphasizing how dark it was getting. He wouldn't be surprised if a thunderstorm was imminent. She had said there was a signal back at the road, but now he began to wonder whether by 'the road' she meant the lane where his car was parked, or the main road (well hardly a main road, but a wider lane than the other one) from which they had turned into the single track lane which led to the parking place. He tried to remember how far away that turn-off was. Distances which seemed relatively short in the car transformed into major hikes on foot. He wouldn't have time to go any distance, if he was to have any chance of returning to the cottage before she had noticed that he was gone.

Hang on, though, don't be a moron. Once you reach the car, you can drive somewhere until you find a signal. That was it. He'd be OK once he reached the car. Jude would never know that he'd been anywhere, because she couldn't see or hear the car from the cottage – not even from the upstairs windows. Better still, he could fake up an excuse for going back to the car which had nothing to do with using his phone. He could tell her that he'd forgotten something. What? What would be in the car? Road map. That's it. He could say that he needed to look at the map because he was planning to take her somewhere special next day, and without an internet signal, he couldn't check the route online. Where? Where was there in Cornwall to go? Land's End. That's it. I wanted to stand at Land's End and look out across the ocean with you, because . . . because that's how wide our love is. Bugger – was that a spot of rain?

He glanced down at the phone in his hand again, and saw the bars in the top left-hand corner blossoming upward, like the answer to a prayer. He stopped and attempted to gather both thoughts and breath, while he waited for the phone to connect him to Chaz. It rang at least half a dozen times before Chaz's familiar voice came on the line, the clarity of it surreal somehow, as if Chaz was standing just behind the nearby hedge, spying on him.

'Hello?'

'Hi. It's Mark Medlicott.'

'I know who it is. What do you want?' Chaz's impatience betrayed the fact that the call had come at an inconvenient time.

'I need a couple more days—'

'No chance.' Chaz cut him off mid-sentence. 'Time's up. Where are you? It sounds like a fucking wind tunnel.'

'I'm in Cornwall. On honeymoon. Jude and I got married this morning, which is why I need a couple more days. Until I can get back up to London. After that I can pay the first instalment no problemo.'

'I told you. Time's up. I've got a contact in Cornwall. Where are you?'

'Sorry. You're breaking up.'

'Don't try that one with me, you—'

Mark pressed the button which ended the call. He stood looking at the phone for a few seconds, then quickly turned it off, just in case Chaz pressed the recall button. At that moment the isolated spots of rain turned into a sharp shower. Mark swore under his breath and began to retrace his steps towards the cottage, but he had only gone a matter of yards before he could feel that the back of his shirt was already drenched and adhering to his back. This sodding rain would ensure that he was soaked through by the time he got back and that meant Jude would know that he'd been out to make his phone call. The road map – that was it – his excuse for going out to the car. He turned and headed for the lane again, which meant that the rain was pelting in his face.

In his enthusiasm to gain the shelter of the car, he broke into a run. It only took him a couple of minutes to reach the parking space, but he was out of condition and snorting like an old cart horse before he had gone more than fifty yards. He kept his head down for most of the way, watching out for his footing on the uneven ground and trying to keep the water out of his eyes, and it was not until he had almost reached the edge of the field that he slowed and felt for the key fob in the pocket of his jeans. It wasn't there.

He stopped in his tracks, scarcely aware now of the uncomfortable sensation of icy raindrops meeting bodily heat, overwhelmed instead by a wave of confusion, shock and something he did not want to acknowledge as closely akin to fear, because in the same moment that he discovered the loss of his car key, he had also seen that his black BMW was no longer standing in the centre of the double parking bay, where he had last seen it when making a second trip to unload luggage. Since then, someone had repositioned the car to one side of the gravelled area, leaving room for a second vehicle.

What the hell was going on here? He turned back along the path, his mind in turmoil. The car was not where he had left it. How could that have happened? Was he going out of his mind? Well of course not. *She* must have moved it.

He had hoped to get his phone call made without her knowing about it, but now that he was soaked through, there wasn't much chance of that. Nor did he know what to say to her about the car. He was reluctant to confront it head on, because there was a definite risk that he might lose his temper with her and it was important to avoid a row. He was still in a quandary when he got back to the cottage, letting himself in via the kitchen door, and finding the room was empty. She was probably still upstairs, putting her things away.

Jude entered the kitchen a couple of minutes later, just as Mark was towelling his hair dry with a clean tea towel, which he'd found in a drawer. He had abandoned his wet shoes on the mat, but his operations with the tea towel were cascading droplets of water across a wide radius.

'What on earth – have you been swimming or something?'

'No. I went to get something from the car, but I couldn't get into it, because my car key has gone from my pocket.'

Was that the briefest flash of alarm in her eyes?

He was giving her a chance to explain, but the fleeting expression of anxiety seemed to confirm that he had something to worry about. He noticed that instead of explaining the absence of his car key, she countered with a question.

'What did you want from the car?'

She was trying to divert him, but he wasn't having any of it. 'Never mind that. Where's my car key? And why have you moved the car?'

'There's no need to shout.'

As they faced one another across the kitchen, he sensed that for once she had nothing at the ready. When she spoke again, it sounded lame.

'You know I said that we liked to leave space for another car . . . I mean, suppose we needed an ambulance or something—'

'Don't be ridiculous,' he snapped. 'You took the key out of my pocket when we were making out, then you sneaked down to the lane and moved the car without telling me. Which not only takes some doing, but is a pretty funny way to carry on. I didn't even hear you go out. You're expecting someone.' He jabbed an accusatory finger at her. 'Who's coming? It's not Rob, is it? And where is my key?' He cast around the room as he spoke, but the missing key was nowhere in sight. The feeling of alarm which had gripped him on first observing that the car had been moved, returned like a cruel hand, twisting his guts. The situation was too weird. Jude's initial insistence that they needed to leave room for another car had been distinctly off-beam, but her behaviour in moving the car without telling him was seriously worrying. A variety of factors, including the unknown distance between himself and the nearest other human habitation flooded into his mind, muddying his thought processes.

'Don't let's make a big thing of this. Get your wet things off and I'll pour us another drink. There's plenty more champagne. Or – I know – why don't I make some really good martinis?'

His mind was racing, but he tried to steady himself. Two possibilities, he thought. Either she's a complete, bunny boiling nutter, or there's something much more sinister going on that I haven't got a handle on at all. In the same instant that she was speaking, he recognized her persuasive tone for the one she had always used when she needed to divert him, manipulate him. He had never really picked up on it before, but this was the second time she'd tried it in the space of a couple of hours. Again that sense that there was something very wrong with all of this. His instinct was to get the hell out of it, but of course that was ridiculous and anyway, not an option until he could access his car.

'Where is my car key?' he asked again.

'What on earth do you want your car key for? It's pouring with rain out there. Tell you what, let's go upstairs together and I'll help you out of those clothes.'

The seductive note in her voice only served to set off more alarm bells. 'Get away from me.' He spoke so sharply that she instantly withdrew the arms she had reached out in his direction.

'Mark, please. What's wrong? We're on our honeymoon.'

That pulled him up short as the implications

flooded through his mind. The need to keep her onside. Chaz with his blasted contacts in every corner of the UK. It was all going wrong. He didn't know why. He didn't know what to do next. He was standing in damp socks, on a chilly slate floor, his clothes soaking wet, trying to dry himself with a ruddy tea towel of all things. For a second, he was afraid that he might give way to tears.

As he hesitated she began to speak again. 'I'm sorry I moved the car. I didn't think it would upset you. You know I'm a bit OCD about stuff sometimes.'

'So where's the key?' He took his cue from her, softening his tone, affecting to be apologetic.

'Oh, I don't know,' she said airily, making a big show of patting herself down. 'I must have put it down somewhere upstairs. It'll turn up. I'll come upstairs and look for it, while you change out of those wet things.'

'I hope you haven't lost it,' he said. 'I haven't brought the spare down with me.' He knew that his acting skills weren't up to much. She wasn't convinced. She knew that he knew that the key was not lost. She knew perfectly well where she had put it, but was unwilling to tell him for some reason.

'It can't be lost. The key's just mislaid somewhere in the house. We'll probably find it somewhere really obvious in the morning. I don't want to waste ages looking for it now.'

'It won't take ages, will it?' His words came out far too loudly, the way fake jollity always did. 'Not if it's somewhere obvious.'

He headed upstairs to the master bedroom, where he divested himself of his shirt, dragging it over his head when he'd undone half the buttons, then peeling the cold, wet denims from his legs. She had followed him upstairs and was making a big show of hunting for the missing key.

'I'm really, really sorry,' she began. 'I shouldn't have moved the car. I know it was stupid. And now I've gone and mislaid the key.'

The word 'mislaid' jarred. It sounded to Mark like a lift from a script – an expression she wouldn't normally use in ordinary conversation. At that moment she turned to face him, holding out her arms, and he could see why she had been easy to fall for. She had such a kissable mouth, and he might have been tempted to forget all about the moved car and missing key, to ignore that sense of impending danger which continued to nag at him, but was surely based on nothing more than a spell of nerves after talking to Chaz, but then the remembrance of Chaz brought him up short. There had been a reason for all those hours spent wooing her, making love to her, and the time was fast approaching when he had to start making it pay. The fact that she appeared to be genuinely contrite about the stunt with his car, coupled with Chaz's absolute refusal to countenance any further delay made it time to act.

'I'm sorry too.' He advanced to meet her invitation, enfolded her in his arms and held her close. He could feel her breath on his left shoulder. 'The truth is that I'm a bit uptight.' He spoke softly, his breath coming back at him, out of her hair. 'That call I had to make. I've had a terrible run of bad luck and I desperately need some ready cash . . .' He paused, aware that the rhythm of her breathing had changed.

There was a silence, during which he slid his right hand upwards and began to gently caress her neck with his fingertips. He noticed that contrary to his usual experience, she neither moaned, nor relaxed at his touch.

After what seemed like a long time, she said, 'Are you asking me for money?'

'Only temporarily. I'm ashamed – really embarrassed – we've only been married a matter of hours . . .'

'Can't you ask your own family?'

Her query threw him off balance. He couldn't decide whether it would be better to move towards an increasingly intimate situation or not. He was already undressed. Was it more or less sleazy if he pressed his financial claims while they were in bed together? Would bringing her to the state of frantic desire which he had so often achieved in the past make her more easily persuadable?

'But you're my wife. My very closest family.' He took her chin between his finger and thumb, intending to tilt her face to a better angle for another kiss. In moving her head, he caught a glimpse of them both in the long mirror, every inch the honeymooners, heading for an early bed, but the vision was abruptly altered when she pulled away.

'You never mentioned before that you had money troubles.'

'It's only a short-term problem.'

'How much of a problem?'

'Jude . . .' He attempted to kiss her but she took another step back, putting several feet between them.

'How much of a problem?'

'I only need a few thou to see my way clear.'

'I'm not in a position to lend you any money.'

He dropped his hands to his sides and stared at her. He had been expecting some sort of resistance, but something in the way she spoke suggested that she meant what she said. It was not that she needed persuading, because she was reluctant. It was because she genuinely couldn't give him the money. But that surely wasn't right?

He tried again. 'Is it Robin? Does he have a controlling interest in things?'

To his surprise and alarm, she laughed out loud.

Thirty-Six

Peter had offered to drive to the hospital as a matter of course. He reckoned that a single G and T would not have put him over the limit, and even if it had, so long as he didn't do anything stupid, he was unlikely to be breathalysed if he flashed his warrant card and explained that he was taking a colleague to the hospital, to visit a relative in a critical condition.

Hannah told him not to wait for her, but accepted gratefully when he said that of course

he would, telling her to take as long as she needed
– all night if necessary. He watched her disappear
towards the main entrance, then sat in the car,
on the hospital pay and display, watching other
people come and go, while trying to divorce his
mind from what Hannah and her family would
be going through inside. It was a private, family
time into which he had no intention of intruding.
'A matter of hours,' the consultant had said.

Hannah's sister was the reason they had come
together in the first place and her dying would
make a difference. Or would it? He and Hannah
fitted comfortably together. Physically and generally. He had grown to like Hannah as a person,
rather than as a colleague. The private Hannah
was far more sensitive, intuitive and gentler, than
the workplace Hannah. He might – given time
– grow to love her. Maybe that was how these
things happened. Or not. Hannah was an unknown
quantity. They had never talked about what was
happening between them, except to reach a vague
understanding that he would stick around and
be supportive in the short term. Was that all she
wanted of him? A comfort blanket to tide her
over a difficult time?

For all that he had got to know her better,
he had no idea what was going on in her head.
The job forced you to cultivate a public face. In
the course of his service, he had learned to
suppress any visible sign of all kinds of emotions,
including horror, disgust, surprise and even mere
curiosity. Whatever your head was saying, you
could not afford to let your face give you away.
So yes – she had let down her guard and cried

on his shoulder, but she had given away very little apart from that.

How long did it take to get over the death of a beloved sister? Forever, if the relatives of murder victims, hit-and-runs, fatal accidents were to be believed. But Hannah was not banking on him sticking around forever. She had even encouraged him to accept Ginny's offer and join the band. That didn't exactly sound as though her heart would be broken when the time came to say goodbye.

For all that they got along, perhaps they didn't have that much in common? He had his music and vaguely supported Arsenal, whereas Hannah liked watching Ipswich Town and occasionally played netball with some sporty friends. Netball! He remembered when glimpses of the Year Eleven girls playing netball in those short skirts had provided the highlight of a school day. Come to think of it, a glimpse of Hannah's long legs, and her skirt flying up as she jumped to catch the ball . . . steady boy. Don't want to turn into a dirty old man before you're thirty. He put Hannah, netball and women in general out of his mind, watching as an elderly woman coped with a wheelchair-bound man, a few vehicles away from him. He thought of going over to help, but he knew that people did not always welcome an offer of assistance from a stranger.

The sky had grown darker and a few isolated spots of rain appeared on the windscreen. It had not been the best of summers and looked as if it might turn out to be a wet autumn. Peter turned his mind back to the conversation they had been having before Hannah received the summons to the hospital. With the arrival of the call from her brother-in-law, they had abandoned the topic of the Thackeray kidnap, focussing instead on the practical issue of reaching the hospital as soon as possible, and accomplishing most of the drive in silence. It had been hard to know what to say. Platitudes about everything being all right were inappropriate. As he continued to observe the steady trickle of patients and visitors returning to their cars – the more able-bodied quickening their steps at the impending threat of a shower, the aged or infirm making much slower progress, turned in on themselves, their need to focus completely on the operation of moving from A to B all absorbing – he found himself wondering where Jude Thackeray and her brother were at that precise moment.

He had never particularly liked the brother. Not that likes or dislikes meant anything very much. You couldn't like everybody and Ling had always tutored them to accept that gut feeling and instinct were double-edged swords. A copper persuading himself that someone was a wrong 'un had led to many an unsafe conviction, and the point about an unsafe conviction was not only that an innocent person got locked up, but what was worse in the long run, a guilty one went free. 'Never mind, "I think", or "I suspect", get me some hard evidence,' Ling always said. '"I think" is no bloody use at all.'

So he hadn't liked Rob Thackeray. So what? It could have been social prejudice, as much as anything else. Robin Thackeray had that rich boy look which tended to wind him up right away. Blue jeans worn with a noticeable belt, an immaculate white shirt, open at the neck, expensive cufflinks and a fancy watch. Brushed-back hair, good teeth, suntan. The smallest hint of encroaching weight above that brown leather belt suggestive of good living. A guy who'd grown up with a sense of entitlement.

Would Rob Thackeray have harmed his sister? Not personally, of course. Suppose he had paid a hit man? Peter Betts cast his mind back to an early case conference when that theory had been among the suggestions on the table, but he knew that it was a needlessly elaborate idea that didn't really work. If Robin Thackeray had wanted his sister dead, he needn't have bothered with an elaborate preamble. A professional hitman could have broken into the cottage, abducted Jude and got the business done in a matter of hours, making it look like a burglary gone wrong.

The Thackeray money. What was it that Hannah had spotted about the money angle? He noticed that he always thought of her as Hannah these days, rather than as McMahon.

After almost an hour in the car park, he became conscious of the fact that he was very hungry and thirsty. He couldn't leave the car for long, because he didn't want Hannah to return to a locked car and be left standing out in the rain, but he figured that there was probably some kind of vending machine near the hospital entrance, so he slid out of the car and sprinted across the damp tarmac, rejoicing that he was possessed of the health and strength to dodge the slow movers on their walking frames and sticks. Inside the hospital entrance he encountered a young couple pushing yet another guy in a wheelchair. You don't know what you've got till it's gone. Seize the day. He thought of the latest message from Ginny, assuring him that he still had plenty of time in which to decide. That had been more than a fortnight ago. Ginny was still waiting for his answer.

Thirty-Seven

'So?' Jude prompted.

They were sitting facing one another on separate couches in the sitting room of the cottage. A meeting of sorts – like an interview, Mark thought, fraught with discomforts which were entirely incidental to the hardness of the furniture. His back still felt vaguely damp under a hastily donned shirt, his chinos were still creased from the suitcase. Jude had retained a physical distance between them as he got into some clothes, then suggested that they should go downstairs, so that he could explain his problem. There had been no further mention of mixing martinis.

Mark had readily agreed to this, because he reasoned that she was just kidding when she said she couldn't help him out. Everyone's knee-jerk reaction was to say that they couldn't spare a dime. She'd got all sorts of money behind her. It was probably no more than a question of a phone call. All he had to do was get her onside.

He had assumed his naughty little boy face and told her a tale – largely true – about a run of bad luck. How he had been given some bad advice from someone he'd mistaken for a friend, and it wasn't until he was in up to his neck, he said, that he realized he'd fallen in with loan sharks.

Up until now he had kept his eyes on his fingers, drumming compulsively on his knees – a nice touch, he thought – making him look nervous and contrite, unable to look her in the eye, but now he risked a glance at her face, from under lowered eyelashes. She was watching him, her face absolutely expressionless. He re-focussed on the fingers, endlessly performing piano scales against his patellae.

'I had no idea what I was getting into. They've started to get nasty. Threatened to harm me – threatened to harm you.' (This was a lie but it seemed like an inspired touch, on the spur of the moment.) He paused, glanced up again, but she remained impassive. 'I need to pay them off.'

'So you thought that if you married me . . .'

'Oh no, Jude, darling.' He made to get up and go to her, but the wooden expression on her face changed his mind and he decided it would be better to stay put. 'I adore you. I'm the luckiest man in the world. I would never have married you if I hadn't been in love with you. Surely you know me better than that?'

'What I don't understand,' she said slowly, 'is why you can't get money from your own family? Your father left millions.'

'How do you know what my father left? We've never discussed that.'

'Perhaps we both did our homework before committing.'

'Then you did yours badly. My father's estate was worth a lot because it included all of his business assets – a factory and machinery isn't the same as hard cash. Anyway, he left all that side of things to my brothers. I told him I wanted out of the family business years ago – in fact I never went into it. The old man expected me to. Monty and Michael became directors virtually straight from school, but there was no way I wanted to be stuck up in Yorkshire, worrying about the price of acetylene or ball bearings.'

'So you got nothing?'

'I got a little – and I invested it, but as I've already told you, a lot of things went tits up and—'

'Don't you have any life insurance – something you could cash in?'

'What would I want with life insurance? I'm only thirty-four for goodness' sake.'

'So basically, you've got big fat nothing and you need me to help you out?'

She rose to her feet and he sprang up alongside her, arms outstretched, but she waved him away, almost imperiously. 'Leave me alone,' she said. 'I need to think.'

The rain had stopped, but it was still grey and damp outside. He followed her into the kitchen and stood watching as she shrugged on a coat and pushed her feet into some shoes.

'Jude.' He was about to try another appeal. Offer to go out for a walk with her, or better still beg her to stay inside. Maybe re-ignite that suggestion of a couple of martinis. After all, she was supposed to love him. For better, for worse. Not that you actually said any of that stuff at a register office wedding.

'Don't even think of following me.' She flung the words over her shoulder as she left, slamming the cottage door behind her. He hastened back to the sitting room, attempting to watch her from the patio window, but she disappeared round the side of the cottage, heading in a direction which led to neither the parking place nor the path down to the shore.

Once out of his sight Jude quickened her pace, glancing over her shoulder every so often, to make sure that he was not following. She headed for a grassy knoll to the north east of the building, where she and Rob had discovered by experimentation that there was a phone signal. Much nearer than the lane, you sucker, she thought.

It was only when you reached the summit of this miniature hill, that it was possible to see the lean-to construction of stone, topped off by sheets of rusty corrugated iron, which had been built into the northern side of the slope, a ramshackle affair, its previous use un-guessable. She and Rob had agreed that its hidden location in comparative proximity to the cottage would serve their purposes very well. It provided the perfect place for anyone who wished to stay concealed nearby, yet sheltered from the weather. However as the rain was still holding off, there seemed no reason to retreat inside and after a final glance to confirm that Mark had not followed her, she glanced at her phone to check the signal, then instigated her call.

The moment she heard a voice on the line, she plunged in: 'We've fucked up. Mark hasn't got a bean. Not even life insurance. We're totally screwed.'

'Who the hell are you talking to?'

She gave a yelp of surprise, instinctively cutting off the call as she turned to see Rob emerging from behind the wall of the redundant barn.

'I said, who are you talking to?'

Jude stood rooted to the spot, staring in disbelief, as Rob advanced the couple of steps it took to bring him right next to her. Whereas swift reaction might have availed her some advantage, hesitation was fatal. He grabbed the hand which held the phone and twisted her wrist so hard that she shrieked and relinquished her grip. In a second he had grabbed the phone and turned his back on her. She knew instinctively that he was redialling the last call. She tried to reach around him, lunging at him in a vain attempt to regain the phone, but his body was broader and his reach several inches longer, rendering her efforts as ineffectual as a butterfly fluttering into the trunk of an oak.

She guessed that he had achieved a connection, because she heard him say, 'Who's this?' as he elbowed her away, hard enough to make her stagger and slide on the damp grass.

'He cut me off,' he said as he swung around to face her, deliberately dropping the phone on the ground and stamping his heel on it twice. Even from several feet away, she could see that it was broken. 'Who is he?' he asked.

'Who?' Her voice sounded hoarse and she knew

it was a stupid question, but she was at sea, with no idea what to do next. None of the careful planning had covered this eventuality. Run. That was the answer. Get back to the cottage and bar the door. Get to Mark's car keys and drive away – drive anywhere. It made no difference now, with everything going so completely wrong.

He anticipated the move and grabbed her even as she attempted to sprint away. 'Who were you talking to?' he thundered.

In the past she had always been the one who needed to urge him into action. She knew that he was capable of violence, but until now she had never had any cause to be afraid of him.

'Get off me!' She struggled to pull free, but he tightened his grip, using his free hand to deliver a stinging blow to her face. When she cried out in protest, he struck her again and began forcing her down the slope in the direction of the cottage, while she continued her futile attempts to pull free.

After a few yards their feet became entangled and to save himself from lurching over completely, he flung her to the ground. Landing face down, Jude took a second or two to recover: she pushed herself up onto her knees, then froze when she caught sight of what he was holding in his hand. Silver grey, shining dully in the last of the daylight, there could be no doubting the veracity of her eyes.

'You've got a gun,' she whispered. 'Rob, where did you get a gun?'

'Insurance policy.'

'You wouldn't shoot me.' It was not exactly a statement, not exactly a question.

'Don't bank on it.'

'You love me. We're in this together.' She attempted conviction, but it wasn't easy, with that mesmerizing cylinder, not four feet from her face.

'I'll ask you one more time. Who were you talking to on the phone?'

She took a deep breath to steady herself. 'I can't tell you.'

A fresh thought appeared to strike him. 'Where's lover boy?'

'Who?'

'The bridegroom. That prat, Medlicott.'

'He's waiting for me, back at the cottage.' She paused, before adding, 'Unless he's followed me after all, and seen you waving that gun around. In which case there's just a chance that he's done a runner, got as far as his car and rung for the police.'

'Get up . . . Come on . . .' He didn't wait for her to obey, impatiently dragging her to her feet and pushing her ahead of him again, while she complied as best she could, weaving a course which mostly enabled her to keep the weapon in his hand in view. So far as she was aware, Rob had never handled firearms. Neither had she, though a teenage flirtation with crime fiction had left her with the impression that a gun could easily go off by mistake, if it fell into the wrong hands.

As they passed the sitting-room window, she noticed that Mark had switched on the table lamps. He was hunched on one of the lumpy sofas, with his back to the window, but something – perhaps the sound of their feet on the paving stones of the patio – made him glance up; and though she doubted that he had seen the gun, her own dishevelment, coupled with the unexpected presence of her supposed brother, replaced the expression of dejection on his features with one of alarm. As they entered via the kitchen door, she thought of yelling out to him to run for it, but there wasn't really time. He was still in his original position when Rob flung the sitting-room door open so violently that it crashed against the inner wall and bounced back towards them, only failing to hit them when it was kept at bay by Rob's outstretched foot.

'What . . .?' Too stunned for more, Mark watched in astonishment as his new brother-in-law hurled the woman who had lately become his wife onto the sitting-room rug, then applied a hefty kick to her backside which made her cry out in surprise and pain. Mark had jumped to his feet as they entered the room, but any gentlemanly instinct to intervene in this unexpected family drama was stifled at birth by the sight of the elegant little handgun, which his brother-in-law was toting in his right hand.

Reaching into his left-hand pocket, Rob withdrew a handful of cable ties and tossed them onto the coffee table. Jude, who had twisted around to face him, was attempting to inch her way towards the wood burner, with a view to maximizing the distance between them, but halted abruptly when Rob ordered her to stand up. She glanced across at Mark, but he seemed mesmerized by the gun.

'Tie his hands.'

213

Now Mark finally looked at her and she read the confusion in his eyes, alongside an undoubted level of fear.

'DO IT.'

She hesitated for another fraction of a second, then slowly bent to extract a plastic tie from among the little group which lay scattered on the table. She worked in slow motion. Trying desperately to come up with something – anything – to get herself out of this. Mark untied could be an ally. Mark tied up was useless.

'HURRY UP.' Rob lunged as he spoke, lashing out at her again.

As she pulled Mark's hands behind him, he found his voice at last. 'Jude? Robin? What the hell is going on . . .?'

She couldn't see the gun, but out of the corner of her eye, she saw Rob raising his arm. 'Please hold still and let me do this.' There was no concealing the fear in her voice. 'I'm afraid he might shoot us both if I don't.'

Mark evidently sympathized with this conclusion, for he made no further protest, obediently bringing his hands together behind him, while she wrapped the tie around his wrists. Her hands were shaking as she tightened it. If she pushed him forward hard enough, might he cannon into Rob, taking him unawares long enough for her to make it out of the room? Crazy idea, crazy, crazy. A stunt like that and they could both end up dead. With Mark's hands secured, she stepped aside, job done.

'Right, you sit down.' Rob accompanied this instruction with an aggressive jerk of the gun in

214

Mark's direction. He appeared to have grown into his role, confident in his ability to control them while holding the trump card. 'And you—' he indicated Jude – 'stand over there with your back to me and your hands behind you.'

Quick as a cat, Jude leapt for the door, but Rob was too fast for her, grabbing the arm of her coat. She managed to wriggle out of the coat, but he swiftly grappled her into immobility, the gun to her temple.

'Try anything like that again, and I'll kill you.' He released his grip slowly, ready to apply restraint if she attempted flight again, but she put up no further resistance, though she managed to cast a look of mute appeal in Mark's direction as she turned to face the wood burner. Rob would have to put down the gun and turn away from Mark, because tying someone up was a two-handed job. If Mark could manage to throw himself forward and get Rob on the ground, while she still had her hands free, maybe she could grab the gun and turn the tables. After all, hadn't Mark had a public school education, where they stuffed you full of ideas of chivalry or better yet, dog-eat-dog survival skills? If ten years of school fees hadn't garnered you a bit of initiative then what the heck was it all for? Surely this was exactly the sort of thing which had made the upper classes into leaders of men?

She held herself taut, in readiness to respond in a millisecond when Mark made his surprise attack, but nothing happened. As she mechanically obeyed Rob's orders to turn around and sit

215

on the other sofa, facing her hoped-for rescuer, she recalled that Mark was not after all upper class, but merely the son of a jumped-up, self-made industrialist. As if from another plane altogether, she noticed that she was entertaining some pretty bizarre thoughts, given her situation.

'Don't move, either of you.' Rob's voice was perfectly steady as he addressed them both. 'Now then—' he turned his eyes exclusively on her and she flinched as if struck – 'I've asked you a question and I want an answer. You might recall us playing a little game once, where you had to pretend to hold out on me when I wanted some information. I'm going to give you a few minutes to consider your options, then when I come back you can choose how things are going to be, because either you tell me who that guy on your phone is, and what the fuck is going on, or we can resume the process of extracting information as practised back in Elmley Green – only this time, it won't be a game. Get it?'

She had turned her head away, but he grabbed her hair and forced her to look up at him. 'I said, get it?'

'Yes,' she whispered. 'I get it.'

A solitary tear found its way into the corner of her mouth, its salty tang mingling with the unmistakable taste of blood where he had already hit her.

216

Thirty-Eight

Stefan balanced his phone on the palm of his hand, watching as if he expected it to make a sudden move of its own volition, but the phone remained still and silent. He had cut the call off the moment he realized that it was a man's voice on the line. Medlicott, he assumed. He'd never heard the guy speak, and even if he had, he probably wouldn't have recognized his voice from no more than a snatch. 'Who's this?' An angry voice – aggressive. Something must have gone wrong. He must have caught Jude using the phone and grabbed it from her, to see who she was calling. Stefan ran through the sequence again. The phone ringing, his own 'hello', followed by the interrogatory two words. Once he had cut the call off, the phone had not rung again. That must mean that Jude had sorted it. Jude was quick off the mark and always knew what to say.

Even so, the situation didn't sound good. No, that was an understatement. The situation sounded dire. Jude had said Medlicott had no money. That surely couldn't be right? This was their big one. The one which would allow them to retire. Alongside the sensation of icy fingers making a lingering descent of his spine, came the remembrance of his dream. The careful operation of building something up over time, only to see it crumble before his very eyes. It was creepy, very,

217

very creepy – and he didn't even believe in that sort of thing.

How could they possibly have made a mistake? The old woman in Florida, well that had been another balls-up of the first order. Then again, how could they have guessed that the house and all the contents were entailed, so that the will leaving them everything she owned amounted to virtually squat? 'Think of it as a trial run,' Jude had said. At the end of the day, they had come out of it better than even, and no one had entertained the slightest suspicions that the old dear's accident had not been what it seemed.

Jude had talked her way around everything of course. She'd always been brilliant. A real loss to the stage. The ideas were mostly hers too, with him adding mere refinements. They had been working together for more than ten years, mostly pulling operations on ex-pats and the occasional gullible Americans, and they had only come badly unstuck twice, once over the old dame in Florida and now this . . .

The trouble was that this was supposed to have been the big one. There was no way that they would be able to find a new victim and play the same scenario out again. Not in Britain, anyway. They had played their hand and lost. Or so it appeared . . . yet even now, he couldn't quite believe it. He tried to work out what must have happened – not over Medlicott's lack of fortune, that post-mortem would have to wait for another time – but how had Medlicott come to overhear Jude, then get hold of her phone?

More importantly, what did Jude expect him to

do now? He looked down at the phone, but it remained obstinately silent. Clearly he could not call or text her. They had an absolute rule against that. Presumably she would wait until the coast was clear and then call him again. Of course, that sort of opportunity might not arise for hours, and in the meantime, would she be expecting him to start putting the plan into operation?

He sat on the edge of the bed, and attempted to consider the problem from a variety of different angles. Only a couple of hours earlier, she had texted to confirm their arrival at the cottage. How could everything have changed in the space of two hours? Could Jude have been telling the truth about Medlicott having no money? Or was it some kind of elaborate double bluff that he couldn't quite figure out? If it was true, then Medlicott was of no further use to them, and his continued presence on the scene was no more than an unwanted complication. If she was wrong . . . well either way, the imperative to get rid of Medlicott probably still existed.

For the moment however, there was nothing lost by simply waiting, in case Jude got the opportunity to communicate with him again. He knew Jude of old. She could talk her way out of anything. He had to trust her to work something out.

Thirty-Nine

As soon as Rob stalked out of the room, Mark turned to Jude but she silenced him with a look, and he realized that she was listening in order to work out where the thug had gone. They heard him enter the kitchen, come out again and begin to mount the stairs, and as the heavy treads ascended, Jude whispered, 'Can you reach your phone?'

'No.' He replied at the same volume. 'I left it in the kitchen. Can you get yours?'

'He's broken it.'

'What the hell is going on, anyway? I always thought your brother was a bit weird, but I didn't realize that he's a complete nutter.'

'He's not my brother.'

'WHAT?'

'Keep your voice down. We have to get out of here . . . Oh God, he's coming back.'

The thunder of Rob's descent was unmistakable and seconds later he strode into the room. He had put the gun away, but there was a visible bulge of a holster under his jacket. In place of the gun, he had a cigarette lighter in his hand, which he flicked into life as he approached Jude, who instinctively cowered back as far as the sofa cushions would allow her.

'Look . . . Rob – why don't we sit down and talk about this?' Mark wished that his voice carried a bit more conviction. The world was falling apart in a rapid and confusing way, but maybe it would still be possible to inject some rationality.

Rob paid him not the slightest attention, not even bothering to turn his head. 'Now then, Princess.' He continued to advance until he was almost toe to toe with Jude, and holding the flickering lighter flame within inches of her nose. 'You'd better start talking, unless you want me to make a mess of that pretty face.'

'I will, I will. Please, get that lighter away from me.'

Making no attempt to reduce the distance between his victim and the flame, Rob said, 'You can start by telling me who you were talking to just now on the phone.'

'His name is Stefan.'

'Who the fuck is Stefan?'

'Rob – please – I—'

From his position on the other sofa Mark saw Rob move forward and in the same instant heard Jude's shriek.

'Stop it, leave her alone,' he shouted, but fell instantly silent as he realized that Jude was already sobbing out a monologue which he also needed to hear.

'Stefan is a friend. He was in on things. He's been in from the start. I wanted us to have back up, in case Mark put up a fight. Stefan was going to help make it look like an accident.'

At this point Jude's account was interrupted by a series of sobs and wails as Rob, apparently losing interest in the cigarette lighter, set about her with his bare hands. 'Liar!' he yelled. 'Liar, liar! I knew there was something. That's why I decided to come down a few hours early. It wasn't just Mark who was going to have an accident, was it? This Stefan is there to do me as well.'

Mark observed this activity with what might have appeared to Jude as frozen detachment, though his mind was in turmoil as he attempted to process the information. Rob was not Jude's brother. The two of them had planned for him to have 'an accident'. But unbeknown to Rob, a third person called Stefan was also involved and he had intended that Rob should also perish in this 'accident'. The exact details were both confusing and irrelevant. The key point seemed to be that he was currently tied up in an isolated property, and the only people who knew his whereabouts were an unknown bloke called Stefan, a madman with a gun, and a double-crossing bitch who had tricked him into matrimony – and essentially all three of them intended him dead. A question earlier that afternoon regarding his life insurance policies or lack of them abruptly acquired a sinister significance.

Rob paused his onslaught to snap out another enquiry. 'Is it true what you were telling him? That Medlicott has no money.'

'That's absolutely true,' Mark cut in, deciding that it was time to get involved. It was a risk, of course, directing the vicious attention which had previously been focussed on Jude back to himself, but perhaps if he could make Rob see that there was no profit in killing him, the guy might have a rethink and calm down. 'I'm afraid I suffered some bad losses – investments that went wrong, a few misplaced bets – and I'm quite badly in debt, actually.'

'He married me for my money.' Jude's voice sounded shrill, as if the humour of the situation – her newlywed husband's utter folly – was in itself a cause for hysteria.

'So we've done it all for nothing.' Rob digested the information as an alchemist, the results of whose life's endeavours has just turned into base metal. He turned on Jude again. 'What about this Stefan? When do you expect him to turn up? I warn you now, if you try to lie to me again, I'll kill you.'

'Why? Why? There's no point harming me. I love you, you know that.'

'Then why Stefan? That's who you're screwing now, isn't it? You disgust me. I ought to kill you right now.'

'No – please.' Jude was shrieking now. 'I'll tell you the truth. I swear I will. Stefan is coming tonight. I was going to let him into the house. He was going to help you deal with Mark.'

'Like hell he was. I think it's pretty obvious that having dealt with him—' Rob jerked his head momentarily in Mark's direction – 'he would be ready and waiting to try to deal with me, when I turned up a few hours later.' He ruminated on the point for a moment, looking from one to another of his captives.

Mark attempted to adopt an appropriate expression, nothing too challenging or too craven, while he tried to remember how to breathe, and wondered whether Rob was contemplating which one of them to shoot first. Across the room he could see that Jude had fallen sideways across the couch. There was blood on her face and fear in her eyes. He remembered that she was supposed to be, in fact legally was, his wife. He knew that he was not feeling everything that a good husband ought to feel on seeing his wife repeatedly pummelled by a violent ruffian. On the contrary, he tended toward the opinion just expressed by the man who he had, until a short while ago, assumed to be his brother-in-law: that she was a conniving bitch. Nevertheless, he suspected that in their current circumstances, she might be the closest thing he had to an ally. It was definitely something to bear in mind.

'So,' Rob finally spoke again, 'what's the plan now that Stefan' – he managed to invest the name with all the enthusiasm of a vegetarian confronted by a plate of medium rare steak – 'has found out that Medlicott's nothing but a useless sack of shit?'

'I don't know,' Jude whimpered. 'I honestly don't know.'

'You must know. You told him that Medlicott had no money. What then?'

'That was it. You came out from behind the wall and I cut off the call. Then you called him back. The next voice he would have heard on my phone was yours. He would have known that it had all gone wrong.' She collapsed into a bout of sobs, trying to bury her face in the cushions, but Rob grabbed her by the hair again and forced her to look at him.

'What was the back-up plan? Does he come

straight here? Head for the hills? What happens now?'

'I don't know. I don't know. We didn't have a back-up plan. He might come here. He might wait for me to ring again. I just don't know.'

Rob glanced towards the window, where dusk was deepening into darkness.

'Has he got a key?'

'No. I was going to let him in.'

'Which door?'

'The kitchen.'

'What was your signal?'

'What?'

'The signal. The signal you'd arranged, so that he would know the coast was clear.'

'I don't know what you mean.' Her words were punctuated by another stinging blow across the side of her face.

'Don't mess with me, Jude. I know the way you think. What was the signal you'd arranged with him?'

'The lamp in the front upstairs bedroom window would be on,' she said. 'Everything else would be in darkness.'

He hesitated, clearly looking for flaws. 'So if it was dark, how would you see to let him into the kitchen?'

'I wasn't going to wait in there for him, I just had to leave the door unlocked. There's quite a bit of light in the kitchen anyway, from the clocks on the oven and the microwave.'

Mark noticed that she was struggling to speak. Possibly Rob had dislodged a couple of teeth. He tried to suppress the thought that it was no more than she deserved. A would-be murderess, as coldly calculating as her brother – no wait, he would really have to keep remembering that Rob *wasn't* her brother.

'OK. Get up both of you.' Rob reached into his jacket and removed the gun from its shoulder holster as he spoke.

Mark stared at him, immobile. This was it. The coward dies a thousand deaths. Hadn't some brute of a PE teacher once mocked him with those words, when he funked it during some sort of outward bound exercise? Well, chucking yourself off some cliff, rigged up with abseiling gear was no preparation for this. 'Look,' he said hesitantly. 'Why don't we calm down and try to talk about this—'

'UP!' Rob roared and this time Mark struggled to his feet without any further attempt at argument, his secured hands providing an awkward encumbrance which set him off balance.

On the opposite side of the room, Jude needed to be half-dragged to her feet and propelled towards the door.

'You first.' Rob jerked his weapon in Mark's direction. 'Out of here, up the stairs, into the main bedroom. Don't try anything clever.'

His relief that they were not to be immediately shot rendered Mark only too willing to lead the way. As for trying anything, he could not even think of anything stupid to try, let alone anything clever. He walked ahead of the others, stepping slowly and carefully, lest a minor slip suggested to Rob that something clever, stupid, or in any way contrary to his instructions, was afoot. It

226

was dark in the rest of the house, but Rob switched the lights on as they went along, activating the switch just inside the bedroom door last of all.

'Lie face down on the bed, both of you.'

As they obeyed, Mark could feel a sick sense of panic rising up through his chest. Wasn't this a typical position of execution? In his mind's eye he could see their bodies, lying still as if in sleep, with their blood seeping steadily down through the bedding until it reached the carpet. He waited, flinching as he heard a click behind him, but it was the light switch, plunging the room into darkness. He heard the door close and a key turn in the lock. He had noticed the key in the old-fashioned lock much earlier, considering it one of the few touches which gave the place character. When he had first spotted the key, it had been on the inside of the door, but Rob had evidently transferred it to the outer side of the lock, and having used it to secure the room, his feet could now be heard descending the stairs.

Deep breaths. Take deep, steady breaths. Ironic, he thought, that they were lying alongside one another on the king-size bed where they had been intending to spend their honeymoon together. He had envisaged that first night in any number of ways, none of which had included a scenario anything akin to his one.

Forty

Hannah's first text appeared while Peter was still hunting down a cup of coffee.

May be several hours. Do you want to go?

He did want to go, because let's face it, who wants to sit for hours in a hospital car park, but then he considered the wording of the message. It didn't say *Go home, I'll get a taxi.*

He texted back: *Will wait for you here.*

Hannah's reply came back immediately: *Thanks. xxx.*

Whatever the future held, this was what Hannah needed him for right now. Unquestioning support with generous sex as an antidote to heartbreak and pain. He found himself humming 'What's love got to do with it?'

Back in the car, nursing a paper cup of thin, vending machine coffee which tasted like mud, he continued to observe the comings and goings in the car park. Patients attending for routine appointments had been replaced by visitors, with the average age range dropping accordingly. Sitting in the car for hours reminded him of doing surveillance work. Not that he had ever done very much of that. At around nine o'clock he spotted a familiar face heading away from the main building and for a moment his mental antennae twitched, but even old lags like Bazza Chivers sometimes went on an innocent errand to visit a sick relative. Bazza was a wrong 'un. You knew it the minute you set eyes on him. It was the complete lowlife cocktail with Bazza, from the abundance of tattoos, and a hostile facial expression, to the chemical content of his inside pockets.

Robin Thackeray could hardly have been more different in appearance. And yet . . . and yet, there was still something wrong about the bloke. It was not the obvious, lifelong ruffian-type wrongness of the kind which exuded from Bazza Chivers. You could have dressed old Bazza up in an Armani suit, put a fat wallet into his top pocket, seated him on a stool in a cocktail bar, with an heiress at his side, and he would still have been recognizably a wrong 'un. The set of his mouth, the tattoos on his knuckles, his rough, ungrammatical utterances, in fact his entire being would still have given the game away in an instant.

Peter opened the car door wide enough to pour half the contents of his coffee onto the tarmac (even alternating with bites from a Snicker bar hadn't been enough to make it palatable) then shifted into a more comfortable position, as he pictured Robin Thackeray. The guy didn't exactly look out of place in the clothes he wore, but there was something . . . He was supposed to be Jude Thackeray's brother, but he didn't look like her and more tellingly, he didn't sound like her. Whereas she had retained a nice English accent, he had adopted an American drawl, which might easily have been concealing something else. He was one of those people who seemingly drifted through life with no visible means of support. He described himself as a company director, with various interests in the UK and abroad. Money and business interests which the Thackerays claimed they had mostly inherited from their parents. Had that checked out? Or was that what Hannah had been about to tell him? That maybe the Thackerays' money, like their friends, relatives and ex-lovers, didn't actually check out at all? They had enjoyed the use of several properties, but had anyone actually checked whether all those properties belonged to them?

For a second he almost texted Hannah to ask if she could spare him a few minutes outside. He stopped himself just in time. He must be getting tired to even let such an idea cross his mind. That was it, he thought. He was just tired and basically being stupid, circling around and around something that wasn't even there. What would be the point in pretending to wealth you didn't possess, staging a kidnap, beating one of the participants black and blue, then disappearing into the ether again? It wasn't an insurance scam. They hadn't even tried to sell their story to the papers. It would have been an expensive stunt to set up, difficult to pull off, and in the final assessment, utterly pointless, which was probably why old Lingo hadn't wasted too much effort on looking into their financial standing.

He remembered a fleeting discussion about the possibility that their money had emanated from criminal activities, which would have opened up all kinds of cans of worms, with the kidnap maybe some sort of gang-related episode with a hidden agenda – but none of the evidence had fitted with that, the Thackerays didn't feature on any criminal database, and so as far as he could remember, the idea hadn't been seriously pursued.

In real-life investigations, motives were seldom complex. For all his instincts that there was something odd about Robin Thackeray, Jude must after all have been the victim of a straightforward conman. A dangerous man, he reminded himself, as a heavy shower of rain began to drum on the roof of the car. A man that was still out there. Someone who might be spending that very evening sliming his way into the affections of some other wealthy woman. And Lingo's team were no nearer to catching him than they had been at the start.

Forty-One

Mark lay completely still and quiet until he was sure that Rob must have reached the ground floor and be out of earshot. Adversity makes strange bedfellows. He remembered hearing someone say that once, though the occasion and the context were lost to him. Time to set aside, for the moment, the uncomfortable facts that Jude had tricked him into marrying her and apparently been involved in a conspiracy to murder him. At the moment they were indeed bedfellows in adversity and this made her the nearest thing he had to a friend.

First he had to get her onside – and although time was short, a bit of sympathy could pay dividends. Turning his head to face her, he whispered, 'Jude, are you all right? Has he hurt you badly?'

'I'm not great. My mouth is bleeding. He may have broken some ribs.'

There was something definitely not right with her voice, he noticed. Aloud he said, 'Did you bring any nail scissors?'

'What?'

'Nail scissors. We may not have much time. Mine are in a leather case, zip fastener, really awkward to get at.'

'Mine are loose, in the top drawer of the dressing table.'

'Which side?'

'Right.'

He noted that she didn't waste any more time asking questions.

'You're hurt,' he said. 'You stay where you are for now and I'll get them. Then I'll give them to you and you can cut me free.'

She didn't attempt to query this, but merely whispered, 'Try not to make any noise. The kitchen's right underneath us.'

'OK.'

He found that rolling onto his back was surprisingly difficult, with his hands secured behind him, but once he had made it as far as a sitting position, it was easy enough to slide his feet onto the floor and stand up. He moved cautiously towards the dressing table, feeling his way and taking his time. He didn't want to trip, or knock

232

something over. It was vital that Rob shouldn't realize that he was on the move. He managed to locate the handle of the drawer without too much difficulty, but found that he had to bend his knees in order to get a grip on it, and the act of sliding the drawer out when he had his back to it proved awkward. Once he had it open, his fingers quested blindly among the contents until he managed to locate the unmistakable shape of a pair of scissors.

'Got them,' he whispered.

'Well done. As you've got the scissors, why don't you cut me free first?'

'Because I don't trust you to cut me free second.'

'Who's to say that if I free you, you'll free me?'

'I give you my word that I will. We have to trust each other.'

'That contradicts what you just said a minute ago.'

'Look,' he hissed, 'are you going to concentrate on getting out of here, or are you going to bicker? Every minute counts if we're going to have any chance. You have to kneel on the bed, with your back to me, then I'll put the scissors into your hand and keep my back to you, while you cut me free. OK?'

'OK.'

He could dimly make out the shape of her, a dark shadow struggling on the pale bedcovers, gasping from the effort and emitting periodic whimpers of pain.

'I can't do it,' she said. 'I can't get onto my knees. It hurts too much.'

'All right. Try rolling onto your back. Then you can slide off the bed and we can stand back to back.' He managed to keep his voice relatively calm, but his heart was racing. He needed her to be able to do this. Any moment might bring the return of that lunatic from downstairs. He watched and waited while she went through a further process of struggling and moaning, until she had eventually levered herself into a standing position, after which they edged closer to one another, until they were ready to effect the transfer.

'I'm holding the blades,' he told her. 'You need to find the scissors, then get your fingers into the holes. Make sure you've got your finger and thumb completely into place, then tell me to let go. We can't afford to mess this up by dropping the scissors.'

It was like one of those bizarre party games, he thought, were you had to pass oranges, or balloons, or do something faintly risqué which involved fumbling blindfolded around a partner's backside, while everyone else looked on and hooted with laughter.

After what seemed like an interminable amount of time she said, 'Let go, I've got them.'

'Right. Now use your other hand to find the tie, position the scissors and cut.'

He felt her fumbling around, at least twice grazing one of his wrists with the blades until she located the tie and attempted to close the scissors onto it.

'They won't go through it.'

'They have to.'

'The plastic's too thick.'

'You need to keep sawing at it. It will go through eventually.'

He tried to sound more confident of this than he actually felt. He had seen similar feats pulled off in the movies, but presumably the script-writers made sure that if Harrison Ford or Tom Cruise was involved, the plastic was thin and the nail scissors extra sharp.

After a few minutes of desperate work with the scissors, during which he had to stifle at least two cries when the points found his flesh, he detected her fingers exploring near his wrist.

'What are you doing?'

'Feeling to see how much I've cut. There's definitely a nick in the edge of the plastic. If you pull your hands as far apart as possible, that will put more strain on it.'

And more strain on me, he thought, as he did his best to go along with her, forcing himself to maintain a position which made the tie bite into his flesh. A nick in the edge of the plastic? At this rate the scissors would wear out (to say nothing of his wrists) before they managed to chop the bloody thing in half.

The tie gave without warning, his hands flying apart so suddenly that it knocked him off balance and he almost fell.

'Now do mine.'

'In a minute,' he whispered. 'First you tell me how things stand.'

'You promised.' The anger in her voice was coloured with distress.

'Sure I did. But it's hard to trust you, after what I've found out tonight.'

235

'You tricked me too.'

'What do you mean?'

'Come off it. You married me for money, I married you for money.'

'I didn't plan to kill you,' he hissed.

'Cut me lose and I'll tell you everything.'

'If you don't tell me everything, I won't help you. I'll leave you here.'

'You can't overpower him on your own. Between us we can take him by surprise.'

'With bashed-in ribs? Anyway, I don't intend to overpower him. I'm going to unlock the door and slip out.'

It was remarkable how much derision she could inject into a whisper. 'Of course you are! The key's on the other side of the door, drongo.'

'I know how to do it.'

'Paul Daniels are we now? Anyway you won't get far, because if you don't take me with you, I'll scream the place down and bring him running, before you have the chance to get as far as the stairs.'

'Fair point.' He felt for her hands in the dark. 'OK. I'm going to take the scissors out of your hands. Hold your wrists still and I'll find the band and start cutting, but in the meantime, you talk. Is this Stefan likely to turn up?'

'When he can't get me on the phone, I think he's sure to.'

'And did you tell Rob the truth about your signal?'

'What signal?'

'The signal that tells Stefan he's safe to let himself into the house?'

236

'Yes.'

'So the parking space was being left for Stefan?'

'No, for Rob. Stefan is coming by boat.'

'Boat?'

'Yes, boat. He'll come into the beach, then climb up the cliff path.'

'And what was Stefan supposed to do, when he got here?'

'Are you cutting at all?'

'You know I am. But I'll stop the minute you start to hold out on me.'

'The idea was that Stefan would be here, hiding in the house. Rob would come and we'd carry out the plan Rob knew about.'

'Which was?' he prompted.

'Don't stop cutting.'

'Then don't stop talking.'

'He might come back any minute.'

'He won't. He's waiting in the kitchen, ready to deal with your other boyfriend when he turns up.'

'The other plan,' she gulped, her voice already muffled by some unseen injury to her mouth dropped even further, so that Mark could barely distinguish her words, 'was that I would suggest a romantic stroll on the cliffs, first thing in the morning. Rob was going to be concealed, a little way down the path and he was going to push you, so that . . . so that you went over the edge.'

'Charming.' He tried to sound calm. He thought that he'd come to terms with the initial shock of discovering that they'd planned to murder him, but hearing it spelled out was chilling.

'Rob thought we'd get away with saying that

it was an accident. You know – that we'd gone out for a walk and you just slipped and fell, breaking your neck. But Stefan was going to deal with Rob as well, then put your two bodies into one of the boats he'd brought and use the other to tow it well out to sea, before shoving you both over the side and leaving the boat to drift. I was going to report you missing, saying that you and Rob had gone out together in this boat that Rob had borrowed. They would search and find the boat, and believe that there had been an accident. Stefan reckoned that he knew where to put the bodies over, so that it would be some time before they washed up on shore – if they did at all. That way the bodies would be too far decomposed for anyone to be sure exactly how they'd died. Even if it looked like there had been foul play, we thought they might assume that the two of you had fallen out and had some sort of fight, rather than suspecting that a third party had been involved.'

'Oh yes,' he said, sarcastically, as a heady sense of hysteria swept through him. 'Well obviously, that was a *much better* plan than just pushing me over the top of the cliffs.'

He continued to work away in silence. In theory, it ought to have been easier to cut her free, because he was able to work facing forward, pinching the tie between the fingers of one hand, while he worked the scissors with the other, but perhaps the scissors had been blunted by their earlier work. 'These are starting to feel loose,' he said. 'I think they might be coming apart. I'm going to try to find mine.'

238

He wasted some time at the dressing table, before remembering that he had left the manicure set in his bag.

'What are you doing?' she hissed. 'Hurry up, will you. Just use my scissors.'

'I've remembered where they are. They're Sheffield steel. Much quicker in the long run.'

At that moment his fingers closed around the leather case and he withdrew it from his bag, unzipping it as he did so. Seconds later he was back at work on the plastic tie.

'If Rob isn't your brother, who is he?'

'His name is Rob McGilligan. I met him while he was on holiday in Florida. That's where we got married.'

'Then our marriage isn't legal?' For some reason, the news that he was not legally shackled to her after all elevated his spirits considerably. 'So where does Stefan come in?'

'Stefan and I go way back. We met each other when we were both travelling. We started to go around together. Then we tried a few things.'

'Things?' he prompted.

'Are you ever going to cut me free? Are you even trying?'

'Keep your hands still. Twisting around won't help. You were saying . . . about you and Stefan?'

'We were looking after this old lady, in Florida, but after she died, things got heavy with the family and we had to leave.'

Mark experienced that familiar feeling of bile rising in his throat. He swallowed hard and said, 'Go on.'

'So we came up with something a bit more

239

inventive. Rob provided the seed money and the muscle. We needed a third party, you see, to help fake the kidnap. If it went wrong, I had a story all prepared . . .'

I bet you did, he thought.

'Rob didn't know anything about Stefan – obviously. He thought it was just him and me, in it together. It was dead easy for him to get documents. He just pretended to be my little brother Robin who'd died. It was just coincidence, him being called Rob, but it made it masses easier, because there was never any chance of me calling him the wrong name.'

Mark was tempted to remark that when it came to lucky coincidences, the devil evidently looked after his own. He was just wondering how long it had taken her to find a sucker like Rob, who was as keen to embark on a criminal career as she was, when another question thrust itself to the forefront of his mind: why was she suddenly so willing to share all this information with him? The answer raced in behind it, like an express train. She knows it doesn't matter, because one way or another, I'm never going to make it out of here to tell anyone what I know. If bloody Rob doesn't do for me, this bastard Stefan will.

'Can't you hurry it up?'

'It's not my fault if the bloody scissors are blunt. Are you pulling your hands as far apart as possible?' He was abruptly seized by a violent urge to follow Rob's example and kick her skinny backside from here to kingdom come. If it hadn't been for his fear that she would make good her threat to alert her erstwhile 'brother', he would have left her there to fend for herself. As it was he would have to cut her loose and take her along when he made his bid for freedom which, given her murderous intentions toward him and the fact that this Stefan character might turn up at any moment and side with her, put the odds very much against a successful outcome. 'You do realize,' he enunciated the words carefully, as if explaining to a child, 'that you've got nothing to gain from killing me now? I haven't got any money or any insurance . . .'

At that moment the plastic tie gave up the unequal battle with the scissors and he had to grab her, before she fell forward.

'Thanks,' she whispered. 'Now, how do we get out of here?'

'Do you think we dare put a light on? This would be masses easier if I could see what I was doing.'

'Would one of the bedside lights do? They're on dimmers and if we put them on really low, I don't think anyone would be able to notice them, just from looking out of the window downstairs.'

'Good idea. You work your way across to the window and pull the curtains across, while I find the lamp.'

'OK.'

Each of them worked their way as silently as possible to their appointed place. His fingers encountered the edge of the bedside table, then quested for the lamp. He was terrified that at any moment he might knock some unobtrusive object onto the floor and give the game away, but he encountered nothing until he found the lamp itself. He slid his fingers up until he reached the switch and the bulb blossomed into life. Jude swished the curtains across in the same moment, hiding their activities from anyone who happened to be observing from the blackness beyond the windowpanes.

'Good,' he said quietly, attempting to sound confident and in control. 'What I need now is a sheet of card or paper, and a pencil.'

'What?'

'Keep your voice down.'

'Sorry.'

'Have you got anything like that?'

'This is a bedroom, not an artist's studio.'

'Then we need to improvise.' He was looking around as he spoke, trying not to notice the mess Rob had made of her face. Violence of any kind unnerved him, even if she didn't deserve his sympathy. Besides which, if little brother – no, no, he wasn't her brother – well anyway, if that thug came back upstairs and caught them trying to get away, Mark had more than a suspicion that the damage Jude had sustained was a mere foretaste of what he could expect himself. 'Can you think of anything?' he asked, desperately.

'What are you going to do? Put a message in a bottle?'

'Do you think facetious remarks like that are going to help? I need something thin and flat to slide under the door, and something long and thin, like a pencil, to push into the lock. The key falls out onto the sheet of paper and we slide it back under the door and unlock the door from the inside.'

'How do you know the key will fit under the door?'

'I don't – but I know there's a big gap.'

'How?'

'Because when women look around a bedroom they see how much hanging space there is, and the nice view from the window, whereas men see things like a screw missing from the handle of a drawer, and badly fitting doors. Will you *please* help look for the things we need?'

'I've got a little pen,' she said, ferreting in the same drawer from which he had earlier extracted the nail scissors, and pulling out a thin, delicate object enamelled in a pattern of dark flowers, with a tassel dangling from the end.

'Excellent.' He tried to achieve a positive tone. It seemed a good moment to foster a sense of team spirit.

The sheet of paper presented more difficulty. She offered to tear a page out of her pocket-size diary, but he explained that it wouldn't be big enough.

'Even though we'll be pushing the key really slowly and gently, to stop it from flying out of the keyhole, we can't guarantee that it will fall absolutely straight, so we need to be able to cover as wide an area as possible – and don't forget, we have to keep part of the paper on this side of the door, so that we can pull it back again.'

'Couldn't we push the key out, then hook it back under the door, using a metal coat hanger?'

He hesitated. The idea was not without merit, but he had to allow for not being able to see the key. Suppose they inadvertently pushed it further away?

'We should keep that in reserve,' he said. 'Surely we've got something that we could use for the key to fall on?'

'Pages from a book?' She proffered a paperback, swiped up from the table.

'Not big enough.'

'Not one on its own. But push two or three under, lengthways, and you've got something as big as a sheet of A4. Pull them in one at a time, and you've got your key.'

She was quick thinking, he had to give her that. He nodded encouragement, while she tore out a page at a time from the latest Peter James thriller, working in elaborate slow motion, for fear of the sound of ripping paper. He took them from her and lined them up carefully, sliding each in turn as far as he dared, out towards the landing. Once four sheets were in place he crouched before the door and began manoeuvring the ladylike little pen, a millimetre at a time into the keyhole. He slowed the operation still further, when he felt the pen encounter the resistance of the key. It was vital that it toppled down onto the paper. If he was over hasty, and the key shot from the lock too fast and bounced out of reach, they were sunk.

The key fell with a faintly audible sound of metal against paper, the noise muffled by the carpet beneath it. He gripped the torn-out page directly in line with the lock and eased it under the door, almost sobbing with relief when the flat metal head of the key appeared on his side of the door.

'Bloody clever,' Jude whispered at his side, like

him, half-disbelieving of their success. 'That was absolutely amazing.'

He decided not to tell her that he had borrowed the idea from an old episode of *Doctor Who*. Instead he straightened up and turned to ask, 'Where did you hide my car key?'

'It's in my coat.'

'Where's your coat?'

She thought for a moment. 'It's still in the living room. It's the coat that got dragged off me, when Rob started knocking me around.'

He hesitated for no more than seconds, before saying, 'We can't risk trying to get it. We need to get straight out of the front door and leg it for the road. If we keep walking, we'll find help eventually. The most important thing is to get away from him.'

She nodded. 'Straight down the stairs and out of the door.'

'As quietly as you can. We must get out without him hearing us.'

'Right.'

He fitted the key with elaborate care and turned it in the lock, before easing the door open. As he stepped out onto the landing, two shots rang out in swift succession.

Forty-Two

Peter was finding it increasingly difficult to stay awake. There had been another text from Hannah, this time urging him to go home, but he knew

245

that wasn't really what she wanted, so he had responded by promising to stay. He had moved out of the driver's seat, where the wheel got in his way, and taken up a marginally more comfortable position, sitting diagonally across the back seats, so that he could stretch out his legs. Even so there was very little room. He was reminded of a conversation they had once had about the lack of space for sexual congress in the rear of a saloon car, which in turn set him back to thinking about their visit to the lay-by in Foxden Woods, in connection with their review of the Thackeray case. It had been the first occasion on which Hannah had propositioned him. That was only a matter of weeks back, but it felt like aeons ago.

When he woke, it was with a painful jerk to his neck. He struggled upright, momentarily confused by the discomfort and darkness. When he checked his phone, he saw that it was shortly after midnight. He had been in the middle of a dream, in which he had lost his warrant card, and although he knew it must have been a dream, he instinctively felt for the familiar rectangle of plastic in his inner pocket. He realized that he must have been thinking about giving up the job – subconsciously, if nothing else – just before he had fallen asleep. The thought of handing in his warrant card must have been preying on his mind. It was the final thing he would have to do. The symbolic act which signalled the end of his police career. He'd heard ex-coppers say they felt naked without it. The card went everywhere with you. It said what you were, who you were – and then it was gone. Would an endless round of 'Valerie', 'Peggy Sue' and 'Crazy Little Thing Called Love' – or as Ginny had put it, a load of oldies for a load of oldies – mostly tracks from before he had been born – really fill the gap?

At that moment he remembered that he hadn't renewed the pay and display ticket on his windscreen, but when he peered forward, he could discern no penalty notice stuck under his wipers. The car park attendant probably didn't work at night. Bloody disgrace anyway – making people pay to park when they needed to visit the hospital.

Now that he had been awake for a minute or two, he realized that though poorly lit, the area wasn't completely dark. Still a rapist's dream, he thought. Plenty of shadows to lurk in, while waiting for some hapless nurse or lone female visitor to walk across the mostly deserted spaces, as she returned to her car. He decided to move to a space nearer the door, not because he was so far away as to put Hannah at any risk, but to save her from having to walk more than a few feet, when she finally emerged. He had just resumed his position in the driver's seat and fired the engine into life when he saw her coming out of the main doors. She paused on the threshold, looking lost and alone. He switched on the lights and brought the car up to the door for her, giving her a long, wordless hug once she had climbed inside.

'Straight home?'

'Yes please.'

Forty-Three

At the sound of the gunshots, Jude grabbed Mark's arm so hard that he all but cried out.

'He's shot Stefan!' Her voice emerged as a weirdly subdued wail, only fractionally louder than the whispers in which they had been communicating before.

As he prized her talons from his shirt, he was tempted to say that of course he has shot Stefan, because you, you daft cow, gave him the information which enabled him to set a trap for this Stefan – whoever he is, or was – and shoot the bloke as soon as he came in at the kitchen door. However with an armed lunatic downstairs and pinpricks of fear racing all over his body, it was clearly not the moment for recriminations and instead he hissed, 'Come on,' then demonstrated the need for urgency by taking off down the stairs at breakneck speed.

In the gloom of the unlit hall, the front door seemed to be a ridiculously long way away. Fractions of seconds stretched into slow motion, like a nightmare in which imaginary pursuers gained ground as his arms and legs mysteriously failed to function. This aberration of time afforded him the opportunity to think. To realize that Jude, grief-stricken though she may have been over the assumed demise of the unseen Stefan, was right behind him. To ask himself how he ever came to be in this predicament. Had it all begun with that under-insured building burning down? The stupid decision to accept a loan brokered by Chaz? Or did it go back even further? To his determination to break away from his father and the safety of the family business? There was even time for him to wonder whether these surreal and terrifying circumstances were in fact no more than a dream.

He reached the door at last. Its solidity brought him up short and in a moment of confusion he couldn't recall how to unfasten it. Jude arrived beside him and said something about a catch. There was always a catch, he thought. Always some bloody catch which tripped a bloke up at the last minute. They were getting in each other's way now, as each scrambled to get the door open. It jolted ajar, only opening a couple of inches before it was brought up short by the tangle of their feet, as they trod on each other in their attempts to step out of the way. Then he heard the kitchen door unlatch and the next second there was another shot, deafeningly close, and they were tumbling out of the door, with Jude grabbing his arm and all but dragging him around the side of the house, saying, 'Not that way,' as he made an abortive dart towards the path up to the field.

He knew at once that she was right. Rob would expect them to go that way and he was only a pace or two behind. There was no point in heading for the lane, because they didn't have the car keys anyway. Rob couldn't shoot at them if he couldn't see them. He wondered how much that bullet had missed him by. Perhaps it hadn't missed at all. He remembered hearing that some people didn't initially realize that they had been shot. He suppressed an instinct to stop and feel for any telltale bleeding, focussing instead on following Jude, who was a little ahead of him, and appeared to know where she was going. Of course she did – this was her childhood holiday home. No – wasn't that just another lie? She probably didn't know where she was heading at all. This appeared to be confirmed a moment later when she fell heavily and he almost tripped over her. He swerved out of the way, making no effort to stop and help her. It was every man for himself now.

A moment later he crashed to the ground himself. So far as he could gauge, he had gone full tilt into some kind of fence. Already breathless from running, the collision knocked the last of the stuffing out of him. He sat on the cold, wet, night-time grass and massaged a bruised patella while taking stock. It was very dark out here at ground level. If he kept still, it was possible that he could remain unseen.

Jude's arrival at his side instantly exploded that theory. 'He's looking for us.'

'I've found a fence,' he said, making it sound almost as if a fence were some kind of useful implement in a contest between unarmed escapees and a pursuer with a gun.

She seemed to think for a moment, then said, 'It runs parallel to the cliff path. There's a gate in it. You remember? We went through it.'

He didn't remember. He didn't care. 'Maybe

we can hide somewhere – until it gets light?' He inflected it as a question. She was the expert on the locality after all.

'On the beach,' she whispered. 'He won't think of us going down there.'

Well who would? He thought. The path down looked bloody dangerous in daylight, so attempting to get down it in complete darkness must rate as suicidally stupid, but then he thought of something else. 'Didn't you say that your friend Stefan was bringing a boat?'

'Yes.'

'So there will be a boat on the beach? A boat we could use to get away in?'

'Yes . . . if he went ahead and brought it.'

'Beach it is then.'

Beach it is then? What was he thinking? Making it sound like some sort of holiday picnic? What shall we do today, children? Oh, it's such a lovely day, let's all go to the beach. He hadn't much fancied that treacherous-looking climb in the daytime, and now he was blithely proposing that they undertake it at night. Beach it is!

Surmounting the waist-high fence was complicated by the fact that it was topped with barbed wire. Mark swore under his breath as he stabbed his hands and tore his clothes, but he eventually dragged himself clear, only to hear Jude whispering, 'I'm stuck.'

'Just pull yourself free.'

'I can't.'

A big part of him said 'just leave her'. It was dark. How could he possibly help her, when he couldn't even see the problem? All the same, he stopped, grabbed her outstretched arms and dragged her towards him. Brute force was often the answer, but in this case it was a mistake. The barbed wire which had been snagged in her jeans now ripped through the fabric and scraped across a good six inches of the flesh of her inner thigh, and though she tried to swallow the involuntary yell generated by this latest assault on her body, the sound she made lasted long enough for Rob to pinpoint their position. The act of freeing her had turned them into sitting ducks and in barely a moment another bullet was whistling overhead, its passage almost simultaneous to the report of the gun.

'Get down,' she hissed.

The instruction was entirely unnecessary, because he had already dropped onto all fours.

'How much ammunition does he have?'

'How should I know?' She sounded half exasperated, half distraught. He could hear her breath coming in choky little gasps. 'I didn't even know he had a gun.'

'How good a shot is he?'

'What? I told you – I didn't know he had a gun. I don't think he knows anything about guns at all. I think we should try to reason with him.'

'And I think we should keep heading for the beach.' He was keeping his voice so low that he couldn't even be sure if she had heard him, but he demonstrated his commitment to the plan by beginning to crawl backwards, ignoring the slimy feel of the damp turf beneath his palms, keeping his face towards the direction from which the bullet had come and his rear towards the edge of the cliffs.

'Rob,' she called.

She was going to try it. Madness. Absolute madness. Their best chance was to try and stay hidden, while continuing to move as far away from the man with the gun as possible, but instead this lunatic was intent on giving away their position. He tensed himself, waiting for another shot to come, but instead he heard her call again.

'Rob . . .'

No answer.

'Rob. Listen to me. There's nothing to be gained from shooting me – or him. Let's talk this out. The three of us.'

Still no reply.

'Rob, please. We've all messed up here. But if we work together we can sort it out – cover it all up. Two more dead bodies isn't going to help you.'

Mark began to move again, continuing to work his way backwards as fast as he dared, figuring that her voice would mask whatever sound his own stealthy movements were making. She doesn't get it, he thought. Alive we're two witnesses to the murder of this Stefan character. Dead, we're two bodies who he might be able to use to stage some scenario in which he doesn't appear to figure at all. He was tempted to shout out to her, but what was the point of giving away his position too, when she was evidently intent on orchestrating her own destruction?

Suddenly he heard Rob's voice, unnervingly near at hand. He had evidently been homing in on Jude's every utterance. 'All right then. Stand up so that I can see you. I need to see that there aren't going to be any tricks.'

'First you have to throw the gun away,' she called out. 'So that we can be sure you aren't going to shoot us.'

There was a pause. Mark stayed where he was, still on his hands and knees, not daring to move a muscle as he peered into the darkness. The only sound now was the whisper of the sea. Little frothy wavelets, rolling up the gentle slope of the beach, dozens of feet below.

Rob's voice came again. 'I'm throwing it away now.' A second later came the very faint thud of a heavy object, hitting the turf. 'It's gone.'

Jude's voice came again. 'OK. I'm standing up now. Mark, you should stand up too.'

He wanted to shout to her but it was too late. He could not see her, but he knew that from the landward side, she would be silhouetted against the paler light of the sky. He did not see her fall, but he heard the single gunshot, and the lack of any cry or protest seemed an ominous confirmation of what he was sure he knew.

It was a stone, you stupid idiot, he sobbed, inside his head. He threw a stone.

Forty-Four

Peter had been bracing himself for Hannah to be in pieces, but she was calm and dry-eyed by the time they let themselves into the house.

'I've already cried so many tears for Clare that I think the well's run dry.' She smiled at him ruefully. Big tired eyes, surrounded by a smudgy combination of mascara and lack of sleep, looking out over a mug bearing the incongruous legend *If it feels good . . .*

He had offered to make tea and a snack as soon as they got back to the house, but it had turned into a joint effort, with him putting the kettle on, while she made toast. Comforting staples, carried into her sitting room, where the living flame gas fire did its best to warm the occupants, swathing everything in a pale glow of pseudo firelight, marginally enhanced by an energy-saving bulb in the lamp.

As they sat next to one another on the sofa, comfortably close, sipping tea, Peter struggled to know what he ought to say. Maybe nothing. Hannah just wanted him there and he knew she was sick of platitudes – people trying to put a positive gloss on something as shitty as your thirty-five-year-old sister dying of cancer. It was not the moment for clumsy attempts at verbal consolation.

It was Hannah who broke the silence. 'It makes you think . . . something like this. At first I used to think how awful it was that Clare would leave behind two little kids, but in these last few days I've been thinking the opposite.' She paused, but when Peter made no attempt to respond, she continued. 'At least she's left a legacy. Two lovely children. I mean, that's the best kind of legacy, isn't it? I've always thought that I would have kids, but being a copper kind of gets in the way.' Another longish pause. 'I'm thirty-one. Thirty-two next month.'

'You're still grieving for your sister,' Peter said gently. 'This might not be the best time to make any big decisions about your own future.'

'It seems like an ideal time. As one life ends, a new one begins.'

The statement hung in the air for a moment before he put his mug on the table and slid his arm around her. 'Two o'clock in the morning isn't the best time to discuss something as big as this. Come on, McMahon. Let's turn in.'

When they got to the bedroom, he could see that Hannah was almost too tired to undress, and she fell asleep within minutes of her head hitting the pillow. He was tired too, but for once sleep eluded him. Instead of achieving pleasant oblivion, thoughts pinged to and fro across his brain like an electronic table tennis match. After about forty-five minutes, he became convinced that he wasn't going to get to sleep, so being careful not to disturb Hannah, he inched the duvet sideways and sat up, preparatory to swinging his legs over the side of the bed.

Hannah stirred beside him. 'Don't be scared,' she said. 'I'm not trying to trap you. You can say no. Or you can say yes, but not be involved.'

'I'm not scared. I'm not even thinking about that. I'm going to get a glass of water.'

'You're a lousy liar, Peter.'

He stood up and walked across to the tiny en-suite, where he was obliged to make good his statement by filling a glass with water and sipping it. He only remembered too late, as the stale, tepid liquid filled his mouth, that he should have run the tap first. He hadn't intended to get back into bed, but knowing that she was awake, probably watching him, it somehow became a point of honour not to acknowledge that unaccustomed insomnia had almost driven him back to the sitting room.

'Peter?'

'Yes.' He faked a yawn, as he climbed reluctantly back under the duvet.

'You won't leave right away, will you? You'll stay until after the funeral.'

'What makes you think I'm in a hurry to go?'

'You only moved in to keep me company, right? While things were tough.'

'Do you want me to leave?'

'Of course not.'

'Then I'll stay – at least until after the funeral.'

He felt her relaxing back into sleep, her breathing becoming regular and even. Probably dreaming about watching him kicking a football about with a toddler in an Arsenal strip. Hold on – where the heck had that come from? (And anyway, it would be an Ipswich strip, if it was her dream.) He tried to clear his mind, but sleep remained elusive. He tried to focus his thoughts elsewhere but everything returned to Hannah. Hannah sitting on top of her desk as they worked their way through the Thackeray review, swinging one foot back and forth, as she said, 'It has always surprised me that the cupboard was empty, ready and waiting for her. Who has an empty cupboard in their house? My cupboards are all stuffed to capacity. Open any of them and something is liable to fall out on to you.'

It was true, he reflected, that Hannah was a

257

terrible hoarder – but it was also true that there was something off-key about that kidnap situation. Hannah again: 'Compared with a lot of victims, she actually got off quite lightly. Think of all the people we've seen, with their faces black and blue, broken ribs. He hardly touched her face, didn't actually break any bones.'

What he had taken as an almost flippant observation: 'It's almost as if he let her go on purpose . . . The way he left the van door open, then let her get away into the woods . . .' abruptly took on the mantle of a shrewd observation.

There were a dozen pieces of the puzzle which taken in isolation could have meant very little: the oddly controlled violence, the oft-made observation that the assailant could have done just as well by forcing his way into the house one night, making Jude Thackeray give him her pin numbers and the combination to the safe, while wearing a Mickey Mouse mask, so that she never got to see his face. There was the apparent carelessness of the attacker in being caught on CCTV at the garage, which in reality could have been just another facet of the plan, providing some hard evidence of his existence which ensured that Jude's story was believed, while giving the police nothing to go on regarding his actual appearance.

That old friend of Nanna Mina's with the odd-sounding name – Miss Salt – hadn't she remarked that Jude had entertained ambitions to be an actress? Wasn't that in line with the exact words Hannah had used to describe the episode in the woods, where Jude had foiled

258

her captor and escaped certain death? 'The last act in the play . . .'

At the time her words had almost annoyed him with their jokey undertone, but lying beside his colleague several weeks later, with a hint of dawn creeping into the bedroom, it finally came to him that everything added up to a situation which had been carefully stage-managed.

Forty-Five

In spite of the sense that his limbs were disintegrating beneath him with fear, Mark forced himself to think. It was obvious that having taken out Jude, Rob would come looking for him next and would start by walking towards the place where he had seen Jude go down. That would entail negotiating the barbed-wire fence, and would bring him to a point only a few yards away from where Mark was crouching now. His best hope therefore, was to put some more distance between himself and Jude. It was no use just backing up towards the cliff edge until he fell over it. He needed to find the start of the path. He tried to remember how far away it was and what it would look like in the dark. He remembered that there had been a couple of raised bumps in the ground, where the path began. Surely they ought to stand out, even in the relative darkness?

He knew that Rob must be coming in his

direction, but he couldn't hear any sound and this encouraged him to begin moving again, starting by edging crabwise and then turning a half circle and crawling directly towards the sound of the sea. He felt even more vulnerable, now that he had his back to his pursuer. You could stride across the grass much faster than you could crawl, which meant that Rob could be right on top of him in no time, but he dared not stand up and make a run for it, lest he provide a target against the sky, as Jude had done.

He tried to put all thoughts of Jude from his mind. The knowledge that Rob had almost certainly killed the unknown, unseen Stefan, had been terrifying in its implied consequences for his own safety, but the idea of Jude lying somewhere nearby, blood pooling around her, the life gone from her body, made him feel physically sick. He had held the woman, made love to her, and whatever scheme she might have been hatching against him, the reality of her death was too awful to contemplate. He tried to push away the thought that his own death must be near. The situation seemed hopeless. Crawling low to the ground, it was impossible to make out anything more than a couple of feet ahead, so what possible hope could there be of finding the path down to the beach, or indeed of finding his way anywhere in particular?

Two more shots, one straight after another, sounded from a few yards behind him. Jude had not been killed by the original shot then? But that evil, ruthless swine had found her and finished her off, at close range – and it was his turn next. In his head, he heard the crowing, distorted voices of a couple of Munchkins from *The Wizard of Oz*, chorusing 'She's really most sincerely dead.' Sick thoughts, crazy thoughts. He had never liked those bloody Munchkins.

Rob, standing six feet tall and knowing roughly where to look, would have the perfect vantage point from which to hunt him down and pick him off. Oh God, how had he ever ended up in this situation? Even when things went bad, even when Chaz had been threatening him, couldn't he have turned to his family, or even gone to the police? The scheme to resolve all his problems by marrying a bit of money seemed so ridiculous now. A big-league con, attempted by a lower league player. A ridiculous gamble. He had always been attracted by a long odds bet. Now his supposed lifeline was dead, one of her accomplices was dead and pretty soon, he would be dead too.

Was it all his fault? If he hadn't embarked on this last, wild throw of the dice, maybe Jude would still be alive? But no, he thought. It was not entirely his fault. She had targeted him too. He could reasonably consider himself a victim – of her, of the man who had posed as her brother, of smooth-talking Chaz and all his bloody contacts and schemes . . . and finally of sheer bad luck. The cards had been dealt and he had picked up an especially bad hand.

He sensed his danger before his adversary made a sound, jerked his head to look over his shoulder and became aware of the dark figure, almost on top of him. He lashed out with his right arm, but met only thin air, doing marginally better when the kick he aimed as he rolled onto his back made contact with something solid. It was only a glancing blow, insufficient to do any real damage, but it was enough to disrupt the dark shape's progress, and forced him to skip back a step.

Mark had never been a fighter, but the instinct for self-preservation was strong. He hurled himself forward at the figure's legs, grappling him to the ground, alternately hitting out and grabbing for a hold. It was too much to hope that Rob would drop the gun, but if he could work his way up to find the hand that held it, wrestle for possession . . . when hope is a slender thread, you grasp onto it as best you can. He thought it unlikely that Rob would risk shooting wildly in the dark, with his target in such close proximity that he was quite likely to hit himself, and this hunch was swiftly proved correct, because instead of employing the weapon for its usual purpose, Rob brought it down between Mark's shoulder blades with sufficient force that he groaned. A second blow found the back of his head with such a sickening crack that Mark wondered whether his skull had been fractured.

The moments which followed were confused. Mark's head was awash with pain and though he battled to stay on top of his opponent, he was conscious of losing the struggle. Rob wrestled him onto his back, then attempted to clamber astride his chest, while Mark flailed against him, feeling as if he was pitting foam rubber limbs against iron girders. He attempted to use his legs, but the effect was something akin to a toddler, drumming his heels on the carpet in a tantrum. Then the carpet abruptly gave way. The earth crumbled and his legs were hanging out over the void. In the same instant Rob, superior position finally achieved, straightened up to take aim and slid backwards with a yell of alarm which seemed to echo on and on, drowning out the sound of falling flesh, bone, turf and earth.

The lingering scream was replaced by the insistent whisper of the sea. Rob was gone. The gun was gone. Mark lay still for the length of time it took for another three or four small waves to break on the sand, after which he pressed his hands gently down onto the turf and inched his legs shoreward. He managed to haul his knees and lower legs clear of the void and levered himself into a sitting position, flexing his legs and drawing up his knees in readiness to slide backwards again, when a second sound mingled with that of the waves. It was the whispered trickle of earth and small stones, followed by a chink as one pebble bounced off another, then the ground gave way again and Mark rode with it, leaning back like a child on a slide in a public park.

Forty-Six

Cats are creatures of habit. The cottage which lay on the far perimeter of Jigsaw's nightly patrol had been shut up and deserted for most of the summer, but he had continued to visit it regularly, much as he returned to other successful scavenging and hunting grounds. In previous seasons, the summer months had been marked by the regular arrival of various humans who had lived in the cottage for a while. None of them stayed very long and all of them disappeared as mysteriously as they had come, but a not inconsiderable number of them had been pleased to see a feline visitor and some of them had been only too willing to share scraps from their suppers, tasty bits of meat and fish, far superior in quality to that which was provided at home.

Being an extremely sensible, experienced patroller, Jigsaw always approached with caution – even when the place appeared to be deserted. He checked for scents, taking care to leave some of his own, just in case any other cat had the temerity to come out here, then kept his eyes and ears open, as he drew closer to the building. Tonight he could see that there were some lights shining inside the place, which nearly always meant humans, though not necessarily the right kind of welcome: strange people were like strange dogs – unpredictable.

There were no human noises coming from the place. (This was also unusual. Humans were noisy creatures, by and large.) Perhaps there was no one around after all. Jigsaw made a leisurely circuit of the house, investigating an outside drain and pausing to rub his scent glands against a doorpost. No sign of anyone sitting outside, but that was no surprise. It was dark and damp after all. However when he looked in through the big windows, he could not discern anyone in the main downstairs room either.

As he reached the open door at the other side of the house, he heard a couple of loud bangs. Being a country cat, he was familiar with distant gunshots, though he knew that they seldom came at night. The open front door interested him far more than the bangs. He had already heard some similar noises earlier on and dismissed them as not of significance from a hunting cat's point of view. The open door represented far more interesting possibilities. It was more often the big glass door at the other side of the building which was left open, but one entrance was as good as another to Jigsaw, who strolled confidently into the hall and entered the kitchen.

This was usually the point where one of the house's occupants reacted with either pleasurable surprise (cue friendly eye contact, and a weave around the ankles) or some degree of hostility (cue swift exit, via the same route by which you came in) but the only human occupant of the kitchen was slumped awkwardly against the kitchen door, with his legs stretched out in front of him, and his head slumped forward. Jigsaw had never seen, or smelled, a person like this before and he slowed his approach, sniffing suspiciously, keeping his ears pricked for any sound and readying himself for a speedy retreat, should this prove necessary.

Dark liquid had soaked the man's shirt and pooled onto the floor, which was sticky beneath Jigsaw's paws. The interesting smell seemed to be intimately connected with the liquid, which reminded him of a combination of fresh road kill and some raw liver which he had once made off with, after someone had left it unguarded on a kitchen worktop. He was just leaning forward for an exploratory taste, when his sensitive ears picked up a lingering scream of distress in the distance. Jigsaw was well used to the eerie night-time sounds produced by the local fox and owl population, the cries of nocturnal hunter and hunted leaving him generally unmoved, but there was something in the quality of this particular scream, which made him decide at once that it was time to leave.

Turning away from the recumbent figure on the kitchen floor, the cat headed back towards the front door, knowing that once outside there were multiple escape routes. It was not an undignified retreat, but he moved in a swift, loping walk, which could convert in a heartbeat to a dash for safety, should this become necessary. As he headed back down the hall and across the slate step which led into the garden, his four paws left a pattern of neat, carmine prints in his wake.

Forty-Seven

Unlike Alice's legendary fall down the rabbit hole, Mark Medlicott's fall down the Cornish cliffs was a short-lived affair, ending almost before it had begun, as the right side of his body collided with a pinnacle of something solid, which brought him up short before he even had time to frame a scream.

He held his breath, waiting for the second, inevitable, fatal slide to begin. Seconds ticked by, possibly minutes, but nothing happened. He was conscious of the ends of his fingers, pressing painfully into the earth and stone, crushing his nails in an attempt to dig into non-existent hand-holds. Eventually he dared to breathe again: a series of cautious inhalations while he took stock of his position as best he could, all the time trying to remain absolutely immobile. His right side and most of his weight had come to rest against a bank of earth, studded with stones, which formed an apparently solid barrier from the level of his upper thigh to at least his shoulder. In the mean-time his left leg was fully extended down a sloping bed of earth, which for all he knew, formed an unbroken route to the beach and might be as dangerously unstable as the ground which had given way beneath him at the cliff edge. It was too dark to make any kind of visual assess-ment, though his ears told him that the water's edge was much closer than it had been a few moments before.

Moving his head by inches, he tried to see how far he had fallen from the top, but the cliff at his back was an impenetrable wall of darkness, and he was afraid to incline his head too much, lest it even slightly alter his balance. He decided that it was out of the question to attempt any improve-ment to his position until he could see what he was doing, not least because his last efforts had precipitated a landslide and all but killed him.

267

The uneasy thought crossed his mind, that maybe, in spite of that terrible, lingering cry, Rob had not made it to the bottom either, but was perhaps sharing his ledge in the darkness, gun at the ready and murder in his heart. Life had lately descended so far into the surreal, that anything seemed possible. Then he heard an alien sound, coming from somewhere far below him. A hideous animal moan which told him that though Rob had fallen much further, perhaps even all the way down to the shingle beach, like Mark, he had – at least for now – survived the experience.

He tried to blot out the sounds by focussing on his own situation. He was not apparently injured – or at least no more than badly bruised. No tell-tale rattle of falling stones or whisper of crumbling earth warned of imminent instability. If he could manage to keep absolutely still until the sun came up, he might be able to see a way up – or down – the cliffs. He had no idea what time it was, but the summer nights were short.

What if there wasn't a way up or down? Suppose he needed someone with ropes, or even a rescue helicopter? Was anyone likely to pass by and spot him clinging there? Fishing boats perhaps? A farmer? Wasn't there something called the South West Coastal Path? This was the south west coast, wasn't it? Friendly hikers to whom he could yell were probably tramping past from dawn to dusk.

Who was he trying to kid? He would end up clinging there until the hours turned into days and delirious with hunger and thirst, he would lose consciousness and plummet to his death on the rocks below. He might as well get the thing over with now. He'd gambled and he'd lost everything. Even if he managed to get safely back to terra firma, Chaz and his gang of thugs were out to wreak revenge for his unpaid debts. That was assuming he wasn't in custody for murder, because on consideration, the situation didn't look good: two people shot, another one pulped at the bottom of some cliffs, and him the sole survivor.

His right side ached where it had been bruised and jarred in the fall, while his head still throbbed from the blows inflicted by Rob. Every part of his body was protesting. Wouldn't it just be easier to give up now? Another series of hideous noises drifted up to him. Rob was pleading with someone – anyone – to come and help him. Mark clenched his jaws together. The guy had shot Jude in cold blood. He deserved to suffer. His continued survival however gave pause for thought. If he threw himself down and the fall didn't kill him, he was going to be in far worse discomfort than he was now. From where he was positioned just now, a suicide attempt didn't look like a smart option.

Forty-Eight

Peter had eventually crawled back into bed at around six thirty, his ability to sleep miraculously restored. By the time he woke again Hannah was already up, showered and dressed. He found her sitting at the kitchen table, with the telephone and a handwritten list in front of her. He recognized it as the list she had already agreed in advance with her brother-in-law, of people she should ring to convey the news of Clare's death. Typical of conscientious, efficient Hannah, he thought, to have fulfilled her difficult commission within twelve hours of the event. When he got nearer, he could see that there was a neat tick alongside each of the names. Impulsively he kissed her on the top of the head. She responded by reaching for his hand and squeezing it.

'How are you feeling?' he asked.

'Not as awful as I thought. I expected to be in floods at this point, but I think it's like I said last night – or was it this morning? There's been such a long lead up, so much grief already. We'll never get over losing her, but somehow the actual moment . . . it isn't as bad as I thought it would be.'

He bent down and kissed her hair again. Close up, she always smelled gorgeous. You could get high, just sniffing her, he thought.

'It's the funeral I'm dreading now.'

'I'll be with you.'

She raised her face, then frowned when he failed to kiss it. 'Don't panic. You can forget what I said last night. I'm not going to trick you into fatherhood.'

'I never even thought about it. I didn't want to kiss you, because I haven't cleaned my teeth in I don't know how many hours and my mouth tastes like the scrapings from a guinea pig's cage.'

'I didn't realize you were familiar with the taste of guinea pig droppings.'

270

'I'm a man of wide experience.'

'Seriously – I want you to forget what I said last night. Forget the whole conversation. I know it kept you awake last night.'

'*Au contraire* – there you are, you didn't know I could speak French either, did you?'

'I'd expect nothing less from a man of wide experience.'

'Well, OK then. As it happens, it was an entirely different conversation with you which kept me awake last night.'

'What conversation was that?'

'It was the conversation we've been having – on and off – for weeks. The Thackeray case. You've made point after point and basically no one – least of all me – was listening. And the trouble is that no one – maybe not even you – completely got what all of it means.'

'Points mean prizes?'

'*Your* points – all those on-the-ball, nit-picking, typical spikey McMahon observations—'

'You do know that I find it extremely sexy when you call me McMahon – I wish you'd do it more when we're in bed together.'

'Please can we stay on track here?'

'Just another observation.'

'Right. What it all adds up to is that Jude Thackeray – and her supposed brother, Robin – may have set the whole thing up.'

'Supposed brother?'

'Granny Mina's friend said she didn't think there was a brother. We need to check that out, because it seems like something else that wasn't looked into properly at the time.'

'We were short-handed.'

'I don't care if we were short-footed.'

'I realize what it all adds up to. If Jude and Robin Thackeray are not what they seem, then they could have set the whole thing up between them. I've gone over and over it all and got to that time and again,' Hannah said. 'But what I don't get is why. What's the motive? They didn't make any money out of it. They didn't want the publicity. It was as much as we could do to persuade them to do a press conference to appeal for information.'

'They said they didn't want publicity, but they got it anyway. Appearing reticent gave them a veneer of authenticity. The seriously rich don't need to sell their story. But suppose you weren't rich at all, but you wanted to attract a man who was. An extremely wealthy man will be wary of even the most attractive gold-digger, looking to snare a rich husband . . .'

'Whereas you would accept someone who had already been publicly identified as a wealthy heiress, as being just the opposite of your traditional gold-digger,' Hannah finished for him. 'It would take some doing, but I suppose the idea would be to keep up the façade just long enough to get a ring on your finger.' She thought for a moment, then added, 'But surely having got your millionaire, you'd need to keep him sweet, unless you wanted to lose him again. And you'd lose him pretty damn quickly, once he realized that he'd been tricked.'

'Are you familiar with the saying, where there's a will, there's a beneficiary?'

Hannah emitted a slow whistle from between

puckered lips. 'If Mr Millionaire made a will in your favour, then died, you could end up getting all the spoils.'

'Precisely. In fact you wouldn't need to make a new will. Marriage negates any pre-existing testaments, so if anything happens to hubby, brand-new wifey stands to gain. Having taken the trouble to plan an elaborate sham kidnap, in which the victim manages to escape at the last minute, it presumably isn't going to be beyond newly-wed wife, assisted by her fake brother, to organize a robbery or an accident, in order to dispose of poor old hubby.'

'Surely they're not dumb enough to think that they could get away with pulling the same stunt twice?'

'Why not?' Peter ran his hand across his unshaven chin. 'If we're on the right lines, then they've already got away with it once, and I don't suppose it's their intention to re-run a carbon copy of the original stunt. They would think of something else.'

Hannah looked thoughtful. 'It's so extreme.'

'It's also bloody risky. All kinds of things could go wrong.'

'Then again, you don't have to be in this job forever to realize that some people will go to the most ridiculous lengths to get money, and come up with schemes so crazy that no sane person would attempt them.'

'If we're right, then the boss isn't going to like the fact that so many things were missed first time around. And if we're wrong, we could end up looking like a right pair of idiots.'

'If we're right, some poor bloke could be in danger right now . . . Did that last remark sound as melodramatic to you as it did to me?'

'Definitely. Except that it may be true. Are you off today?'

'Yeah. I phoned in earlier. Compassionate leave – and as it happens to be your day off anyway . . .'

'Anything in particular that you have to do?'

'Not really. We all said what we had to say to one another at the hospital last night. I've worked my way through the list of people I'd agreed to telephone. Basically, I'd much rather be at work than taking condolence calls at home.'

'Then I suggest we do a little bit of unofficial ferreting. We're going to need more than a few hunches to persuade Lingo that we're really onto something.'

Forty-Nine

'Stay awake, stay awake,' Mark muttered to himself. The effort of maintaining the same position for what seemed like hours was sending his body into involuntary spasms, making his upper body rock backwards and forwards, like the head of a nodding dog on the backseat of a car. Though he doubted whether it was possible for anyone in such an uncomfortable situation to accidentally fall asleep, he was afraid that it might be possible to drift into some form of unconsciousness from sheer mental and physical exhaustion.

From somewhere far below came another series of howls and moans – a mere dribble of incoherent sounds now, with no definite words discernible. Mark longed to scream down at Rob to shut up. The noise had been going on and on. It was serving no useful purpose and was driving him crazy. He remained silent however, because at the back of his mind there lingered a faint doubt as to how badly injured Rob actually was, and whether or not he had lost his grip on the gun. It would be just my luck, Mark thought, to hang on until dawn breaks, only to find myself still in the firing line of a man who's lost the use of everything except his trigger finger.

When the fear of losing mental concentration – and with it, his precarious balance – crept up on him, he tried to focus on something concrete. He attempted to remember every Derby winner for the last twenty-five years, but he got stuck on the one which came between Benny the Dip and Lammtarra. After that he went through every person who had taught him since nursery school, followed by a recitation of the kings and queens of England, from William the Conqueror onwards. He was nothing if not an asset to a pub quiz team, he thought. At one stage he wondered about praying, but he hadn't really given the Deity much consideration since leaving prep school, and thought that promises of turning over a new leaf in exchange for divine intervention would sound particularly hollow under present circumstances.

He tried to decide which direction the cove faced. North west probably. He had watched as the moon climbed briefly above the headland, before disappearing behind it again, and with the resumption of a darker sky, he had become more aware of the stars, but as he knew nothing at all about astronomy, they gave him no help with his orientation. As for telling the time, though he did recall the phrase, 'the darkest hour is just before dawn', he had a distinct suspicion that it came from a pop song, rather than being an actual real-life indicator of the passage of time.

He couldn't ever remember watching the sun come up, but he was expecting something dramatic, so he was surprised when the reality of the dawn crept upon him unexpectedly, with a gradually lightening sky and the realization that he could make out the shadowy barrier of earth and rock which had arrested his fall, and then the faint shape of his own lower body. He stretched out an exploratory arm and counted the grey shadows of his fingers and thumb – confirmation that it was definitely getting light. Soon he could see well enough to distinguish the water from the sand, and make out the crests of the small waves as they tumbled forward, then receded in a mass of white lacy froth, a dizzying distance below him.

He could see now that the section of cliff which had broken his fall was part of a narrow ridge which ran down from the top of the cliff face, ending a matter of inches from where it had brought him to a halt. If he had gone over the edge just a couple of feet further to his left, he would have missed it altogether, which he was forced to assume was what had happened to Rob. It was some while since he had last heard anything from him and though there was now ample light in the sky, he still could not see him. An uneasy suspicion grew in his mind that Rob might have recovered sufficiently to be back on the prowl, and was maybe working his way to a vantage point, from which he could take a pot shot at a helpless target. At the same time, a competing voice of common sense said that those sounds the night before had emanated from a badly damaged individual, who was probably lying somewhere in the area of beach directly below his eyrie, hidden by the jumble of outcrops which criss-crossed the reddish brown cliff face.

If that was the case, then it was unlikely that anyone walking along the cliff top would be able to see Rob either, still less spot himself, clinging part way up. He supposed that he could try shouting for help, but there was no point doing that unless someone was coming. Would he be able to hear anyone walking along the top of the cliffs? How often *did* anyone walk along? No one ever came to the beach itself – Jude had said so and he had no reason to disbelieve her on that point, even if she had lied about so much else. How often did anyone come along the coast in a boat travelling close enough in to notice people stranded on the beach? Maybe not for days. Rescue from an external source appeared to be a forlorn hope.

Though it was not a sheer drop to the beach, the slope immediately below him was far too steep to tackle, and Mark knew that once you began to slide it would be game over. The only other option was to attempt an ascent. He twisted his neck at an awkward angle, and began to contemplate what would be entailed in going up. The surface above his head was pitted and uneven, theoretically providing plenty of foot and hand holds, but how to tell which ones would support his weight and which would give way beneath him? Every move would represent a gamble, and gambling – as things had turned out – clearly wasn't his forte. Still, since attempting to go down was out of the question . . .

Obviously it would be foolhardy to rush into anything. He considered the options again – a process which did not take anything like as long as he would have liked it to. It was getting lighter every minute and apart from the fact that he felt as weak as a kitten, he knew that there was no particular excuse not to get started.

Holding his breath, he began by drawing his left leg up from its position on the exposed slope, marvelling that the limb responded at all, after the deadening cramps which he had endured the night before while trying to retain the same position for so long. Once he had his left foot level with his right, he dug in gently with his heels and inched his backside further up into the small gully between two ridges of earth. It was the same manoeuvre which had brought down the unstable overhang from the cliff top the night before, but this time he achieved it without mishap. He lifted a dirty palm and saw that his hand was trembling.

Another few inches and he felt a good deal safer. He had pulled himself into what amounted to a cup-shaped hollow, where his body was protected from any immediate drop on three sides and his feet were at least a yard back from that treacherous-looking slope. It was as far as he would be able to progress by shuffling backwards. Now the real test would begin, because he needed to stand up, steady those trembling knees, turn to face the cliff and start to climb up the narrow chasm.

'Don't look down.'

He had spoken aloud without realizing it. No harm in a bit of self-encouragement. It wasn't as if he had anyone else on his side. He clambered awkwardly to his feet, then edged around, an inch at a time, until he had completed the half circle and was facing away from the drop. There was a sticky out bit to his left and another foothold a little bit higher, to his right, and yes . . . by some kind of superhuman effort, he managed to make it onto another outcrop, which in turn led to another, smaller, three-sided, cup-shaped place where he paused, his heart hammering, his ears singing, clinging to a lump of turf which presented itself at face level.

He was already sobbing with effort and had probably managed to ascend no more than six feet. Above the turf, he could see nothing further to help him and nor could he be certain of returning to what now seemed the relative safety of his former position. His eyes welled with self-pity. It had been the wrong choice again.

Wait though . . . if he could step around the

side of his current perch, there was a reasonably wide series of lumps and bumps, which led downwards. Getting onto the first one involved almost stepping into thin air, but he made it, then began to follow what seemed like an initially easy route, taking care to secure some kind of hand hold and testing each step with only half his weight before committing.

The sunlight was flooding into the little bay now. From his new vantage point, he could see that a couple of boats – presumably brought there by the mysterious Stefan, were pulled well up the beach, ready and waiting for him. If everything had run according to their plan, one of those boats would have been taken out to sea and abandoned by now, bobbing along, awaiting discovery, a few items no doubt carefully planted to suggest a tragic accident; his own and Rob's bodies dumped in deep water, maybe never found. His imagination instantly conjured images of their corpses, bloated and battered by long immersion and the beach suddenly seemed to come up to meet him, just as his leading foot slipped. No . . . oh no . . . he dug his very fingernails into the cliff face and managed to cling on.

It took several minutes to steady himself before he could manage to move again. The two-tone loafers on his feet were hardly what he would have chosen for a climbing expedition and since the latest near-disaster whatever limited confidence he might have achieved had ebbed away again. However, he made it around a couple more vertical buttresses of earth and rock, before the series of downward hand and footholds petered out.

It now appeared possible to attempt an upward climb again. He knew that there was nothing to be gained from going back, but equally he could see that he was making no real progress in any direction but sideways. At this rate, he would end up alternately scaling and descending in a sideways course along the face of the cliff until he finally ran out of handholds, or alternatively fell exhausted onto the beach.

The latest ascent took him on another zig-zag, with his progress becoming slower and slower. Had there been any opportunity to sit or crouch, he would have taken it, but the cliff here was pitted with a series of narrow shelves and small depressions, which afforded no suitable location for respite. Small plants and tufts of grass, none of them rooted reliably enough to bear the weight of a man, obstructed his progress, some of them seeming to deliberately entangle themselves in his hair. The ache in his tired limbs was a constant source of agony now. Then he saw it – not twenty feet to his left, just beyond the next pinnacle of earth – the path which connected the cliff top to the beach. He struggled towards it, negotiating a large fallen boulder, a treacherously sloping grassy margin, and then he was clambering onto a wooden platform built into the side of the cliff, where he sank to his knees and sobbed in sheer relief.

For a few moments he wanted to do nothing but luxuriate in this place of safety. He could not fall or slide: the earth would not suddenly dissolve from under him as he sat. He rolled from his knees to his backside, noticing that his clothes were filthy. Who cared? The sun was up, the sky was blue, it was a beautiful morning and he was alive. Complications tried to insinuate themselves into his mind, but he was having none of it. He sat and contemplated the bay, allowing the steadying rhythm of the waves to fill his head.

He had reached the path at a point about halfway up the cliff – or halfway down, he thought, depending on your point of view. He did not feel as if he could walk very far, but he consoled himself with the thought that he did not need to, because there were now two forms of transport available to him.

First and foremost there was his BMW, still parked in the layby, though he no longer had custody of the key. What had happened to the key? He forced himself to remember that Jude said she had left it in her coat – a garment he had last seen on the sitting-room floor of the cottage. Jude's body lay somewhere between himself and the cottage, and unless he was much mistaken, there would be a second body in the kitchen. On the other hand, there were two dinghies on the beach, ready and waiting, each equipped with an outboard. He had once taken a holiday with some sailing friends. He knew how to handle a boat.

Of course, Rob was somewhere on the beach too. Rob might still have the gun. Then again, the hideous noises of the previous night, followed by the long silence ever since, tended to suggest that Rob would pose no threat this morning. Logically, Mark knew that the two definitely dead people between himself and the car key presented no threat either, but a part of him dreaded coming face to face with Jude's body. He had schooled himself to be fond of her, to the extent that he had taken her to be his wife. The woman had been absolutely beautiful. He had not been shamming the whole time. Even when he reminded himself that she had been party to a plot which would have seen him murdered by one or another of her pet thugs, it failed to raise the level of his anger to a pitch which blotted out the horror of her being dead. While his own intentions had not been strictly honourable, he had never intended something as awful as that.

He sat for some minutes more before scrambling to his feet and starting to make his way down towards the sea, proceeding cautiously – occasional wooden platforms alternated with semi-natural steps and shelves – it would be awful if he missed his footing now, when the going was comparatively easy.

He did not see Rob until he had almost reached the bottom. His adversary had been transformed into a crumpled figure, sprawled on its stomach, a few feet from the base of the cliff, its head facing towards the sea, its empty hands extended palms down on some of the loose stuff which had fallen with him. There was no sign of the gun.

Mark's instinct was to keep as far away from the figure as possible, but Rob lay on the direct route to the two inflatables, so an element of proximity was unavoidable. He tried to look away, because he expected something pretty hideous, but the reality was far less terrible than his expectations. One leg lay at an impossible angle. There was definitely some blood on Rob's clothing and matted in his hair, and a series of vicious scratches were visible on one of his upper arms, where some of his clothing appeared to have been torn away. As he was noting all this, Mark fancied that he saw the fingers of one hand move. He halted and watched, but when nothing else happened he hurried on, skirting Rob's outstretched legs and feet – one shoe was missing, he noticed – and making it to the boats with only a single glance back. From this angle he could see enough to be aware that Rob's face was a mess. Impossible to decide whether or not his eyes were open.

Suppose the guy was still alive? Mark knew nothing of first aid. He had no phone. He ignored the possibility and concentrated on the boats. There was nothing he could do for the guy, even if he had felt remotely inclined.

Both the craft which confronted him were fairly standard inflatables, which had been tethered together and in turn secured by a long rope which had been passed several times around a large rock, and both were sitting well above the water line. This Stefan character must have been halfway towards being Superman, Mark thought, to have dragged them both that far up the sloping sand. Then he remembered the tide. It had probably been much higher when Stefan arrived. He stood watching the waves for a moment, trying to work out which direction the tide was going in now, but the treacherous, sparkly water seemed intent on playing some mysterious game of its own and his brain refused to compute.

He would just have to shove one of the boats down far enough to get it afloat. He selected the craft which was several inches closer to the water-line, untied it from its fellow, then marched purposefully up the beach and disentangled the rope from around the rock. As he returned to the boat, he steadily wound the mooring line into nice equal loops, finally placing the coil neatly in the bows. His sailing acquaintances would have been proud of him, he thought.

Pushing the boat down the sand proved almost impossible. It slid a reluctant inch, then stopped, like a creature which has dug its heels in and refuses to move any further. Struggling with the dinghy reminded him afresh of just how tired he was, and how much his body ached.

He tried a different tack, grabbing a section of the thin nylon rope which was looped around the sides and dragging the thing around until its bows were facing the water. This was marginally easier and he began to make slow progress. It occurred to him that he was going to get wet before most of the dinghy did, so he took off his shoes and socks, and chucked them into the bottom of the boat, before renewing his efforts.

He soon found that fooling around at the seaside while wearing trunks or shorts was one thing, and trying to launch a small boat off a beach, single handed, encumbered by ordinary chinos was quite another. He had to go in up to his thighs and was splashed well above the waist, before he managed to coax his reluctant vessel onto the water. The waves were dragging at the sand beneath his feet, and he nearly lost his footing, eventually all but tumbling head first into the boat, when he finally swung the stern out onto the water.

Oh well . . . that was OK, because he couldn't go anywhere without being in the boat. He steadied himself and clambered over the central wooden seat to better reach the outboard. There was a second plank seat at the stern of the boat, ideally placed for the steersman, and Mark positioned himself on it, grateful for the stability it afforded. The outboard had been lifted up so that the propeller was clear of the water, but when he released the lever and tilted the motor and attached propeller down into the water, they snapped into place with gratifying efficiency. Now it was just a question of getting hold of the pull cord and sparking the thing into life. It was a bigger piece of kit than the one he remembered on his friends' boat, but that didn't matter, because the principle was surely the same.

He took the loop on the end of the cord between finger and thumb and withdrew it hard and fast, to the full extent of his arm. Nothing happened. Bugger. Outboards were always fiddly, temperamental things. He tried again . . . and again . . . this time nearly jarring his arm in its socket. Then it occurred to him that there was something different about this outboard. It wasn't emitting that stutter of hopefulness, which died away with each false start. It wasn't making a noise at all. The engine needed to be switched on, before it would start. He looked more closely and immediately saw the place to insert the key.

He knew that there was no point trying to look

for the key in the boat itself. Firstly because there was nowhere in the boat to hide it, but secondly because the skipper would habitually remove the key whenever he left the boat tied up – even when leaving it in a remote spot where no one else was likely to come. Mark had never actually launched a boat on his own before, but even so, only an imbecile, he thought, would have forgotten about needing a key.

Earlier doubts regarding the state of the tide now seemed ridiculous – it was undoubtedly ebbing. He noted with rising panic that even in the short time that he had been fiddling about with the outboard, a combination of the tide and a light breeze blowing off the land had carried the inflatable quite a distance from the shore. He wasn't much of a swimmer and there might be dangerous currents to contend with, as well as the tide. He glanced desperately about. Not only was there no key, but there were no oars either, probably because the thing was too large to be rowed. Apart from the mooring rope (whose nautical coils now all but mocked his general lack of seamanship) and a plastic milk container, which had been cut down to serve as a baler, there was no other equipment at all, save for one small wooden paddle, probably better suited to fending off, than for any attempts to propel or steer his oversized coracle.

Fifty

'Holey moley, Batman! Why on earth didn't anyone check all this out before?' Hannah sank into the driver's seat and flicked the car's ignition into life.

'People off sick, people assigned to other jobs, court appearances taking you off an investigation for a week at a time, crossed wires, missed communications, downright lack of communication . . . Do you want me to write you a list?'

'I know . . . but it's taken us no more than a few computer searches, half a dozen phone calls and some flashing of warrant cards in a couple of estate agents' offices to unearth a lot of information which puts this whole investigation into a totally different light.'

'We're a good team, Hannah.'

If there was a particular nuance to his tone, she didn't appear to notice.

'I'm not denying it. But it's taken us less than a day, for crying out loud. It's a set-up. The Thackerays lied. Jude Thackeray's real baby brother, Robin John Thackeray, died before he reached his first birthday. Goodness knows who that guy calling himself Robin Thackeray is, but it sure as hexes isn't Jude Thackeray's brother. None of those properties belonged to them, they were all rented. We already know that these people couldn't produce anyone

288

who'd known them while they said they were living abroad . . .'

'Tomorrow we've got to take this to Ling.'

'Ling isn't going to like this,' Hannah said rather grimly, as she took a right at the traffic lights.

'Too right. I feel a massive arse kicking coming on for somebody.'

'What I mean,' Hannah said, patiently, 'is that Ling isn't going to like the fact that this all went tits up on his watch. This woman and her so-called brother have made complete fools of a team which was ultimately being led by him. The Old Man won't like what it says about his leadership – or in this case – lack of it. He may well be inclined to shoot the messengers.'

Peter said nothing, because he knew that she was right. He had always admired the boss, but the point which she was making had already occurred to him and he also recognized that she was right about the Old Man's pride, and the fact that he took no prisoners. It didn't help matters that they'd been pursuing the investigation on their own time, when the gaffer had expressly told them to leave it alone, and that in Hannah's case, she was supposed to be off on compassionate leave. The triumphal fireworks which had metaphorically accompanied their discoveries abruptly fizzled out. He could see how when it came to outlining their activities to Ling, it would look suspiciously like a couple of junior detectives setting out to make their commanding officer appear incompetent.

'Maybe you could tell him,' Hannah suggested.

'You've got nothing to lose. Not if you're going off to be a rock'n'roll star.'

'I'm not sure that a residency on a cruise ship comes under that particular heading – even if I go.'

'You should go. You've got no ties. There's nothing to keep you here.'

He glanced sideways at her, but she was concentrating on the traffic. There was a Tesco home delivery van parked on a double yellow line, causing all sorts of problems. Had there been a slight catch in her voice? She'd asked him to stay until after her sister's funeral, but did she maybe hope that he might stay longer? He would need to give Ginny an answer very soon. Instead of a vision of Ginny, belting out 'Don't Get Me Wrong', he saw Granny Mina, eyes twinkling mischievously above a hand of cards. 'Stick or twist?' Should he gamble? Take an unknown card, which just might turn out to be an ace? But that meant discarding something else from his hand. His warrant card, represented by the trusty Jack of Spades? Or maybe Hannah, a Queen of Diamonds?

'You're very quiet.'

'I was just thinking.'

'About the Thackerays?'

'About a card game that I used to play with my grandma.'

'Great to know that it's something important.'

'Should we pick up a take-away?'

'Only if it's an Indian.'

'I can live with that.'

Hannah broke down unexpectedly, while they

were eating their onion bhajis. As soon as he realized that she was crying, Peter abandoned his half-eaten starter, pushed back his chair and went to her side.

'It isn't fair,' she sobbed into his shirt. 'Why Clare? It isn't fair.'

Having no ready answers, he merely held her a little closer for a moment or two, then freed one hand and took advantage of the reach which had always made him a natural for goalie in the school team, in order to draw a box of tissues into a more convenient position for her.

'Sorry,' she mumbled, between dabbing her eyes and blowing her nose.

'I told you before, you don't have to apologize for being upset.'

'I don't know how I would have got through this without you.'

He wasn't sure what to say to that, either. It's my pleasure was the phrase which came immediately to mind, because it mostly had been, but that sounded particularly crass and inappropriate.

'I'll never forget this.'

'Nor will I.'

'When I'm here alone, solving all the crime and locking up the bad guys,' she attempted a laugh, 'and you're lazing on some Caribbean beach by day and playing duets with another woman by night, I'll be thinking of that night when you made love to me, as the dawn came up over the gasworks.'

'What night was that?'

'Well, it wasn't a specific occasion. I'm employing what's known as poetic licence.'

'For goodness sake, Hannah, don't ever give up the day job to be a romantic novelist. Anyway, chances are I won't be going to the Caribbean.'

'I thought that's where you said this ship was supposed to be going?'

'I did. It is. I mean that I might not be going with it.'

'But it's the opportunity of a lifetime – you said so yourself.'

'I know. But maybe there are too many reasons to stay.'

'We'll have the Thackeray case cracked before you go.'

'I wasn't talking about the Thackeray case.'

Fifty-One

It was still reasonably light when Jigsaw reached the point on his nocturnal rounds where he had been spooked by that strange cry the night before. (His timing's varied, though his route did not.) He approached the cottage near the cliffs with his usual caution, but nothing seemed to have changed since the night before. The door by which he had entered some eighteen hours earlier was still wide open and his sensitive nose picked up the same kind of smell, if much staler, which had been discernible during that previous visit. He could hear a couple of flies whining around inside.

Jigsaw did not like flies (in his extreme youth

he had been known to chase and catch the ones which made the mistake of entering the house). It was not the flies however, which made him hesitate. Just as before, there was no sound of voices, or indeed any of those other noises which he associated with human occupation of the house. No humans meant no titbits. Jigsaw was used to coming by and finding the house closed up and silent, but it was outside his experience to find the place open, yet surrounded by this odd atmosphere of desolation. He had not survived through fourteen summers without developing good instincts and tonight something told him that no good would be achieved by making a diversion into the oddly quiet house. As a matter of form he scented the post of the still-open door, then turned east towards the rough bank near the little strip of woodland, where he still occasionally managed to pick off an unwary rabbit kitten.

It was not going to be his night, when it came to the rabbits however, because the advancing dusk was hastened by a raincloud which brought a sharp shower, sending the rabbits underground and causing Jigsaw himself to seek shelter under the gorse bushes as best he could.

Out in the field between the house and the sea, just a few yards landward of the coastal footpath, yet entirely hidden from it, Jude Thackeray's body took the full brunt of the downpour. Streaks of blood, long since congealed, were diluted by the rain and ran in pale pink rivulets down the sides of her face and into the grass.

Down on the beach, the hair and clothes of a second human form quickly became so saturated that a witness – had there been one – might have imagined that the outstretched body had just been dragged from the nearby waves.

The rain storm lasted for almost twenty minutes. Once it had passed over, Jigsaw went immediately on his way again, this time heading for home, high-stepping to avoid the long damp grass, which wet his undercarriage, and twitching his ears in annoyance when drips fell on him from the surrounding bushes and trees.

Fifty-Two

'Bettsy! Ling wants everyone in the briefing room.'

Peter glanced up at the office door in order to acknowledge the heads up, but Joel McPartland had already disappeared down the corridor. Blast. He hadn't even realized that the gaffer was in the building. An eight thirty summons might portend almost anything, but it would certainly mean a delay before he could get the Old Man on his own and have a conversation about the Thackeray case. In the end it had fallen to him to broach the subject, because Hannah was still on compassionate leave. She had initially wanted to come back into work, but he had persuaded her that working voluntarily on the Thackeray case was one thing, whereas coping with whatever the job might throw at you, while still in a pretty emotional state over your sister's death, was something else again.

As he made his way to the briefing room, Peter wondered if something big had kicked off, without him noticing. He was usually on top of anything that made the local news, but he and Hannah had been somewhat preoccupied over the last forty-eight hours and although he'd had the radio on as he came in, he hadn't really been listening. Too busy rehearsing the conversation with Ling, he thought, to say nothing of thinking about his long overdue response to Ginny. (She had told him that he still had time to consider it, but he knew that he ought to have had it settled one way or the other by now.)

The prospect of heading off to the other side of the world on someone else's dollar didn't seem half so appealing as it had five weeks before, when it wouldn't have created such a big Hannah-shaped hole in his life. He had begun to reassess the importance of music in his wider scheme of things. To be a proper musician didn't you have to put it first, second and third in everything you did? He loved to play, but had he ever been that serious? Only the other night, he had ducked out of his session at Mel's Bar, where he had an informal arrangement to play every second Wednesday that he could make, because he thought that Hannah needed him more than the patrons of the bar did. When she'd asked him if it wasn't his night for Mel's, he'd told her that there had been a call to say they didn't need him. (Police service was a great enabler when it came to putting out the straight-faced, plausible lie.)

Whatever his own feelings for Hannah, he knew that it would be wrong to put her under any kind

295

of extra emotional pressure right now. Even so, he had come very close to telling her how he felt the previous evening. The trouble was that every time their conversation strayed in the direction of the future, she invariably went out of her way to make it plain that theirs was a temporary arrangement between good friends (who just happened to sleep together and have the best sex imaginable). It was hard to tell her how he felt anyway, because he wasn't entirely sure. He had never been in any kind of serious, long-term relationship. At least two previous girlfriends had attracted him in a full-steam-ahead, bells-and-whistles kind of way. So much so, that at the beginning of those relationships, if some wizened old gipsy soothsayer had approached him to confide in either case that, 'This is the one', he would have believed it wholeheartedly, but of course there had not been any wizened old fortune tellers with crystal balls and nor had it taken very long to realize that each of those relationships wasn't going anywhere that he wanted to be.

Usually, he thought, you started out optimistic-ally, thinking that a strong mutual attraction might lead to something permanent, whereas with Hannah the circumstances had been turned on their head from the outset by her determination that it would be a strictly temporary arrangement, in which neither party needed to pretend to be in love, or profess themselves willing to make any kind of commitment.

The thing was that being there for Hannah, holding on to her, caring for her, felt right. He didn't want it to end, but soon it would be Clare's funeral and that was the point at which Hannah would expect him to back off and move out of her life. She might actually need him to leave, he thought, so that she could draw a line under this difficult time, which she would always associate with the loss of her sister.

How did Hannah really feel about him? Did she share his growing conviction that they were now much more than good friends? He had come very close to asking her, but it seemed unfair. She was still grieving for her sister and emotionally vulnerable. Besides which, he didn't want to make a complete prat of himself because at the end of the day, if he didn't go off to play rock'n'roll with Ginny ('running away with the circus' as Hannah had once put it) he and McMahon would still sometimes have to work together.

Maybe that was as good a reason as any for going off to join the band. Hannah was an attractive woman, whose body clock was ticking, and that inevitably meant her hooking up with some guy soon. How was he going to feel when he saw Hannah with someone else? Basically, he thought, by comparison with her, I'm a knuckle-dragging Neanderthal, who wants nothing more than some good, old-fashioned commitment.

He was one of the last to arrive in the briefing room, where a large contingent of CID had already packed into most of the available space, sitting and standing, some chatting in groups, others texting or talking into phones. Peter joined the latecomers, leaning against the wall at the back. The gathering put him vaguely in mind of the beginning of a lesson, before the teacher arrives. A couple of the younger lads were even indulging in some horseplay, shoving one another about.

The gaffer's arrival put a stop to all that. He entered accompanied by his own private thunder cloud. Class in session, Peter thought.

Graham Ling had a newspaper in his hand, folded open at an inner page. Knowing that he had their full attention without even asking for it, he began to read without preamble. 'Kidnap victim Jude finds happiness. Tragic heiress Jude Thackeray, who suffered a horrific ordeal at the hands of a crazed kidnapper, was secretly married to her new love, business man, Mark Medlicott this week, in a romantic ceremony with just two close relatives as their witnesses. A police source said they are still no closer to apprehending anyone in connection with the case.' He stopped reading and scanned the room at large. 'What idiot has been making comments about the Thackeray case to the press? How many times do I have to tell you that we never put out anything as negative as that? It makes us sound utterly clueless.'

No one spoke. 'McPartland here, tells me that some girl claiming she was a witness at the wedding has been posting the story all over Facebook and Twitter. Doesn't McMahon usually keep an eye on that stuff?'

'McMahon's on compassionate leave, sir.' Old Lingo didn't generally stand on ceremony over being called 'Sir', but there were occasions when it was expedient to maintain the formalities and Peter decided that this was one of them. 'And there's something I need to speak to you about urgently, sir.'

'Is it about McMahon?' Ling snapped, and Peter was aware of an exchange of knowing looks between a pair of colleagues within his line of sight.

'No, sir. It's about the Thackeray case.'

'What about it? Don't tell me it was you who made this half-witted comment to the press?'

'No. It—'

'Come on then, spit it out.' Ling was in a combative mood, which was never the best time to tackle him over anything and certainly not the moment to break it to him that he had overseen a major cock-up in an investigation.

'It might be better if I talked to you later, sir. On your own.'

This created a rustle of mild disapproval, with a camp, barely audible, 'Ooooh, get you, love,' from some unseen wag at the back of the room, none of which improved the senior officer's mood.

'If it's urgent, I want to hear it now. If it isn't, then you can have an appointment for four o'clock, day after tomorrow.'

Peter hesitated. He hadn't prepared himself properly and he knew it wouldn't come out well. 'There's a lot of new information on the Thackeray case. To start with, Robin Thackeray isn't really Jude Thackeray's brother. Jude Thackeray did have a brother, but he died, when he was still a baby. We – that's me and McMahon – think that

299

the whole thing was a set-up. Robin Thackeray did the kidnap, Jude colluded with him and the idea was to make it appear that she was this incredibly wealthy heiress, so that she could marry some other rich dude and cash in. I think Mark Medlicott might be that rich dude and if so, he could be in a lot of trouble, if we don't find him, sir.'

There was a moment's silence.

'Sounds like a load of melodramatic tosh to me,' said Jerry Wilkins. 'You and McMahon been curled up watching *Midsomer Murders* again, Bettsy?'

The remark was greeted by a minor ripple of amusement, though most of those present remained silent, aware that Ling's face had become ashen with rage.

'And just how long have you been sitting on this information?' he roared.

'One day, sir.'

Ling jerked his head from side to side, as if ridding himself of a troublesome wasp. 'Betts, McPartland, Wilkins and – yes – Aitken, you come with me. The rest of you get back to what-ever it is you're supposed to be doing. None of this goes any further than these four walls until I've got some proper confirmation. Not one word – everybody clear on that?'

'Yes, sirs' on various notes came in from all over the room.

It took next to no time to track Katrina Medlicott to the house she was sharing with friends in Belsize Park. The advantages of social media, combined with the fact that vacationing students

300

were unlikely to be out of bed before noon, Peter thought. Unfortunately the journey down took a good deal longer than the trace and when they came face to face with their quarry, the interview itself was not particularly productive.

'Am I in some sort of trouble?' The girl was wide-eyed with a combination of excitement and nervousness. 'I know they told me not to say anything, but I thought it wouldn't hurt to put it on my Facebook page. I wasn't really giving anything away – not really. I thought my friends would think it was romantic.'

'You're not in any trouble,' Peter assured her, for at least the third time. 'But it is important that you tell us everything you know. We have to find your Uncle Mark and his wife. It's really important.'

'Have they done something wrong?'

'It's a question of everyone's safety,' Joel put in.

'Are they in danger? Mark and Jude? Is it the man who tried to get her before?'

'We're not at liberty to explain any details,' Peter said. 'But it is very important that you tell us where they are, if you know.'

'I never said anything to the papers when they rang me. Some of them have printed stuff that I never said.'

'That's OK, Katrina. We know that journalists make things up. But if you could just tell us everything you know about Jude's and Mark's plans. Where they were going for their honeymoon, that sort of thing.'

'I don't know very much.' She spoke with

evident disappointment. Both men sensed that this was a state of affairs which she genuinely regretted, since it meant that all the excitement of being interviewed by a couple of visiting police officers, was likely to be short-lived.

Peter tried again. 'How long had you known in advance that your uncle was going to get married?'

'No time at all. He just texted me out of the blue, asking me to skip my classes that morning, so that I could be a witness at his wedding. He said it was a secret. They were going on honeymoon first and would tell the rest of the family and everybody when they got back. Of course Uncle Mark couldn't have been thinking, because I didn't actually have to skip any lectures, because it isn't term time at the moment. I just came back down early to hang out and have some fun before—'

Peter cut across to ask, 'Did you know that he was seeing Jude Thackeray?'

She laughed. 'I only see Uncle Mark once in a blue moon. He doesn't even do Family Christmas, if he can avoid it. I think he'd chosen me to be a witness because I was the only family member within two hundred miles, so no, I'd never set eyes on her until she showed up at the register office.'

'So it was just the bride and groom, you, and the bride's brother?' said Joel.

'That's right. Not the sort of wedding I'd choose.'

Peter gave her no opportunity to enlarge on a vision involving clouds of tulle, a large marquee

302

and a lorry load of champagne, cutting in quickly with: 'So this honeymoon your uncle mentioned . . . Did he say where they were going?'

'I asked. I was trying to make conversation. You know, before we were called into the room where they did the actual ceremony. Actually it felt a bit awkward. I didn't know her, or her brother. It was a bit of a weird situation. I didn't know what to say. I just said any old thing, you know, like "Mum'll be pretty mad that you didn't do it properly so she could wear a big hat!" I mean actually, I don't believe Mum will give two hoots. Uncle Mark is Dad's brother and Mum has never much liked him to be absolutely honest. You're not taking this down are you? I mean she wouldn't want that said in public – major family embarrassment! My Auntie Rachel—'

'Getting back to the honeymoon,' Peter interrupted firmly. 'You asked them where they were going, and they said . . .?'

'Cornwall.'

'Just Cornwall?'

'I know! I mean I was expecting Barbados, or Aruba, or maybe one of those islands in the Indian Ocean. When my cousin Jamie got married, they went to—'

'What I meant,' Peter attempted to stem the flow again, 'was did they specify *where* they were going in Cornwall?'

'No. She just said "Cornwall".'

'Cornwall's a big place. Try to think back. Did they give you any idea at all whereabouts in Cornwall they were heading?'

'Nope. Just Cornwall.'

Peter tried one last time. 'Can you think of anything else at all that they told you about their plans that might be helpful – anything at all – even the smallest remark?'

Mark Medlicott's niece put her head on one side and considered for a moment. 'Sorry,' she said at last. 'I can't think of a thing.'

'I don't know what she aims to be when she's finished university,' Peter commented, as he relayed the gist of this interview to Hannah, later that evening. 'But one hopes that her wish list includes transformation into an intelligent human being.'

'Of course, we might be wrong,' Hannah said.

She was lying comfortably in the crook of Peter's arm, nursing a mug of coffee, while he played idly with a tress of her hair.

'Let's hope we are – for Mark Medlicott's sake anyway.'

'Nothing more from the States?'

'Not yet. Though we've already got quite a lot to support our theory. The fact that the pair of them are evidently not brother and sister, have faked a lifestyle, carried out a sham kidnapping, and appear to have targeted a young bloke from a wealthy family, is pretty suggestive.'

'Mmm.' Hannah stretched.

He loved the way she did that – one limb at a time, like a cat unfolding from a good long sleep in the sunshine.

'Credit to old Lingo, he's throwing everything at it. Descriptions of them and Medlicott's car out everywhere. The boys in Cornwall are going to start making enquiries with hotels, cottage agencies . . .'

'Across the whole of Cornwall? That will keep them busy.'

He decided it was time to turn the talk away from work. 'Did you manage to get everything done?'

'Flowers ordered. Funeral booked. Number of cars and identities of pall bearers agreed.' Hannah recited the litany sadly. 'Basically far too many of us, all trying to help. In the end I think poor John just wanted to be left on his own. We all want to support him, be there for him and for one another, but the bottom line is that Clare has gone and none of us can bring her back.'

'I know I never met your sister,' Peter said carefully, 'but I'd like to come with you to the funeral.' When this was met with silence, he ventured, 'I'd like to be there to support you. That is . . . if you'd like me to.'

'It's a full Catholic mass.'

He tried to read her voice. Was she welcoming the offer or not?

'I'd really appreciate it if you came, but . . .' she hesitated.

'I was brought up a Catholic,' he said.

'Brought up?'

He laughed. 'I haven't been to confession in a while.'

She laughed too. 'Neither have I.'

'I emailed Ginny this afternoon and told her that I've decided not to join the band.'

'Oh.'

'Oh? Is that all you're going to say?'

'What did you want me to say? What time is it, anyway?'

'Ten to eleven.'

'Presumably that's the answer to my second question?'

'Yeah.'

'I'll have to get to bed in a minute.'

'You're definitely going back in tomorrow?' he asked.

'There's no point staying home, mooning about. I've done everything I can towards the arrangements.'

'You've been brilliant.'

'So everyone keeps saying. I get ten out of ten and a gold star for being super-efficient in the face of tragedy,' Hannah said, a shade bitterly.

'What do you mean? What's the matter?'

'Sometimes I wish I was less . . . well . . . maybe more like Clare. I never missed the train, lost the bus fare, or forgot my lunch money. She was always the loveable, ditzy one. In the end everyone likes you better for it. If they'd all had to choose between us, they'd have had to choose Clare: lovely daughter, loving wife, brilliant mother.'

'I'm sure that's not true.'

'I've missed too many family Christmases, spent too much time loving my job and not enough loving my family. Truth is, Peter, I'm thinking of going in another direction. I've been thinking about it a lot, and I don't see the police as part of my long-term future.'

It was the perfect cue, he thought. But do you see me as part of that future? He was about to frame the words when his phone rang. He located it by feel and brought it to his ear.

306

'Peter Betts . . . Yes . . .? OK . . .' He glanced at his watch. 'Just us? Not Ling? . . . Oh yes, I'd forgotten . . . I'm not sure how long it'll take to get there, I'll have to check . . . Right.'

He turned to Hannah, who had raised herself to a proper sitting position and was looking at him enquiringly. 'Developments in Cornwall. Ling wants me to go down there.'

'I want to come.'

'He's sending me and McPartland.'

'That's not fair. It was you and I who did the original review – *and* came up with the new evidence.'

Peter hit a couple of buttons on his phone, then waited for a reply.

'McMahon wants to come too. It seems only right . . . She's the one who made the break-through in the first place. If it hadn't been for her, we'd still be taking the Thackeray kidnap at face value . . . OK.' He turned back to Hannah. 'He's checking with Lingo and ringing me back. Made some smart alec crack about pillow talk.'

'Who cares?' Hannah sprang off the sofa. 'One way or another, I'm coming with you, whatever Lingo says about it.'

Fifty-Three

Introductions had been made, pleasantries and professional courtesies exchanged, loos offered and coffees ordered. Time to get down to business.

307

'It's still a developing picture,' DI Treffry said. 'As you know, it took us a day to get anything out of him at all, but then he suddenly started to talk and he hasn't stopped since. So far, every-thing he's told us has stacked up. One deceased male with gunshot wounds in the house. One deceased female – also gunshot wounds – in a field not far from the house and finally, one male with serious injuries found on the beach and airlifted to the Royal Cornwall Hospital, where he's yet to regain consciousness.'

'Do they think he will?' Hannah asked.

'Who can say? You know what doctors are like – you can never get a straight answer out of any of them.'

'Obviously you're very welcome to go down and take a look at the crime scenes, once SOCO have finished. Can't say how long that's liable to take either at this stage. Big area, no clearly defined perimeters and resources cut back to the bone. We haven't formally interviewed our Mr Medlicott yet. Doctor's examined him and pronounced him fit, and the murders are on our patch, but in the light of the circumstances, we've held fire until you got here.'

'Much appreciated.' Peter put every ounce of sincerity into it. They might all be on the same side, but no one liked to have their toes trampled on by some force from the other side of the country. 'So can you tell us the story so far: how Medlicott came to be here and what he's told you?'

'It's got to be one of the funniest set-ups I've ever come across.' Treffry allowed himself a

308

chuckle. 'I mean it's a funny old world, down here in the south west. We've had the naked cyclist . . . didn't that make the news up your way? No? Oh well, just a local interest story, I suppose. We had the two old biddies who tried to poison one another, after a bust-up over the arrangements for the Women's Institute Harvest Supper . . . didn't hear about that case either, I suppose. There's the armless body reported floating off Padstow which turns out to be a mannequin – make up your own punch lines for that one . . . and now this. I mean, it's not even a traditional love triangle, is it? Given that there were four of them.

'Anyway . . . our PC Avent is a keen fisherman on her own time. Got a little boat she has, in part shares with her brother, and on mornings when she's not on duty she goes out to check their pots.'

'Pots?' queried Hannah.

'Lobster pots. So she's motoring along, beautiful morning, hardly any swell, and she rounds the headland and spots this little boat in the distance. She can see right away that there's something not right, so she goes over for a look and finds your Mr Medlicott, waving to her like a madman and trying to control this bloody great inflatable with a single paddle. Obviously he's very pleased to see her.'

'He didn't try to get away?'

'Not likely. If you'd been adrift off the Cornish coast in a dinghy, *you'd* be pleased to see PC Avent rock up, fisherman's overalls and all. First thing he says to her, is, "Have you got a phone or a radio? I need to talk to a policeman."'

'That was the first thing he said?'

'According to Avent, yes. So she said, "As it happens, I am an off-duty policewoman." To which he says, "Yes, of course you are. You would be. Well, I need to report a murder. In fact, several murders." At which point, Avent decides, judging from the state of the bloke and the way he's talking, that he's probably a loony tune, and that it would be safer to have him stay in his own boat, while she gives him a tow back to the harbour: radioing ahead to let us know that she's bringing him in.'

'Did she have much conversation with him on the way back?'

DI Treffry regarded Hannah pityingly. 'Ever tried shouting from one boat to another, when you're travelling at ten knots, with a diesel engine going full tilt? We'd got officers waiting on the quayside by the time Avent came alongside, but Medlicott didn't give us any trouble. As soon as he was in the car, he started to talk about these murders again. Said he'd got important information and wanted to speak to "the top man", as he put it. He was cautioned, obviously, but he didn't seem to care. Didn't ask for a lawyer, didn't take up the option of a phone call. Seemed very anxious about anyone knowing where he was. Said a couple of times, "I'll be safe here", as if he thought there was someone coming after him. Trouble was, after dropping it on us that he needed to report some murders – plural – he suddenly said he didn't know where to tell us to go. Then he said maybe he'd imagined the whole thing. Let on that he couldn't

310

recall what his name was and asked us if we'd keep hold of him, until he regained his memory. As you can imagine, by now it isn't just Avent who's starting to think that he might be a sandwich short of a picnic.

'Needless to say we got in a social worker and a trick cyclist. At this point he shut up altogether. Basically did nothing but drink tea for the next few hours. We didn't know what to make of it. Nothing on him to say who he was. And then the message from your lot lands on the desk and I went in and put it to him, polite as you like, that he was Mark Medlicott and he just said, "Yes, that's right", and he started talking again, as suddenly as he'd stopped.

'The story was a bit of a jumble. Reckons that his wife, Jude, was shot by her brother, Robin Thackeray – though just to confuse matters, he also said that this Robin Thackeray *isn't* actually his wife's brother. Robin Thackeray is also supposed to have shot another man, who Medlicott only knows as Stefan – and by the way claims to have never set eyes on at all. Only knows this Stefan was shot because he heard it happen, apparently. Finally, to stack up the body count one further, he claims that while Robin Thackeray was in the act of attempting to kill him too, they both fell over the cliff, and Robin Thackeray was killed. Of course he's not correct about that, because when we eventually found the guy on the beach, he was still – just about – alive.'

'Eventually?'

'It took a while, because our friend, Mr Medlicott, reckoned that he couldn't remember

311

the name of the bloody house, or exactly where it was.'

'Useful memory lapse?'

'He seemed genuine enough. Tried hard to describe how you got to the place and looked at maps with us, trying to pinpoint it. We knew where Avent had picked him up and there aren't that many deserted beaches and hilltop cottages along that stretch of coast, but it caused a bit of a delay.'

'And he hasn't gone into any more details yet?'

'Not yet. But if you're ready to go, we'll fetch him into the interview room and get started. I've offered him the services of a local solicitor, Mr Carveth, because it keeps us covered. Weird thing, Medlicott wasn't keen. Said, "I can't afford to pay for a solicitor." I said, "If that's so, then I expect Legal Aid will probably pay for you."'

'What's his status? He isn't under arrest, is he?' asked Peter.

'Here voluntarily, helping with enquiries. Most people's first question is how long we're going to keep them here, but he's just the opposite. Doesn't want to leave. He's an oddball, is our Mr Medlicott.'

Mark Medlicott was waiting for them in the interview room, dressed in a white paper suit. His blonde hair was badly in need of attention from a comb. As the officers entered he stood up and shook hands with each of them. His solicitor, Mr Carveth, shuffled belatedly to his feet and proffered his own hand, as if the unexpectedly enthusiastic level of courtesy displayed by his client had put him under an obligation to offer the same.

They went through the appropriate preliminaries, all identifying themselves for the tape, shuffling into chairs which had to be positioned at awkward angles, with rather too many officers crammed into an inadequate space.

'We are investigating the deaths of two individuals and the serious injuries sustained by a third,' DI Treffry said portentously, like a narrator, embarking on the prologue of a Shakespearian drama. 'We would like you to tell us, in your own words, what you know about these incidents.'

The man in the white paper suit nodded. He folded his hands together on the table in front of him, looked at Treffry, down at his hands, back at Treffry and then down again. At last he looked up and, taking in the room at large, opened with the words, 'I'm sorry, I don't seem to know where to start.'

'How about you start right at the beginning.' Treffry managed to sound a lot kinder and more patient than he actually felt.

Observing from a corner of the room, Hannah was struck by how pathetic the guy looked. This was not merely someone who had come through a frightening ordeal. This was a man who had suffered a crushing defeat of some kind and was now utterly lost.

'I don't know . . .' Medlicott continued to hesitate. 'It starts with my needing the money, I suppose. And that starts from deciding not to go into the business . . . with my father and my brothers. Bad decisions. Always bad decisions. There was this other girl, you know. Poppy. Lovely girl. Rode in point-to-points. I think

313

something could have come of it, if I'd stayed in Yorkshire. She's married to some other chap now. Farmer of sorts . . .' He trailed into silence. 'This isn't what you want to know about. I can see that, of course – but it's context, you see. I want you to understand . . . how it all started . . . where it all began . . .'

Catching Treffry's eye, and sensing his assent, Peter said, 'Suppose you tell us about meeting Jude Thackeray? Would that be a good place to start the story from, at least for now?'

'Yes.' Mark nodded. 'Jude Thackeray. I met her at a race meeting in May. Newmarket. The Two Thousand Guineas. I recognized her face from the papers and I engineered it so that we'd be introduced. I started dating her. I won't pretend that I loved her. It was a sordid business. I needed to get married, you see – to someone who had money – because of Chaz.' He paused to look around the circle of faces, as if he half expected recognition of the name, but when he got no reaction, he went on. 'What I didn't realize was that she . . .' He broke off, shaking his head. 'It just sounds so crazy . . . I can't see how anyone is ever going to believe me.'

Peter Betts leaned forward a fraction. 'We know far more about Jude Thackeray than you realize, Mark. Just keep talking. There's every chance that we'll believe you.'

Fifty-Four

'I wish a few more of our cases required close liaison with our brother officers in Devon and Cornwall.' Peter positioned his fork and spoon neatly on his empty dessert plate and lifted his napkin to his mouth. 'That's the best meal I've had in ages.'

'If we can hang things out long enough tomorrow,' said Hannah, with more than a hint of sarcasm, 'you might have time to fit in a clotted cream tea.'

'We're booked into separate rooms,' he said, unnecessarily.

'That would be because colleagues of the opposite gender are not generally assumed to be sharing.'

'Mine's a single room.'

She laughed. 'Bad luck. I've got a double.'

They were interrupted by the waitress arriving with their coffee. When she had gone, Peter said, 'It will be interesting to see what turns up about this Chaz Bingham character.'

'Mark Medlicott seems terrified of him.'

'After what the bloke's just been through, I'm not surprised. He's probably terrified of his own shadow.'

As she sipped her coffee he glanced around the almost empty hotel restaurant. It was the sort of place frequented by business travellers as well as tourists. If there had been more time, he would have tried to find somewhere a bit less corporate, a bit more romantic for them to eat, but by the time they had finished at police headquarters, it had been too late to be sure of getting a table anywhere else.

There had never been much opportunity for nights out, romantic meals. Their relationship had not taken a normal course, with flirtatious preliminaries. It seemed as if they had fallen into bed at the end of a working day, got up to go to work together next morning and carried on from there.

'Do you fancy going on holiday?' he asked.

'What?'

'I said, do you fancy going on holiday?'

'With you?'

'No with your netball team! Of course with me.'

'Where to?'

'Anywhere. Cornwall. Crete. The Caribbean. Places that don't even begin with the letter C.'

'You'd fry in the Caribbean. All that fair skin.'

He noticed that she wasn't answering the question. Presumably the netball team option seemed preferable. When she didn't need him anymore, he would have to take it on the chin, as Granny Mina would have put it. The best thing would be to seek a transfer. It would be too hard, if he had to be confronted by a Hannah who had moved on, found someone she really cared for, maybe started that family she secretly longed for. Why was it so hard to say the things you most needed to say? Probably, Peter thought, it was more a

316

case of putting off the moment, because that avoided having to hear the answers that you didn't want to receive.

As she lifted her coffee again, her almond-shaped eyes met his over the rim of the cup and he was unexpectedly reminded of Granny Mina's eyes as she watched him over a hand of fanned-out cards. 'What's it to be? Stick or twist?' That old sense of excitement and uncertainty, of choosing to take a card, not knowing whether it would spell triumph or disaster, until you turned it over and learned your fate.

Now or never. He reached across the table with both hands and clasped the set of fingers which were not involved with the coffee cup. 'I've been thinking,' he said, 'about my empty flat. It's been amazing these last few weeks with you . . .'

He stopped abruptly when he saw that her eyes appeared to be watering. Yes, there was no doubt about it. Tears had emerged and were already leaving parallel tracks down her cheeks. 'Hannah – what's wrong?'

'I'm sorry.' She relinquished the coffee cup and eased her other hand from between his, in order to fumble in her bag for a tissue. 'I'm really sorry,' she mumbled. 'I promised myself that I wouldn't do this.'

'Do what?'

'Make a fool of myself. Make it awkward for you, when the time came.'

'Why? What? What are you talking about?'

'It's probably better if you don't say anything. I know you mean to let me down gently, but . . .' She had to stop in order to blow her nose, which seemed inclined to join her eyes in the operation of manufacturing unwanted moisture.

He had feared a whole variety of possible reactions and rejections, but he had not expected her to start crying. He could see that their waitress and a couple at another table had noticed something amiss and were covertly observing what had all the appearances of a romantic date gone badly wrong.

'Hannah . . .' He lowered his voice. He was no good at this sort of thing and now he'd attracted an audience. 'I didn't mean . . . well, what I wanted to say . . .' Oh, for goodness sake – what did he want to say? Why wouldn't anything remotely sensible or coherent come out of his mouth?

'You mentioned your empty flat,' she prompted, dabbing her eyes again.

'I was going to say that it's a waste,' he said, 'keeping two places on.' He looked at her carefully, trying to divine encouragement. 'The thing is, Hannah . . . The thing is . . .'

'What, Peter?' Her sense of humour was bubbling back. She was on the edge of laughter as she asked, 'What – exactly – is the thing?'

'The thing is, McMahon, that I don't want to move back to my flat, because I prefer living with you. I strongly suspect that I've fallen in love with you. The evidence all points that way on my side, but you keep giving off these other signals.'

'What other signals?'

'You keep on stressing that everything is a temporary arrangement. You won't even let me meet your family . . .'

318

'Only because I didn't want them to scare you away. I'm mad about you, you idiot. I have been for ages, but I thought you were only sleeping with me out of kindness. As for my family, at the first whiff of romance my mum and my granny will be all for making us an appointment to see Father Joseph at St Ignatius.'

'I wouldn't necessarily have a problem with that. I mean, I'd be fine with my son being brought up a Catholic, so long as he wasn't being brought up as an Ipswich supporter.'

Fifty-Five

Mark took a last look around the room before picking up his case. He had found sanctuary here, closeted from the outside world. Beyond the walls of the house, he knew that he was an object of notoriety, and constantly imagined himself being pointed out. People turning to one another and saying, 'That's Mark Medlicott. The bloke who was mixed up with that double murder in Cornwall. Funny business. Can't make head nor tail of it myself.'

Sometimes he heard people whispering. Only that morning, he had heard them whispering about him when he woke up. Except that they couldn't have been, because when he opened his eyes the room was empty and the door was closed, and there was nothing to hear except the sound of the television, intruding faintly from Michael's and Rachel's bedroom where she always had that dreadful, repetitive breakfast programme on, while she had a cup of tea in bed.

He remembered that he mustn't be critical of his sister-in-law Rachel and her lack of taste when it came to either the television, or the fussy decorative scheme she had chosen for the guest bedroom which he had been inhabiting, because Rachel had been so kind to him – tremendously kind. So had Michael, and Monty, and Monty's wife Sally, though the latter had initially been annoyed at his 'involving' Katrina in his wedding plans. As if turning up for half an hour at the register office constituted being placed in some kind of terrible danger.

He had endured a certain number of Prodigal Son type homecomings in his youth, but these had always involved his late father, (though he suspected that his brothers had often been aware of the circumstances). Nothing to compare with this one, of course. It was surely the ultimate humiliation to be driven from a police station, wearing clothes borrowed from one of his older brothers, which were at least a size too small. He had always cared about his appearance. The Thomas Pink shirts, Paul Smith shoes. His embossed leather wallet. No wallet that day, of course. No phone, no credit cards. The police had confiscated all the stuff he had been wearing in the boat, and everything else he had brought down from London was corralled at the 'crime scene' until further notice, while they proceeded with their investigation. In the meantime he couldn't just walk out wearing a paper suit. It wasn't Milan Fashion Week, after all.

It had taken him several hours to come round to it. Hours during which the police officers, while remaining polite, had pressed the questions ever more firmly. Who would he like to call, so that they could collect him? Who would be able to bring in some clothes for him?

He hadn't been able to call a friend, because he wasn't sure who his friends were anymore. Too many of them led back to Chaz, or to one of Chaz's contacts, and he couldn't afford to have Chaz find out his whereabouts. In the end he had crumbled in the face of the persistent sergeant who brought him cups of tea, and said that he would ring his brother, Michael. (His parents had been into alliterative names – his eldest brother, poor devil, had been called Montague, in honour of their maternal grandfather.) In the end, he had spoken to Rachel, wife of Michael and in the course of a confused conversation had managed to get it across to her that he needed someone to pick him up. 'Yes, from Cornwall . . . yes, I know it's a long way.' When he told her that he would also need somewhere to stay, she immediately did that family thing of saying that of course he could stay with herself and Michael as long as he liked, which he had instantly recognized as a platitude, born of good manners, rather than sincerity.

The conversation with Rachel had been followed up soon afterwards by a call from his brother. When they told him that Michael was on the phone, Mark had steeled himself for a hostile interrogation, followed by some harsh and well-deserved criticism, but his brother had only

321

seemed interested in whether he was all right and had promised to get there as soon as he could. It was this final shock in a topsy-turvy world, Mark thought, which had reduced him to crying aloud down the phone.

He had been reluctant to leave the small, anonymous room which had been set aside for him to change into his brother's clothes at the police station, lingering in there just as he was lingering in the guest room now. He remembered the paper suit lying discarded on the floor, like a shed skin: the ghost of a person he had temporarily become. Another person had replaced the ghost. A non-person, wearing borrowed clothes a size too small. A new person.

If only it had been true – but you can't just change your clothes and walk away. While he had been there at the police station, it had felt almost safe. Even reliving the nightmares of his short-lived, so-called marriage for the Cornish policemen and their friends, had been better than contemplating the horrors which lay in the future, where Chaz and his friends still awaited.

The scary policemen, who had appeared on the scene much later than all the others and said they were from the Met, had been very interested in the subject of Chaz. Among the dizzying numbers of police officers with whom he had been confronted, starting with the woman in the yellow oilskin trousers, whose patrol vehicle appeared to double as a fishing boat, and ending with the uniformed bloke who'd made it perfectly plain that he couldn't stay in the police station forever, Mark had liked the Met chaps least of all. The nicest officers seemed to be the pretty one and the bloke with a haircut which reminded him of Tin Tin. They were off-comers too. They had told him where they came from, but he couldn't remember now. It had been hard to keep track and he hadn't always been paying attention.

He glanced around the guest room again. He had become fond of the view from the window. The trees at the edge of the garden. The birds which visited Rachel's feeders. Having arrived reluctantly, he now found that he didn't want to leave.

There had been a family council of war, soon after his arrival in Yorkshire, and the brothers and their wives had initially agreed, between the four of them – he had taken very little active part in the discussion – that he should stay with Michael and Rachel, at the very least until the trial was over. That would take ages, of course. Monty had talked it over with Old Hargreaves, who'd looked after the family's legal affairs for years, and he had opined that it could take anything up to a year for the thing to come to court, with the situation exacerbated by the condition of the accused, who was still being treated in hospital for his injuries. (Old Hargreaves had also been very helpful in getting the London flat that he could no longer afford onto the market.)

In the meantime Michael had suggested that when Mark felt a bit more up to it, he might like to see what went on at Medlicott & Sons. 'There would always be an opening for you . . . if you wanted to take it up.' Needless to say, he hadn't felt up to it. He couldn't even manage to focus on Channel Four racing, let alone the prices of castings and spare parts for crushing machinery.

They hadn't understood, of course, with their kindly suggestions of rebuilding a life for himself up there in the north. How could they possibly understand that Chaz would find him up there, or indeed wherever he went? Chaz had friends everywhere. And of course it had barely taken Chaz a couple of weeks to discover his where abouts and contact him, with a request that they meet down in London. Michael and Rachel hadn't known about Chaz at that point. The police had not wanted him to talk to anyone about Chaz and that suited him just fine.

After a last glance out at the blue tits jostling on the bird feeders, he opened the door and took the stairs slowly down to the hall, where Rachel was waiting for him.

'Take care of yourself.' She hugged him, as he stood alongside her, suitcase at his side, hesitating like a kid setting out for his first term at prep school. 'We're very proud of you, you know. It took a lot of courage, to do what you did.'

Mark accepted the praise in silence. He knew that it was a waste of time trying to disabuse Rachel of her conviction that he had turned out to be some sort of hero. He had worn the wire to the meeting with Chaz because the two scary-looking policemen from the Met had put it to him in a way which suggested that he had very little choice. They had explained it all to him, in a sympathetic sort of way. How Chaz had stitched him up. Lent him money, gained his trust, then fooled him into betting on the wrong horse.

Handed him a spade with which to dig himself into an ever deeper hole until the next obvious step to escape the rearrangement of his features had been to engage in a spot of drug smuggling. He had done exactly what the police had asked of him. Allowed Chaz to outline a scheme in which he apparently agreed to collect a package from Turkey, as a favour for his friend.

According to the scary-looking policemen (Smith and Jones? Crockett and Tubbs? Morse and Lewis?) Chaz and his various mysterious friends were involved in a whole lot of things which were of interest to scary-Metropolitan policemen in general, and to Starsky and Hutch in particular. Race fixing was just the tip of the iceberg. And according to Carter, or was it Reagan? Or maybe it was Tango and Cash, or even Buzz Lightyear and Sheriff Woody, his getting Chaz on tape that day at the Bannister Club, was going to provide a crucial piece of evidence which would see Chaz going to prison for a considerable period of time.

Unfortunately it was pretty well understood by everyone involved (including Captain Beaky and Reckless Rat, or whatever their damned names were) that as well as Chaz himself being very unhappy about this, Chaz had a lot of friends who would have a significant level of interest in Mark's whereabouts, between now and Chaz's coming up for trial, and possibly for quite some time after that. As a result of this, they had offered Mark a place on their Witness Protection scheme, and this was what now entailed him packing a case and heading off with either Beaky or Rat (he had never particularly differentiated between the two of them) to an unknown location.

'When you're able to come back,' Rachel was saying, 'you know there is always a room here for you.'

She was getting teary now. A good woman, Mark thought. A kind woman. Michael was lucky. He had chosen well.

He nodded and returned the hug, kissing her on the cheek. He knew that he wouldn't be able to come back. Probably not for years, if ever. Rat – or was it Beaky? – had picked up his case and was carrying it out to the car. A plain, unmarked car, which might have been a taxi cab. Mark followed him, wondering where they were going. Somewhere which was probably not as nice as the spare bedroom, with its floral curtains and dried flower arrangement, and pretend hatboxes, arranged in graduations on the overlarge dressing table. When the initial revulsion had worn off, he had become very fond of the spare bedroom. He knew every inch of the wallpaper pattern, the shape and shade of every shadow that fell when the bedside lamps were lit. He had had plenty of time to get to know it all. He did not sleep anymore.

Fifty-Six

Peter stretched out a hand without opening his eyes and explored with it until he found the edge of the sun lounger, then the softness of the sun-baked beach towel and finally the warm smooth texture of Hannah's skin.

'Do you want another beer?' she asked.

'No thanks. Anyway, I'll have to move in a minute.'

'Why?'

'The sun's moved around. I need to get back under the umbrella.'

'I told you that you'd fry in the Caribbean.'

'It's worth it for the scenery and the rum punch.'

'It certainly feels a long way from Great Yarmouth.'

'It *is* a long way from Great Yarmouth.'

'Can I mention a work thing?'

'No.'

'OK. Can I mention a wedding thing?'

'Only if it doesn't involve bridesmaids' dresses, or flowers. You know I'm no good at that sort of stuff.'

'Actually, it involves the local paper.'

'Which local paper? Not that awful free thing?'

'Yup. The Crappy Chronicle, it is.'

'Go on.'

'Mum wants to get their reporter to cover the wedding. She says it will be newsworthy – two members of the local police force getting married.'

'Oh please, no. Not one of those terrible pictures with a load of leering coppers, making us walk under an archway of truncheons?'

'You know they're going to do that anyway, don't you?'

'Are you sure you wouldn't prefer the Register Office?'

'It's too late to back out now, Mum's ordered the cake.'

'Oh well – that obviously makes all the difference. Tell you what, seeing as how the cake's ordered and you and your mother have had your way over just about every detail, from button holes to invitation lists—'

'You've chosen the band, *and* they're going to let you rip up a few numbers with them.'

'True enough. But let's just agree that you've chosen pretty much everything else – suppose I say "yes" to notifying the local press, on condition that when our firstborn son arrives, we call him Thierry Henry.'

'Not a chance.'

'Emmanuel?'

'Emmanuel!'

'Emmanuel.'

'As in Petit?'

'*Oui.*'

'*Non.*'

'Ian Wright Betts?'

'Not on your life. Anyway, we might have a girl first.'

'Dennis? As in Bergkamp?'

'You don't give up easily, do you?'

'That's because I'm a good copper, Hannah. What do you think about Charlie George Betts?'

'Charlie George?'

'Scored the winning goal in the 1971 FA Cup final. It's a nice combination. Good enough for the royals . . .'

328